The author of this book is not a religious expert nor psychologist. Suggestions given on the importance of forgiveness come from personal knowledge of scripture and the author's own life experiences. The intent of the author is only to offer information of a general nature and to show its effect on the main character in this particular story.

Mountains of Trouble is a work of fiction, inspired by the life of a woman with courage and resilience.

Print ISBN 978-1-09833-268-6
eBook ISBN 978-1-09833-269-3

Mountains

of

Trouble

Clare L. Bills

To Ken,

the cheerleader of my life,

and to Rose, Jacob and Isaac

Chapter 1

1912

Escape may sound extreme, but Cora was fleeing for her life. Eluding the farmer, his children, and, ultimately her own mother.

Marry a man sixteen years her senior? Rear his five urchins? Slop pigs and chase chickens 'til her teeth fell out?

Never.

Cora wanted more. She had no idea what lie ahead, but she longed for a life where she was a major player and not a mere marionette.

She stowed her suitcase, then settled onto the worn leather seat. But her mind wouldn't settle. Was she too hasty in committing to the teaching position? No! No. Too late for second guessing. She was Kentucky bound and determined to make the most of it.

"Well, well, Missy! Don't come runnin' back to the farm if things don't turn out." The words pierced Cora's heart as she rocked back and forth with the sway of the southbound train. Did Ma mean Cora could never come home? Well then, so be it! She would miss Pa and her sister Alice, but not her overbearing critical mother.

She strained at the scratchy collar of her muslin blouse loosening it a bit. Glancing around her to be assured no one was watching, she hitched her calico skirt up to her calves and fanned her legs with it. Endure this stuffy locomotive and then her life was her own.

She hoped.

"This'll likely be your only chance at marriage," Ma said when Cora refused to marry the widower.

"I don't love him."

Ma snorted. "Love! When you has enuf to eat, that's love."

Love? Really? Then Cora wanted no part of it. The notion of sleeping next to, being intimate with, a man she barely knew repulsed her. No better than a prostitute!

She felt sorry for his children. They needed a mother. But didn't she deserve a life?

"You'll marry some hillbilly, mark my words." Ma never saw beyond the fencepost. Never hoped for a better life for herself or her daughters.

Cora wasn't looking for a man. She had battled her mother to stay in school every year until she graduated high school. She longed for freedom and hoped teaching was her pass.

She fanned herself with the copy of *Sister Carrie* Alice pressed into her hands as they hugged goodbye. How had Alice found the money? Her heart ached at the memory. But better to think of the adventure ahead.

Famished, she tucked into the lunch bag Ma had oddly insisted on packing for her. A single slab of dry whole wheat bread and raw potato peels wrapped in old newsprint were inside. Thanks, Ma. Cora nibbled on the bread but couldn't bring herself to eat the soggy peels meant to be pig slop. She pushed Ma's anger out of her mind, along with her hunger. She'd been hungry before. Ma sent her to bed without supper for arriving late for the afternoon cow milking or reading in the meadow instead of weeding the garden. But no more. A new life awaited her. A life with mountains, rivers and valley, instead of the monotonous corn fields now blurring by the dusty window.

Read, she thought. Books transported her. From now on, she vowed, she would read every evening. She was finally in charge of her life.

Hours later, as she searched for a handkerchief in her handbag, her fingers landed on two oatmeal cookies wrapped in a note from Alice. "Don't forget me, dear sister. I miss you already." Bless her. Cora ate the cookies slowly to make them last. Cookies and bread her only nourishment until when exactly? She wasn't sure, but there was no point thinking about it.

The cornfields of Iowa gave way to the wheat fields of Missouri. Cora changed trains and went east to Lexington, Kentucky. Tree covered hills pushed upward. The unexpected beauty outside the last leg of her trip calmed and distracted her from the smelly train, incessant heat and her grumbling stomach.

When the train squealed to a stop, she stepped off and nervously scanned the handful of people waiting on the platform.

"Cora?" A bulging belly of a man approached, trailed by a buxom woman in a sapphire blue dress cinched at the waist.

"Pastor Rehmann?" Cora asked.

"Yes, Martin Rehmann here. Glad to meet you." He thrust a large, soft hand into Cora's which she cautiously shook, self-conscious about her callouses. "And this is my wife, Minnie."

Minnie smiled and offered a gloved hand. "Pleased to meet you, dear. We've been looking forward to meeting you for weeks. Why the last person we met from Iowa was, let's see… the grandson of a cousin of a missionary. Or was it a son-in-law? Last name was—"

"—ah, never mind Minnie." Pastor Rehmann's pock-marked face peered at Cora under her bonnet. "Can you really be 18?"

Cora's cheeks reddened. "Yes, people tell me I look young, but I've brought my graduation certificate." She opened her handbag in search of it.

Minnie put her hand on Cora's. "We can look for it later dear. You must be starvin.' I've planned a supper at our home. Then after you set a spell, we'll go see the school and get you settled into your cabin."

Cora warmed to Minnie instantly. Her sympathetic eyes and easy smile seemed genuine. Strands of chocolate brown hair mixed with sprinkles of grey escaped from under her flower laden straw hat. The breeze threatened to undo the braided bun at the nape of her neck.

Minnie tucked her arm into Cora's elbow and led the way to a carriage painted with elaborate scrolls. Inside the bench was cushioned, unlike the utilitarian buggy they had in Iowa. Pastor Rehmann took off his tall felt hat and set it on the seat next to him, opposite the women and summoned the driver to take off.

"How was the train ride, Cora?" Minnie asked.

"A bit hot. And long. Until the last leg. I relished the changing landscape. First time I've been out of Iowa."

"Is that so? My, my, you're a long way from home."

"Yes, ma'am."

"Please call me Minnie. I do hope we can be good friends."

"Yes, ma'am…Minnie."

"So, tell me, did you leave any siblings behind in Iowa?" Minnie asked.

"Just one sister, Alice. She's a bit younger." It felt so odd to have adults asking her questions.

Minnie smiled and soft lines fanned around her eyes. "Does she hope to be a teacher too?"

"Oh no, Minnie…ma'am. Alice has a way with animals and wants to live on a farm."

Pastor Rehmann stroked his mustache thoughtfully. "God gives talents to each according to their abilities. What's drawn you to teach?"

"I've always loved school. My teacher sometimes let me help the young'uns with their letters or sums. I was so pleased when they caught on."

Pastor Rehmann nodded. "Yes, your teacher, Miss Daisy Dell, wrote a kind letter on your behalf. She said you were her brightest student yet."

Cora blushed. "Thank you."

"Which subject do you enjoy most?" Minnie asked.

"English. Once you know how to read, it opens the door to all subjects." Cora's face was serious as she tried to convince them she was capable and ready to take on a classroom.

"I hope your students share your enthusiasm for learning," Pastor Rehmann said. "The Mission serves families with little means."

"Many parents can't read or write so they may not see the importance of sending their children," Minnie broke in.

"We hope with time that'll change and with more education—" Pastor continued.

"—it'll improve their lives," Minnie finished. "Why just look at Jim Bob Taylor. He graduated college and is working in Lexington in an office. No one would have guessed it. The youngest of twelve children, but he—"

"—I don't think Cora needs to hear about Jim Bob," Pastor Rehmann said with a smile. He took out a linen handkerchief and mopped his brow. "Summer heat," he explained.

"He's always warm," Minnie whispered to Cora. "Why just last week he got a heat rash all over his—"

"—that's enough dear," Pastor said quickly, clearing his throat.

Cora blushed and squelched a giggle.

"Yes, Jim Bob was fortunate, but some think there is little point to educating the young, especially girls," Pastor said.

"But we think everyone should have an education," Minnie said.

Cora nodded. She knew firsthand what a struggle it could be. As the buggy plodded along, she wasn't sure what to say. Unused to carrying on conversations with adults, she looked at her hands awkwardly. Her parents had discouraged all but the most rudimentary discussions and never allowed her to contradict them. Nod and smile, nod and smile, she was taught.

Pastor Rehmann picked up his hat and threaded the rim through his fingers unconsciously. To avoid staring at him, she looked out the window and stifled a yawn.

"You must be exhausted," Minnie said.

"Oh, excuse me ma'am, Minnie. Yes, a bit, but I'll be fine." Her hand flew to her lap to smother the growling in her empty stomach. If Minnie noticed, she didn't say anything.

Cora nodded off for a brief moment and then gasped when she awoke to see how close they were to the side of the mountain. She gripped the edge of her seat as they rounded narrow dirt roads. "Is this safe?" she said in a near whisper.

"Our driver is very careful," Pastor Rehmann said confidently.

"I suppose this is the first time you've seen a mountain?" Minnie asked, her ample bosom bouncing with the ruts in the road.

"Yes, Southern Iowa is hilly, but no mountains." She hung onto the bench with one hand clutching her handbag with the other.

Cora was relieved when they approached a quaint town in a valley. The horses stopped in front of a sky-blue cottage sporting white shutters and a welcoming front porch.

Cream colored walls and lacy curtains created a refreshing respite inside. Next to the parlor was a separate room for dining. Cora peeked at a table set with delicate dishes adorned with pink flowers, so unlike the heavy brown crockery used on the farm.

Minnie bustled around the kitchen like a bee flitting on a patch of marigolds. Pastor Rehmann motioned Cora to sit opposite him. The high back of the overstuffed chair dwarfed her. She sat upright, legs crossed at the ankle, not touching the floor.

Pastor Rehmann's large frame crowded his chair. "We'll eat in a bit, but first I wanted to give you a clearer idea of this area and the mission schools' peculiarities."

"Peculiarities?" Cora clasped her hands together to keep from fidgeting with her skirt.

"Our school year starts in July, and we take a break in January and February." Beads of sweat shone on his brow.

"Because of the cold?" Cora asked, resisting the urge to swing her feet.

"Yes and no. The school has a stove for heat, but many of the children don't own shoes. Walking on the cold ground is too difficult, so we take a break until March and finish the school year in May."

"We were poor, but I never knew anyone without shoes."

"The families here live on very little. As for you, your contract is for eight months, and you'll be paid $52 for each of the months you teach. However, you may remain in the cabin all year at no expense." He swiped his brow with his handkerchief. "Now, there may be students in your first grade who are nearly as old as you are."

"How is that possible?"

Pastor Rehmann folded his arms over his belly. "Students have to pass a final examination and attend 80 school days before being promoted. Families often pull children from school during harvest or planting tobacco crops. The school shuts down during cold months. If they come to school for only a few months, they take longer to finish their grade."

"Sometimes years," Minnie declared from the kitchen. "Remember that one boy, what was his name? He was fifteen and still in the first grade."

"I believe you mean Frank Desjardin."

"Yes, that's him. Son of a school board member to boot!" Minnie shouted over the frying chicken. The clang of a spoon on a metal pan added to the commotion. "He gave up and dropped out."

"This is why we opened a mission school here," Pastor Rehmann said.

"The state schools are too far away?" Cora asked.

"Exactly. There are few schools, and the students are spread all over the mountains. The Appalachian Mountains have a unique culture and with it, their own form of poverty."

Minnie popped into the parlor. Flour covered her apron, and bits of potatoes were stuck in her hair "The last teacher stayed only a year. Annabeth. From South Dakota. Daughter of a merchant. What was it they sold Martin?".

"Clothing, Minnie." He took a breath and turned back to Cora. "I hope this doesn't scare you off."

Cora assumed he meant the local culture and not Minnie's appearance. "I want to teach – and to help in whatever way I can." She would try to make the best of whatever odd circumstances presented themselves, but would she be able to teach boys nearly her age?

"There are many ways to help folks. I hope you find it as rewarding as Minnie and I have. We came from a large parish in Missouri six years ago. When we heard about the poverty here…"

"…we wanted to be of service. We weren't blessed with children, so these folks have become like family to us," Minnie called out from the kitchen.

Cora shifted in her chair. Between her exhaustion, hunger, and the litany of peculiarities, her head was spinning. Would she be accepted here? Mercifully Minnie interrupted her worrying.

"Dinner's ready," Minnie carried in a plate of fried chicken, flour still dusted on her nose and chin.

Cora stood to help bring in bowls of glazed carrots and mashed potatoes. The mess Minnie made of her kitchen stunned Cora. Potato and carrot peels covered the countertop. Piles of dirty dishes lay in the sink. She smothered a smile and took her place at the table, noting the aroma of freshly baked dinner rolls.

Pastor Rehmann reached over, smiled, and brushed the flour off Minnie's face before he said grace. He passed serving dishes. The rolls were flaky, the chicken crisp and the vegetables tender. Cora was surprised at the luscious meal, but ate sparingly, not wanting them to think poorly of her.

"More potatoes, Cora?" Minnie asked as she stood to serve her.

"No, thank you," Cora said.

"Nonsense," Minnie said as she spooned another mound on Cora's plate. "You haven't eaten enough to keep a bird alive."

"Oh... no...All right, thank you."

"Now, Cora, do you have any more questions for us?" Minnie asked as she added another drumstick to Cora's plate.

"Is there space for a garden?"

"Yes, the land behind the cabin," Minnie said.

"Out of sight from poachers," Pastor Rehmann added.

"Deer and rabbits were our worst poachers on the farm," Cora said.

"Hungry folks will be here," Pastor said.

"And deer and rabbits, too," Minnie inserted.

"And coyotes at times," he said lightly.

"Now, Martin, don't you go scaring her."

"Animals don't frighten me. We had coyotes on the farm at times," Cora said.

"Then you'll be fine dear," Minnie said as she went back into the kitchen.

Minnie brought in a shortcake covered with strawberries. "The strawberries are ripe for the picking, so enjoy!" Minnie said.

"Delicious!" Cora said after her first bite.

"Wonderful as always, my dear," Pastor Rehmann smiled and patted his belly. "I blame her for my increasing size."

"Oh, Martin, don't be silly."

Cora smiled at their teasing.

After lunch, Minnie pressed a basket into Cora's hands. "A few things to get you started. Jam and bread, vegetables, and strawberries."

Cora blushed. "Thank you so much." She couldn't look Minnie in the eye. Such unexpected kindness was foreign to her.

Minnie and Cora climbed back into the carriage, and this time Pastor Rehmann took the reins as they drove the short distance to the school.

Pastor Rehmann helped them out of the carriage and unloaded Cora's single suitcase.

Cora stared at the white clapboard school sitting back from the dirt road.

"What do you think?" Minnie asked.

"It looks like my school back home." A comforting sight.

Inside, a black potbelly stove dominated the middle of the room while a wooden teacher's desk sat empty. Cora traced her fingers along it, picturing what it would be like to be the one sitting at the desk, instead of in front of it. A black chalkboard covered most of the back wall and windows dotted the others.

"Lots of windows!" Cora said.

"Yes, it helps on hot, stuffy days," Minnie offered.

Was the Kentucky weather much hotter than Iowa's? Cora wondered.

"Start each day with a pledge of allegiance, then a song, followed by a Bible reading and the Lord's Prayer," Pastor Rehmann said as he pointed to a metal bell in a corner.

Wooden desks were lined up in neat rows, two students per bench seat.

Cora sniffed at an unfamiliar smell.

"Linseed oil. To control the dust, we oil the floors. You'll need to wash 'em every week." Pastor Rehmann said as he walked over to a bookshelf made of orange crates. "Teacher's manuals here and textbooks for each grade."

She glimpsed the piles of books, eager to examine them, but knew she'd have time later. Near the door, two water buckets stood– one with a metal dipper.

"The coal is under the building, and the bucket is outside," Pastor Rehmann said. "Make certain the school is warm enough in the winter months," he said as he shifted from foot to foot, mopping his brow.

The room was stifling. No need for the stove anytime soon.

Minnie took off her bonnet and used it to fan herself.

Pastor Rehmann took a sheet of paper from inside his vest and handed it to her. "The elders of the mission requested this list of rules of conduct for all teachers."

"Rules? Oh. Thank you," Cora said as she tried not to show her disappointment. Another set of rules.

"She can look at them later," Minnie said and turned to Cora. "Shall we look at your cabin?"

"Yes, please," Cora's eyes lit up. Her heart fluttered at the thought of her own cabin.

A gentle breeze provided a respite as they walked across a grassy stretch.

"Space for the children to play games," Minnie said. Cora glanced around but saw no swings or other playground equipment. She kept the observation to herself.

Pastor Rehmann stayed back while Minnie and Cora stepped onto a creaky porch sporting an empty rocking chair. Minnie opened the door, and Cora surveyed the one-room cabin. A single bed covered by a quilt rested in one corner.

"I made that basket weave quilt for the cabin," Minnie said.

"It's beautiful."

"Do you like to quilt? The Lady's Aide gets together Saturdays to quilt. You should join us," Minnie offered.

"Ah, well, I don't think I'll have time to quilt with lesson preparation and papers to grade," Cora said. "But thank you."

Near the bed was a reading nook with a cushioned chair and tiny table with a kerosene lamp. The kitchen area had a wood burning stove, large sink, and three cupboards. Two narrow countertops were enough space to roll out bread, biscuits or the occasional pie crust.

"I took the liberty to put a few plates and things in the cupboards for you," Minnie said. "Check the garden out back, to see if anything's coming up. The last teacher had carrots, potatoes, green beans, tomatoes, but I think she harvested them all."

"Never mind Minnie," Pastor Rehmann interjected from outside. "Time to let Miss Cora explore on her own."

"I'm sure I'll be very happy here," Cora said as they moved outside.

"The well out back supplies water for both the school and your cabin. Use the school outhouse along with the coal," Pastor Rehmann added.

Cora nodded. Wells, outhouses, wood burning stoves. Just like home.

"We'll let you settle in," Minnie said and surprised Cora with a quick hug. Cora held herself stiffly.

As the plodding sound of horse hooves faded, Cora stepped through the cabin letting her fingertips explore the bumpy texture in the walls and wood countertops as she relished the blessed silence. She peeked into cupboards and filled a bucket with water from the outside well. After pouring a glassful, she sank into the rocking chair on the porch and opened the rules for teachers.

"1. You will not marry during the term of your contract.

2. You are not to keep company with men.

3. You must be home between the hours of 8 pm and 6 am unless at a school function.

4. You may not smoke cigarettes or pipes, nor chew tobacco.

5. You may not dress in bright colors.

6. You may under no circumstances dye your hair.

7. Your dresses may not be any shorter than two inches above the ankles.

8. To keep the classroom neat and clean you must sweep the floor once a day, scrub the floor with hot soapy water once a week; clean the blackboards once a day. On cold mornings, start the fire at 7 am to have the school warm by 8 am when the students arrive."

She cringed when she read the list. She had no interest in men, bright colors or smoking, but would they monitor her hours and the length of her skirt? Did this mean she would never marry?

Barefoot students, months without pay, poachers and boys of 15 in the first grade. It was a lot to take in. But she was here, and she'd make the most of it. This was an adventure, after all. Just turning out a bit different from the way she pictured it before she left Iowa.

Back inside, she noticed two ladder-back chairs next to the kitchen table. Two! Perhaps a friend would join her for a meal. The thought excited her as if the extra chair was a promise of friendship. But not a male friend. No problem. She never attracted attention from the opposite sex. Her nose was too big, her skin too pale, her bosom unremarkable. A figure more like a boy. She wasn't complaining. Who wants to be tied to a farm the way Ma was? Up with the roosters, kneading bread, feeding chickens, making soap, scrubbing clothes, and cleaning chicken coops. Always tired and invariably angry. No thank you.

Impulsively, she darted outside to inhale the Kentucky air and chase away her anxieties. She inhaled the potpourri of lush bluegrass and unfamiliar wildflowers. She set off on a brisk hike, watching for coyotes or other wild animals, but saw nothing but a few grey squirrels.

Later, she retrieved a stack of teacher's manuals and carried them to her cabin. Might as well get started on lesson preparation. Classes started in a week. What would the week bring? Worry crept in like an unwelcome guest. Would there be long endless days alone? Invasions of wild animals? Hunger? She had little money, so once Minnie's gifts were gone, she would have to forage for food.

And she was tired. Bone tired. What if her mother was right? When Cora told her she was leaving to become a teacher, Ma was less than enthusiastic. "You teach? You ain't got a proper education!"

The weight of her worries made her head spin. She collapsed in a chair, opened the first textbook and escaped into sleep.

Chapter 2

"Quiet please. Quiet!" Cora yanked on the metal bell. The throng of students turned her way.

"Good morning! My name is Miss Cora Harper, your new teacher." She shouted from the top step outside the schoolhouse hoping to look taller. Or confident. Or smarter. She felt none of these after chasing mental demons for hours the night before. Her stomach was in a state of turmoil either from nerves or a lack of breakfast. Standing on tiptoes she was determined to take charge of the boisterous mob.

"Please enter with your brothers or sisters and tell me your names." She felt like a child playing the part of an adult, clutching her pad of paper and pencil, but hoped no one saw through her façade. In spite of the sticky heat and humidity, they seemed eager to get inside.

Ragtag groups of barefoot children traipsed past her, eyeing her warily. Cora tried to focus on their eyes, not smudged faces, soiled clothes, and matted hair.

"We be the Rigsby's." His voice cracked. "I be Lenny, and these here be Penny, Denny, Benny, Glenny, Kenny, and Jenny. Our lil brother Henny's at home."

"My goodness!" Cora said writing quickly.

"We be Richard, Robert, Ruth, Ray, Roy and I'm the oldest. Russell Reynolds." Dark brown eyes, partially hidden behind long hair, focused on the ground.

"Right!" Cora stifled a grin.

"I'm Rose Freeman, and these be my sisters: Lily, Violet, Aster, and Daisy." Her chin pointed to each as her head nodded.

"No brothers?" Cora asked.

Rose answered, "No we is all girls."

"We ARE all girls," Cora corrected.

"You is too?" Rose asked.

"No, say, 'We are all girls, not we is all girls.'"

"But Mama's spectin agin. So, we maybe will has a brother. But ifin it's a girl we be namin' her Tulip." Blue eyes sparkled.

"What if it's a boy?"

"We be callin him, Thistle." She seemed to stifle a grin.

"I see." Was Rose teasing?

Identical twins strutted up. "We be Ella, and Stella Gilbert and these uns be our big brothers: Wilbur, Clayton, Gilbert, Hubert, Chester, Wilbur, and Buford," said Ella.

"Two Wilburs?" Cora said as she wrote the names on her paper wondering how she'd ever learn which was who and who was which.

"Mama done run outta names," Stella said.

"And Gilbert Gilbert? Have I got it right?" She asked a large boy of about 15. He nodded and looked away not meeting her eyes.

Ralph, Gertrude, and Carl Clinton strode by next, followed by Robbie, Walter and Ethel Smith.

George, Florence and Henry Lester were the last sibling group.

A tiny girl with soulful eyes and long eyelashes walked alone. "I be Sara Rigsby. I don't has no brothers or sisters," she whispered.

Cora stooped to look at her eye-to-eye. "I don't HAVE any brothers or sisters," she said with a smile.

"You neither?" Sara said, her dark eyes searching.

"Well yes, I have a sister. But you should say 'I don't HAVE any siblings.'"

"What be a sibling?"

"Brother or sister," Cora responded.

"But I told you already I don't has none a them," Sara frowned.

Cora reached over and tucked a stray hair behind Sara's ear. "Yes, you did. Are you related to Denny and Lenny and the other Rigsbys?"

"They be my cuzins," Sara said brightening.

"They ARE my cousins," Cora again corrected.

"Yers too?" Sara asked.

"Well no, not mine. They're yours."

"I knowd that."

"I KNOW that." Cora couldn't stop herself.

"Well if you knowd it, how comes you keep asking me?" Sara pursed her lips.

Cora straightened. "Let's go inside and join the others." Grammar lessons would start immediately.

"Welcome. Please put your lunch pails in the coat closet. And remember which is yours." Old lard buckets, used as lunch pails, were stowed away.

Cora fanned herself with her notepad. It was already sticky. She reviewed the names. Thirty-six students from eight families.

"Let's start with the pledge of allegiance."

A small American flag perched in a corner and the children turned to it and said the pledge, then sang "My Country Tis of Thee." Cora asked for a volunteer to read a brief passage from the Bible, but no one offered. She read the passage and led them in the Lord's Prayer.

Cora brought small groups to the recitation table to assess reading skills and assign spelling words to study. She organized students by grade, rather than age. There were 12 in first grade - the largest number - and two in the eighth grade, the smallest.

"Memorize your spelling words. Each Friday afternoon we'll have spelling bees."

The morning flew by. The students seemed to pay keen attention. Why did she worry?

"Great work this morning. We'll take an hour break for lunch each day. Please collect your lunches and—"

They bolted from their desks and dashed to the coat closet, pushing and pulling at each other. The Russell children argued with each other over which lunch pail belonged to who. Cora was stunned speechless. The eight Gilbert children headed for the door.

"No lunch today?" Cora asked them.

Ella answered, "We just live ore yonder, so we be home for lunch."

Eventually, the pushing stopped without a major fight, and they settled in with biscuits and jam, sausage and other lunch items. Cora brought a slice of bread and jam and carrots from the basket Minnie gave her. She hoped it would be enough to hold her until supper.

"Please wash your hands in this bucket after using the outhouse," Cora instructed.

Sara's nose crinkled up, so Cora rubbed her hands together as she pointed to the bucket.

"Oh, you means warsh," Sara corrected her.

After lunch, they played "Red Rover, Red Rover," "Ring around the Rosie," and "Tag" out on the grass. There were no balls or jump ropes. Cora longed to join in but felt the need to maintain an air of authority.

"Miss, Miss Cora, you're it!" A small boy ran past her and patted her skirt.

"It's Miss Harper," she said and ignored the invitation to chase him. He stopped and looked back at her.

"But your name be Cora!"

"Yes, Cora Harper."

He shook his head and found someone else to tag. With recess over, hot, sweaty bodies lined up and marched into the sweltering school room. At least they were out of the intense sunshine, Cora thought. But she was alarmed to see them slurping from the water dipper.

All afternoon the students struggled with what to call her. Before dismissing class for the day, she made a few announcements.

"I've decided you may call me Miss Cora, as this seems to be your tradition. Tomorrow, please bring a cup from home. When we all use the same dipper, we share germs, and if anyone is sick, we can all get sick."

Wilbur Gilbert, large eighth grader, spoke. "But Miss Cora, we be mostly kin to each other, so we already share germs."

"We ARE kin to each other," Cora said.

"You ain't kin to us!" Wilbur wrinkled his nose.

Cora took a breath. "Please bring a cup tomorrow, and we'll learn more about germs then."

Wilbur shrugged his shoulders and looked at his brother Buford, and they both shook their heads.

"School is dismissed. I'll see you—"Again pandemonium ensued as they pushed and shoved on their way out the door.

"—tomorrow. And don't forget your lunch pails," Cora shouted over the din.

It took an hour to clean the room and blackboard, put away textbooks and empty the water buckets. Something needed to change.

She headed to her cabin and explored the small area behind her garden looking for vegetables. A spade would have been helpful, but she used a kitchen spoon to dig and found a few small potatoes. Supper. A slice of bread and a few strawberries completed the meal. She wondered when her first paycheck would arrive. And where she'd find a grocer.

That night Cora made a list of "chores" for the children to share, hoping to gain more control and put order into their days.

Tuesday dawned bright and sunny, and again the students were ready when she rang the bell. As they filed in, she noticed few brought cups for water. They began with the pledge, a song, scripture reading, and prayer.

"Before we start our lessons today, I want to assign chores which we'll all share. But we won't be sharing the dipper in the water bucket. How many of you remembered to bring a cup?"

Eight hands rose.

Denny Rigsby offered, "My ma says we cain't spare cups to go to school."

"Is this what the rest of your mothers said?" Heads nodded.

"I'll show you how to make a cup out of paper. Remember the bucket with the dipper is the only one you use

to fill your cup. The other bucket is for washing your hands after you use the outhouse. Today we'll talk about germs—"
Lessons began.

Late Friday afternoon of her first week of classes, Cora was alone in the school finishing grading papers.

A young woman stepped in.

"Hi! I heard there was a new teacher and I wanted to welcome you. I'm Sylvia Anderson."

"Thank you! Are you another teacher?"

"No, I'm a missionary." Light blue eyes sparkled from beneath a white bonnet. "I live down the road and serve the people in this community."

"But you don't speak like them!"

"No," Sylvia laughed. "I'm from Minnesota. My parents were missionaries, and I moved here with them. They're back in Minnesota now, but I stayed because I love it. The people are so kind, and I love the mild winters and beautiful mountains!"

"I'll look forward to mild winters."

"Are the children treating you well?"

"They are. But everything is so different from Iowa where I grew up."

"Like to go for a stroll? Maybe I could answer questions."

"Another time perhaps. Too many papers to grade and lessons to prepare." And Cora was aching for a cool bath and time to read.

"Perhaps I'll see you Sunday at services," Sylvia explained where the local church was and strode off, her dark blue skirt swishing around her ankles.

By Saturday afternoon Cora was stir-crazy wishing she knew where Sylvia lived. Too much alone time, even for her. She chided herself for shying away from Silvia's invitation. Why was it easier to say no?

Stay busy, she told herself as she scrubbed her clothes by hand and fashioned a rope line to hang them outside to dry. She baked bread and worked in the small garden out back, looking for signs of life. Her supplies were dwindling, and she needed food. Still, the day stretched endlessly. Tomorrow she would break out of her shell and seek adventure. But she worried that Sylvia would find her dull or immature. Cora was never much good at making friends. It was easier to keep a distance.

Sunday Cora walked along the dirt road until she found the small church nestled in the woods. Minnie dashed to greet her at the door with a quick hug, which Cora stiffly received.

"How was your first week?"

"Busy. It went by quickly, but I have a lot to learn to stay ahead of so many students."

Minnie laughed. "No time to be homesick."

"No." Cora wouldn't admit to the loneliness. Or hunger.

"Well, today is a day of rest, so enjoy yourself," Minnie said. She took Cora by the elbow until they stood next to a small woman with dark brown hair holding an infant.

"Cora, this is Dorothy Davis. She and her husband live just up the hill and then to the east about three quarters, no three-eighths of a mile, and I think then you go south, or maybe west and turn right past the Chestnut tree."

"Oh my! Hello," Cora said. "Is this your first child?"

"Dorothy and her husband just had their seventh child," Minnie nodded to Dorothy.

"Eighth," Dorothy corrected dully.

"Are any of them school age? I don't recall any Davis children."

"We ain't sendin' 'em to school. Teachin' 'em at home."

"I see," Cora wanted to ask more, but Minnie was as impatient as a bee in a field of Black-Eyed Susan. She took Cora's elbow and led her to another weary woman dressed in a faded cotton dress.

"Marilyn, this is Cora, the new teacher I told you about. Marilyn lives in the valley past the horse pasture and beyond to the tobacco field. Her husband's aunt has a son-in-law who works at the machine shop here in town. He can fix anything!"

"Hello. That's certainly useful," Cora smiled and put out her hand, but Marilyn only looked down.

Sylvia appeared, and Minnie started again.

"Cora, this is Sylvia. She lives…"

"Yes! Hi again Sylvia," Cora said brightening.

"I see you two young ladies have met! How perfect. I'll leave you in good hands." Minnie went back to her post at the entrance of the small church.

Cora turned to Sylvia and whispered. "You saved me. Thank you!"

Sylvia laughed quietly. "Oh yes, the Minnie treatment. She means well, bless her heart."

"I'm sorry I didn't accept your invitation for a walk Friday."

"I have time today if you want."

"I'd like that!"

As worship ended, they filed out together, and Sylvia turned to Cora. "Where shall we go?"

"Wherever you like. I'm eager to see more of this area," Cora answered.

"Since neither of us has hiking shoes, let's walk in the woods, rather than the hills." She pointed south, and they headed away from the church.

"Next time, I'll wear proper shoes to scale some mountain paths," Cora said. They rambled through a winding path.

"When no one's watching, I tuck the back of my skirt into the front of my waistband to create bloomers which work better on mountains." Sylvia's blond curls bounced in the back of her bonnet.

"How do you know no one's watching?" Cora asked.

"I don't, and I don't care." Sylvia's eyebrows arched.

"Missionary workers must not have as many rules as teachers."

"Oh yes, plenty of rules. Dress modestly. Don't fraternize with men of any age, no smoking or drinking, that sort of thing. But not as strict as rules for teachers. They're in dire need of missionaries, so if I bend a rule now and then, they overlook it." Sylvia stopped and looked at Cora. "Of course, I still don't drink, smoke or keep company with men. Those are the elders' biggest concerns."

"Ah, so you can show a bit of ankle and dress in bright colors without being burned at the stake?" Cora teased.

Sylvia smirked. "If by bright colors you mean pastel blue, then yes. The mission elders are most comfortable when I wear drab brown, but it doesn't suit my coloring. I prefer blues and greens." She peered at Cora under her bonnet. "How about you? I'll bet you look smashing in red with your dark hair and eyes."

"Red! Oh, I never had the nerve. No place for fashion on the farm."

"You grew up on a farm?"

"Yes, we raised cattle, pigs, goats, and chickens."

"Any horses? I always wanted a horse."

"Pa had a few, but mostly to pull the buggy and the plow. We also raised corn, soybeans, and sorghum. And of course, a huge vegetable garden to see us through the long winters."

"Sounds like a lot of work. I was raised in a small town. Our dog, Prince, was the only animal I ever got close to."

They resumed walking until Cora stopped and whispered, "What is that red bird over there?"

"Vermilion Flycatcher. The male. Isn't he beautiful! The female flycatcher is grey and brown."

"She's rather like me then. Dressed in drab colors and happy in the shadows." Cora smiled as they looked for the female bird.

"You'll love the colorful birds here."

"The people are quite colorful as well. I have a family of girls all named after flowers!"

"The Freeman family."

"You know them?" Cora asked.

"I know most of the families around here. I visit as many as possible to see how I can help. Mrs. Freeman is expecting another baby soon, so I'll watch the girls after the new one arrives."

"What do you know about the rhyming Rigsby's?"

"Oh yes, Benny, Denny, Lenny, Penny and the rest."

"Three in the first grade! I can't keep their names straight."

"Like many around here, they raise tobacco. But their father drinks heavily, leaving little money for food. I bring them produce from the church garden when it's available."

"No wonder they come to school barefoot. I've never seen poverty like this. I thought we were poor in Iowa, but we always had food and shoes," Cora said.

"Would you like to come with me to visit a few families?"

"Really?"

"Yes, of course."

"It might help me understand them - and not just their speech!"

"They have a unique way of speaking." Sylvia chuckled.

"So hard to understand. Asking them to spell it out doesn't help because of the way they put words together and add syllables."

"Uf dah!"

"What?"

"Exactly!" Sylvia broke into a laugh. "In Minnesota, we have a few unique sayings too. I suppose every region does."

"But when you combine the phrases with their pronunciation, it's difficult for an outsider to communicate. Now, what was it you said?"

"Uf dah! It's an expression we use for 'wow' or 'exactly' or 'oh my.'"

"My new favorite saying. Uf dah!"

Sylvia stopped and picked a few berries, and offered them to Cora.

"Blueberries? Thank you."

"Huckleberries. Similar. They grow wild all around here, and they're edible."

They came to a clearing, and Sylvia pointed. "My cottage is about a quarter of a mile up the path and I'm ready for lunch. Care to join me?"

"No, but thank you. I'd better make sure I'm ready for the week. Trying to stay one step ahead is a challenge."

"Maybe next time. The path to your left will bring you back to your cabin," Sylvia said.

"Thank you," Cora said. "Let me know if you plan to visit any of the parish families this week."

"I will," Sylvia waved and strolled off.

A twang of regret hit Cora. She was starving, and lunch with Sylvia sounded fun, but saying "no" was always easier than "yes." She headed home to cook a few potatoes. And then went on the hunt for more huckleberries.

Week two she was determined to learn all the student's names. They each made a name card and placed it on the front of their desk.

"Grade one, please come to the recitation table and bring your name cards."

Twelve students approached. From tiny Sara to Ella and Stella they squeezed around the table taking turns to read a few lines out loud.

"Stella, your turn," she said.

Several of the children giggled as "Stella" started to read. Cora looked closer and noticed "Stella" was wearing green. She was sure she'd been wearing pink when she came in and realized the twins were having a bit of fun. Cora pretended not to notice.

In the afternoon while working on arithmetic problems, Cora noticed the girls changed their name cards again. She devised a game for each grade where the student who answered the most math questions received a small sweet. Stella won the competition, but her name card still read "Ella." Cora fooled her by giving the treat to the real Ella who hadn't known as many answers.

Stella protested, "Wait, I won."

"Yes, but you haven't been honest with me about your name today. From now on, no more switching name cards." And Cora promised herself to study their faces more closely.

"I don't know how to tell the Gilberts twins apart, and now they're using it to play games in class," Cora told Sylvia when she popped in after school.

"Rascals! Speaking of the Gilberts, I'm planning a visit to them soon. Want to come along?"

"Yes, I'd like to meet their parents."

"Prepare yourself. The way they live may shock you."

"What do you mean?"

"The residents of these Kentucky mountains are some of the poorest in the entire United States. Sometimes the conditions still make me shudder."

Chapter 3

Days later, Cora and Sylvia picked their way along a rocky path and found the unfinished clapboard home built into the hill. Chickens roamed outside, along with two mangy dogs. Children were engaged in a version of baseball, using rocks instead of balls and a stick for a bat. Cora stepped gingerly onto the porch careful not to fall through the rotting boards.

"Mrs. Gilbert?" Sylvia called.

A barefoot woman wearing a dirty blouse and long skirt peeked out the torn screen door. Greasy hair was pulled into a long braid. Sylvia introduced Cora, and Mrs. Gilbert invited them in and motioned for them to sit on straight-backed chairs, the only furniture other than a wooden table with benches all around. A sink and wood burning stove sat at the back of the room. Unfinished walls were plastered with bits of newspaper. The stench of unwashed humans filled the space. Cora spotted one of the twins with a toddler on her hip.

"Ella or Stella?" Cora whispered to Mrs. Gilbert.

"Don't much matter." Mrs. Gilbert gummed from a toothless mouth. "Ebery body gets thoseuns mixed."

"That must have been difficult having twins. I'm making a list of all the student's birthdays. But the girls weren't sure of theirs. Do you recall what day they were born?"

"Sometime in Spring. March I believes. Got too many to keeps track of dates."

Their awkward visit was brief. Once outside, Cora breathed deeply, shaken by what she had witnessed. She and Sylvia walked back to her cabin in silence.

"Your cabin is lovely, so tidy and clean."

"Thank you. I need order." Cora put a kettle on for tea. "Sylvia, I had no idea of the condition of my student's homes. No wonder they don't understand when I talk about germs and cleanliness. They're living in squalor. I asked them to each bring an extra cup to school! They scarcely have enough cups to drink out of at home." She set out two mugs of tea and a small plate of oatmeal cookies.

Sylvia nodded. "Education is a way out for these folks if they want a way out. Convince them to stay in school, and you'll help change lives. These cookies are delicious, by the way."

"Thanks. But Sylvia, are they all that poor?"

"Most of them. Some are worse. At least Mr. Gilbert is around for his family."

"Perhaps it would help if he were around a bit less. Ten children!" Cora blushed.

"Cora! You're so naughty," Sylvia laughed.

"On the farm, we kept the bull and male goats in separate pens from the females."

"Is that what you plan to do when you get married? Keep your husband in a separate pen?" Sylvia teased.

"I don't …plan… to marry."

"Not ever?"

"My parents were miserable. I don't know if it was because they weren't suited for each other or because their life was so hard. But I knew I had to get away as soon as I had the chance. There were many things I loved about life on the farm, but watching my unhappy parents was not one of them."

"That must have been difficult."

"It was." Cora was thoughtful for a few minutes as they sipped tea. "What about you? Do you hope to marry?"

"Someday, but not someone from the mountains. An educated man. I'm not in any hurry. For now, helping the people in this community gives me great joy, and I feel called to stay here."

"I know what you mean, but I feel so inadequate. We don't have maps, a globe, or even enough paper for the students. And they have nothing to play with at recess."

"Let's think of a way to raise the funds you need."

"Like what? The people are already so poor I can't imagine asking them to give what little they have."

"There are still townsfolk who might want to help. And women from the church. What about a pie auction? Some of the area schools ask women, and older girls to donate pies, and they auction them off to raise money for the schools."

"We used to have something like that, but we auctioned a box lunch. What a great idea, Sylvia! Will you help?"

"Of course! I can ask the other missionaries to help spread the word, and we can talk about it when we visit the homes."

"I'll make a list of supplies we need so they can see how we'll use the money." Cora felt the blood rushing to her cheeks, excitement mounting. "But who'll auction off the pies?"

"Pastor Rehmann! He has a loud booming voice, and he loves this school."

"Perfect. When should we hold it?"

"Early September? It'll give us time to build excitement."

"And to get everything done in time."

"I know the community will get behind you. The school means everything to folks. Cora, let's spend a couple of afternoons each week visiting folks to explain the school's necessities."

"I can meet more of the parents that way."

Cora awoke the next day with energy that belied the night she'd spent awake, her mind unable to stop planning. She couldn't wait to tell the children about the pie auction.

"Let's make a wish list for the school and playground," Cora suggested after she explained the auction.

Hands shot into the air.

"Rufus?"

"Bat and ball," he offered.

"Good. Ella?"

"Merry go round."

"Might be a bit tricky, but I'll add it. How about a map?" Cora offered.

Heads nodded.

"Or a dictionary?" Cora suggested.

"Jump ropes," Rose and Violet said at the same time.

And so it went. The list expanded along with their excitement.

Cora and Sylvia went to see Pastor Rehmann after school and explained their plan.

"Now that's a terrific idea. Having youthful energy is just what this school needs."

"It was Sylvia's idea," Cora said.

"Let's expand the auction and have families bring picnic suppers to eat beforehand. And invite local musicians to provide entertainment." Pastor was on board.

They chose Saturday, September 8, and the planning began in earnest.

Cora's head spun as she realized they needed to plan, organize, and run a community event that was growing like wild mushrooms in wet grass. She hoped people responded and didn't think it was a foolish idea. In order to raise enough money folks needed to donate pies, attend the evening, and bid on them. But most parents still didn't know who she was. Now on top of her teaching load, she'd taken on more work. In the middle of the night, she wondered what was she thinking? But there was no turning back now that her "hand was to the plow" as her father would say. She missed her father and her sister Alice, but was happy she stepped out for this adventure.

The enthusiasm of the students kept Cora moving forward, week after week. She developed a genuine affection for her students and longed to be able to provide learning tools to propel their desire to keep learning. She and Sylvia also grew closer as they made posters and visited families and businesses to promote the big event.

The school and grounds were spiffed up by volunteers the morning of the pie auction and supper.

Cora appraised the two huckleberry pies she baked from berries she scrounged. She prayed they'd fetch a tidy sum.

Toward evening, families gathered outside the school and spread blankets on the ground. Each brought baskets stuffed with simple fare for their evening meal. Inside the school, tables were set up for donated pies, each presented in a white box ascribed with the baker's name and pie flavor.

Sylvia greeted families and ferried pies inside. "I think you have nearly two dozen already, Cora," she said as she added a peach pie to the table.

Two teen girls produced their offerings and introduced themselves to Cora. Both were graduates of the mission school.

Little Sara Rigsby beamed as she handed a box to Cora. "Blueberry, and I done hepped Mama with the crust."

"I helped Mama," Cora corrected and immediately regretted it.

"You didn't hep Mama," Sara retorted.

"No, you did," Cora said.

"A course I did. I tolds you I done hepped."

"Try saying, 'I helped, not I done hepped,'" Cora said as she stooped down to look at Sara.

"But you wasn't even there!" Sara said.

"You mean, you weren't even there," Cora said.

"But I was there," Sara crinkled her face and frowned.

Cora sighed and took a breath. "Thank you for the pie, Sara."

"You be welcome. But you talks funny," Sara said and skipped back to her parents.

Stella and Ella Gilbert burst into the school with two boxes and plunked them on the table. "They be punkin pies, and we hepped bake em," Stella said.

"And we growd them ther punkin," Ella boasted.

"Wonderful!" Cora was stunned a family of meager means donated two pies. She walked over to Mrs. Gilbert. "Thank you so much for two pies!"

"Wid all those chillens in your school, it be a way for me to hep." Mrs. Gilbert said balancing a baby on her hip.

Cora turned to see ten-year-old Florence Lester offering her box. "Apple. From our trees," she said in a near whisper. Florence's thin stringy hair partly covered her protruding ears.

"My favorite," Cora confessed, and Florence grinned a bit, spun around and retreated to her parent's blanket.

Such love went into each offering. Pies filled the tables and spilled over onto school desks.

"Gooseberry and blackberry," Minnie Rehmann said as she raced in to add her pies to the table. The last to arrive. "Cora, this is a wonderful idea. Let's pray people bring more than spare change!" She reached over and gave Cora's arm a little squeeze.

"That's the hope. But whatever we take in we'll put to good use."

"You're doing a wonderful job dear. I was just telling everyone at the Lady's Aid meeting last week. Oh, did I tell you Mrs. Miller had a fall?"

"Ah, no Minnie. Sorry to hear it."

"Yes, and the Alexander family had more bad news. One of their daughter's in-laws has an uncle whose wife's cousin was diagnosed with the sugars."

Cora's head was spinning. "I'll keep him, or her, in my prayers. I'd better see to the other guests," Cora said and took off looking for Sylvia. Before she found her, a large man with a ruddy complexion dominated by a pickle-shaped nose marched over to her.

"Dickson Desjardin, here. I'm on the school board, Miss Cora. And this here's my wife Phyllis and oh yah, Frank, our son."

Phyllis held out a limp hand and regarded Cora with icy blue eyes. Cora gingerly shook her hand. Behind her, Frank stood with no expression. He was slender with fine features, akin to his mother. The thin auburn mustache was a color match to the shock of curly hair peeking out from his yellow straw hat with the dark brown band.

Cora greeted him. Frank nodded but said nothing as his lip curled a bit to one side.

"Frank's going to play in the band tonight," Dickson said.

"I'll look forward to it," Cora said to Frank who remained silent as his eyes appraised her figure. "It's time to begin." She turned on her heels to make a quick getaway.

As she raced toward Sylvia, Minnie dashed over to her and whispered, "That's Frank, the fellow who was still in first grade when he was 15! And to think his father is a member of the school board."

"I remember you mentioned him, poor fellow. Let's begin the evening."

Pastor Rehmann offered a blessing and families settled on blankets to enjoy supper together.

Musicians from the church, along with Frank, brought out their fiddles and guitars after supper and led them in a toe-tapping round of bluegrass, followed by traditional hymns and a few ballads. Cora watched her students with their families in quiet camaraderie. A twinge of sadness came over her as she realized she had few memories of peaceful family times. Although folks welcomed her, she didn't yet fit in and wasn't a part of the community.

When it was time for the auction, everyone crowded near the schoolhouse. Pastor Rehmann stood on the steps and announced the pie flavors and donors' names.

"Thirty-six pies in all! The same number of students who attend our mission school. Be generous when you bid on them. Let's start with this huckleberry pie made by our teacher, Miss Cora."

Cora blushed a deep red when several young men bid on her pie, including Frank Desjardin, who won the bid. She was relieved she wouldn't have to spend time with him. The box suppers back home were to be shared by the cook and the auction winner, but this auction was different.

Bidding was fierce for pies brought in by the older teenaged girls. A heated volley erupted between two young men for a certain sweet potato pie donated by a pretty girl named Iris. No doubt, part of the flowering Freemans.

Each pie was brought forward and purchased with good-natured comments from bidders.

"Thank you for coming tonight. Together we raised $56 for our schools. God bless you all," Pastor Rehmann concluded the auction.

As he was leaving, Frank Desjardin caught Cora's eye and held up his pie. He raised his eyebrows and curled his lip in a sort of sneer, but said nothing.

"Enjoy it," Cora said evenly and turned quickly to escape. An involuntary shudder went through her.

After everyone had gone home, Cora wrote another letter to her family hoping her mother would soon respond. "We raised more money than my monthly salary. It'll help us purchase supplies for the school, as well as playground items. These poor children don't even have enough paper or a ball for catch." It was her fourth letter, but none were answered. Ma was stubborn, but Cora hoped her anger would diminish with time.

Sylvia helped Cora clean the school and grounds the morning after the auction. "I noticed Frank Desjardin won your pie," she said.

"Yes, kind of an odd fellow."

"His dad owns the mechanic shop in town."

"And he's on the school board. But something about Frank makes me uneasy," Cora said.

"I think he's harmless. Interesting he doesn't look anything like his father."

"I thought so too. Striking resemblance to his mother."

"I've heard others say she spoiled him. But it's probably just gossip," Sylvia said.

"Minnie told me he was still in first grade at 15."

"I've heard that too. Not sure what the problem was. It's not like they pulled Frank out of school to help with crops."

"He plays the guitar pretty well," Cora added not wanting to sound unkind. His father was on the school board. But she hoped she wouldn't run into him again. The possibility was unsettling.

Chapter 4

Packages were piling up like acorns in a squirrel's nest. Cora picked her way through her cottage with the accumulated purchases from the auction money. She wanted to surprise the students by bringing them all out together. Some items she bought at the local general store, but others she sent for in the mail. Early in December, the last ones arrived, and she lugged them all to school the next morning.

"What be in them?" Violet asked.

"It's a secret. If everyone is especially good this morning, I'll open the boxes before lunch."

All morning students were as silent as deer, eyes trained on the mysterious packages in the corner of the room. Cora stopped lessons a few minutes early and put the boxes on the recitation table.

"Are you ready to see what our pie auction money purchased?"

"Yes," they all said. "Open it, Miss Cora!"

She pulled out a large dictionary first. "This will help us learn more words. Whenever you want to find out how to spell or pronounce or learn a new word, you can look in this dictionary."

"What else?" Stella called out.

"Maps of the United States and the whole world. Roy and Ray, will you help me unroll them?"

The Reynolds boys raced to the front of the room and rolled out the large maps.

A chorus of oohs and ahhs greeted the unveiling.

"We'll pin them to the far wall. They'll help with geography and history lessons."

"What else?" Ella piped up.

"Construction paper in all sorts of colors." Each time she pulled out new items, more students left their seats and came close to the table.

"What be that for?" Buford asked.

"For art projects. It's thicker than regular paper. We also have tempera paints and brushes and lots of plain white paper." She placed the art supplies on the table.

Excitement was building. The students surrounded the table like ants around a drop of honey. Cora pulled out a dozen new stories of adventure and mystery and announced their titles as she held each one high.

"The Wonderful Wizard of Oz. The Secret Garden. Anne of Green Gables. Five Children and It. Peter Pan." Collective gasps went up as she displayed each book.

"What else?" Stella asked.

"The Bobbsey Twins of Lakeport. The Railway Children. The Story of King Arthur and His Knights. The Tale of Peter Rabbit. Pollyanna. The Jungle Book. And the last one is the Adventures of Alice in Wonderland."

Some children clapped, others grabbed the hands of a friend excitedly and nodded when a title interested him or her.

"These are the start of our library. I'll read aloud each day for a few minutes after lunch," Cora said. "Which book shall we start with?"

"Wizard of Oz," shouted Gilbert Gilbert.

"Yes!" The others agreed.

"I'll start today then. Good choice," Cora said.

"Anything else?" Gilbert Gilbert asked eying the last package.

"Why, yes," Cora said wanting to drag out the surprise. "The last items are for recess." She reached into the bottom of the deep box and pulled them out one at a time. "A new bat and baseball. Four jump ropes. And a package of marbles."

Cheers went up and Sara, Ella, and Stella joined hands and jumped in circles.

"When can we be play wid em?" the trio of girls asked.

"As soon as you're done with your lunch. I'm so proud of you all for helping with the auction. I want you to enjoy these wonderful gifts."

"It's bettern Christmas." Sara gushed.

"I ain't never seen nothin like it," Gilbert enthused.

"So let's eat!" Cora said, and a stampede of feet headed to the coat closet to retrieve lunch buckets. Except for the Gilbert children who raced for the door to get home and back as quickly as possible.

Everyone gulped lunch, then lined up at the outhouse, washed hands and dashed outside. Older children chose teams for baseball. Cora gave pointers on how to swing a baseball bat instead of an old log. She was thrilled that her bat connected squarely with the ball and she raced to first base, her long skirt flying.

"Ok, well you get the idea," she said breathlessly.

She turned to the Ella, Stella, and Sara who were struggling to jump rope.

"Wrap the rope ends around your hands and jump right now," she said as the rope was passing near her waist. Once the girls got the hang of it, she turned to those standing around watching and drew a circle in the dirt and taught them the rules for marbles. Exhilarated, she was out of breath, and her cheeks were flushed. She chided herself for acting like a child.

She coaxed them to come inside after recess, but they resisted. Until Cora reminded them, they were going to start the Wizard of Oz. That settled it. They raced to their seats as she began the first chapter.

"Dorothy lived in the midst of the great Kansas prairies…"

For fifteen minutes all were as quiet as snowflakes.

"But Dorothy, knowing her to be a witch, had expected her to disappear in just that same way, and was not surprised in the least. That's the end of Chapter two. We'll start Chapter three Monday after lunch recess."

Groans of disappointment rang out, but Cora reminded them their spelling bees were coming next and the week ended on a positive note.

The next day Cora and Sylvia went hiking in the hills, enjoying the weather before it turned cooler.

"I wish you'd been here! It was the most fun I've ever had," Cora told Sylvia. "Students said it was better than any Christmas morning."

"I do wish I'd seen it. Most of these students rarely have a gift on Christmas or birthdays."

"A lot of work, but worth it."

"Speaking of Christmas, what's your plan for the Christmas program?" Sylvia asked Cora.

Cora stopped, and her hand flew to her neck. "Program? Am I supposed to put on a program?"

Sylvia laughed in her lyrical way. "No one mentioned it to you?"

"When I met with the school board last month, they said how pleased they were with the pie auction, but no one said anything about a Christmas program."

"They must not be expecting it then."

"Just when I feel I'm ahead of the lessons, something happens. Ever since I got here, I've felt as if I've jumped onto a moving train." Cora patted her forehead and face with her handkerchief.

"I'm sorry I said anything," Sylvia giggled.

"No, you're right. They deserve a Christmas program, and I need to organize it."

"I'll help if you like."

"Really? Again? I mean, I'd be so grateful."

"Let's have the children put on a nativity play, recite a few scriptures and sing Christmas songs."

"Yes, and since you're the missionary, you can be in charge of the play…and the scripture verses." Now it was Cora's turn to laugh.

"I can come on Wednesday and Friday afternoons to work on the play. We don't need elaborate costumes, but maybe a few women from the Ladies Aide will make simple headdresses and angel wings."

"I'm already overwhelmed with the thought of Christmas and gifts. What to make for my parents and my sister and all the children?"

"Have you heard from your family?"

"No, but I'm hoping by Christmas Ma will soften."

"You don't have to give gifts to all the children. No one expects it," Sylvia said.

"I want to. I'm so attached to each of them. But organizing a play is making my head hurt."

"It'll be fun, Cora!"

"That's what you say. I don't know how I'll fit it all in. Uf dah!"

"I'm so glad I taught you something useful. Uf dah indeed."

"I need to cut this short and head home."

"Cora! I thought we were going to have lunch. I made the vegetable barley soup you like."

"Sorry, Sylvia. No time today. I've got to start working on Christmas. Maybe during the winter break, I'll have time to eat." Cora headed back home, leaving Sylvia shaking her head.

Cora caught Sylvia's arm at Sunday services. "I'm sorry about yesterday. How about you come to my cottage for lunch today, and we can plan the Christmas program?"

"Change of heart?"

"No, a good night's sleep. I feel better about things today. You're right. It'll be fun."

Monday Cora announced the plans to her students and was heartened by their enthusiasm. Even Wilbur and Wilbur, who never seemed excited about anything, said they'd learn songs and help with the decorations.

In the weeks leading to Christmas, Cora and Sylvia assigned the parts of Mary and Joseph, shepherds, angels and the three Kings. Minnie Rehmann and a few other women volunteered to fashion simple costumes. Each morning the students practiced Christmas carols and Sylvia came by afternoons to assist them as they memorized lines and scripture verses. Every child played a part in the pageant, set for the afternoon of Sunday, December 23.

A week before Christmas, Richard Reynolds dragged in a cedar tree. "Pa said we could cut thisun for our program."

"A Christmas tree! How thoughtful. Thank you. And I know just how to decorate it!"

During art, they created construction paper chains to decorate the tree and strung popcorn on long threads and wound them around the cedar tree for contrast and texture. The Lester trio brought gourds from their garden for everyone to paint and piled them on the sides of the makeshift stage, made by hanging old sheets. Others brought in hay from their barns.

Friday before the performance everything was ready except for the costumes. Minnie dashed in moments before the final practice with robes, angel wings, and headdresses.

"I'm so sorry to be late. The Lady's Aide women were working on these when a wild horse came into the community room. It started eating the angel wings and took a bite out of this headdress. Well, Marilyn hollered for her son-in-law's father's cousin who was standing outside on the hill just south of the northeast part of the building to see if Jimmy Don could call Chester who knows a thing or two about corralling horses. Meanwhile, we had to get the quilts out of the way."

"Quilts?" Cora asked and immediately regretted it.

"The three quilts we're making for the benefit for the family who lost everything in last week's flood. The Tuttles. You remember. They live just north of here on the southbound road next to the stand of trees with sour nuts."

"Sour nuts. Black Walnut trees?"

"Yes, yes. Well now you know why I'm a bit late with these, but better late than never, right?"

"Right. Thank you so much." Cora snatched the costumes from her hands hoping to get the rehearsal started before Minnie launched into another story. Musicians from the church volunteered to help lead music and were waiting along with antsy children.

Later, as she left school, Cora looked at the decorations, the stage, and even the horse nibbled costumes, and her heart swelled with pride at all they accomplished with few resources.

No time to rest, there were gifts to finish. Sylvia dropped by the morning before the program.

"It smells wonderful in here! Gingerbread?"

"Old family recipe. I found a cookie cutter at the grocer, so I baked gingerbread people to go into the gift packages for my students."

Sylvia looked around at the piles of apples and oranges and a bag of candy sticks on Cora's kitchen table.

"This is more than most ever have for Christmas, Cora. How did you do it?"

"I've been saving a bit of my wages each month. I want them to have a special treat this year. Want to help me wrap them?"

They cut squares of brightly colored fabric and put the treats in the middle and tied each with a ribbon.

"The boys won't want the ribbons, but they can give them to their sisters for their hair," Cora said.

"I can't wait to see their faces. When's the gift giving?"

"Right after the program tomorrow."

Cora was a bundle of nerves at Sunday services. Minnie greeted her at the door of the church as usual and gave her a little hug, which Cora hesitantly accepted. Then Minnie patted Cora's cheeks. "We'll be at the program this afternoon, and I'm sure it will be a delight. And Pastor and I'd love it if you and Sylvia joined us for dinner Christmas Day."

"Oh! Lovely!" Cora said. She'd been so preoccupied with the program she hadn't thought about Christmas Day. Her first away from home.

An hour before the Christmas program, students trickled in and were transformed into characters for the nativity. Parents streamed in, along with members of their mission church. Cora was relieved the weather was cool with so many bodies packed into one room. Several school board members were among them and then Frank Desjardin stepped in with his guitar.

"Oh! Are you joining us?"

"Yah, I figured ya'd want my help." He gave a half smile/half sneer.

"Let me get you copies of the music." Cora wondered why he hadn't come to rehearsal but didn't feel comfortable asking.

"I don't read, I mean, don't need music. I play by ear."

"OK, well the other musicians are going to stand over there," she said hoping her irritation didn't show.

The nativity play was first, with a few forgotten lines. The older children recited Bible verses, and they all sang Christmas songs. As parents joined in, the room echoed with music.

Before the afternoon concluded, Cora asked her students to come forward, and she presented each with a gift. Several of the older boys were too shy to look her in the eye but mumbled their thanks. Sara, Ella, and Stella showed their enthusiasm right away. "Ribbons!" they squealed and then hugged Cora around her waist.

Next was the parent's turn to surprise Cora. They quietly strode up to her one-by-one and offered her their thanks, along with watermelon pickles, eggs, squash, canned beans and items from their gardens. Mrs. Freeman gave her a small plate of sugar cookies. "The girls heped decorate em."

"I'm overwhelmed with the generosity," Cora told Sylvia as they carried all the gifts back to her cabin. She made tea and the two enjoyed cookies and a chance to catch up. "Did Minnie tell you she invited us for Christmas dinner?"

"Yes. I wasn't sure what I was going to do on Christmas. This is the first since my parents left."

"And my first Christmas away from home." They sipped tea, lost in memories.

"Do you miss the farm?"

"Now and then I think about Alice and my parents, but I'm so busy, I don't have time to miss them very much. How about you?"

"I do miss my parents, but I love it here. And most of the time I feel needed."

"That must be it. I feel needed here. Not just as a teacher, but as a member of this community. I didn't expect to feel this way so soon."

Sylvia nodded. "Will you go home over the long winter break?"

"No, it's too soon to go back. My ma was furious with me for leaving, and she hasn't answered any of my letters. She might try to force me to stay in Iowa."

"Why?"

"Ma was…is…difficult. She likes to control everything… and everyone. She never wanted me to continue with school after 8th grade because she said it was a waste of time."

"Waste of time?"

"She doesn't think girls should receive an education since all they need to do is cook and sew and take care of animals."

"What about teachers? Nurses? Office workers? They all need education."

"Ma's view of the world is limited. And she is the center of it. I'm sorry if I sound ungrateful. I needed to leave before her misery would swallow me whole."

"But she must have realized you might leave to get married someday."

Cora's laugh was brittle. "She always said I was too plain for anyone to want to marry. Alice was the pretty one. And then she tried to marry me off to a widower with five children. I barely knew him!" Cora looked away. "I shouldn't be talking about this."

"You can talk to me about it all you like. I'll hold this in confidence."

"I hope you don't think any less of me for complaining about my mother."

"Of course not. But it does help me understand you a bit better. No wonder you felt you needed to escape."

"When I finally reached 18 and graduated, I saw my chance to control my own life. I made a run for it. Of course, I told them, but Ma was furious."

They sipped their tea. Cora lost in the memory of it and Sylvia trying to imagine what Cora went through.

Sylvia broke the silence. "On a happier note, I thought I'd give you my gift today." She hid her gift among the parent's gifts earlier and now pulled out a small package covered in brown paper and handed it to her.

"May I open?"

"Yes, silly. Open it."

Cora unwrapped the book, "The Story of My Life." "Helen Keller's story. I've wanted to read this. Thank you so much, Sylvia. I'll treasure this."

"I've been so inspired by her story. I know you'll love it."

"Her troubles put mine into perspective. And I have a little something for you," Cora said taking an item wrapped in colorful fabric from a cupboard and handing it to Sylvia.

"Anne of Green Gables. Perfect. How funny that we got each other books."

"Yes, let's trade when we've finished reading them."

Christmas at the Rehmann's was a warm and inviting event. Cora brought some of her homemade jam as a gift and

Sylvia brought a wreath she made out of a branch and colorful ribbons.

After Pastor Rehmann said grace, he looked at Cora and Sylvia and smiled. "I believe God has sent you two like angels to help the good folks of this area. We are extremely pleased with the work you're doing. Minnie and I consider you like daughters."

Minnie looked from one to the other with tears shining in her eyes. "You're truly like family and I'm so thankful you're sharing this meal with us."

"We feel blessed to be here with you, don't we, Cora?" Sylvia asked.

Cora's eyes were damp as she choked her answer. "Yes. Thank you," was all she managed to say aloud. She was uncomfortable with overt displays of emotion, but in spite of it, her heart was full. Why wasn't her mother able to express such love, she wondered to herself.

Chapter 5
1921 – Nine years later

Spring approached like a bear out of hibernation and with it, a hungry restlessness settled on Cora. She finished preparing lessons for the next day and hurried to her cabin for a quick supper. The children were antsy with the windows open and the earth coming to life outside. She didn't blame them. Even though Kentucky winters were nothing compared to Iowa's, the natural rhythm of the seasons existed. And it brought a longing to be outside as soon as spring flowers emerged. She was eager to get her garden planted and to spend more time outside. She thought of the baby animals that would be born on the farm back home and made a note to herself to write to her mother. After several years, her Ma made peace with Cora's departure and wrote to her occasionally.

Cora felt like she was a part of the small community in Kentucky now and enjoyed an amount of respect. Once she thought she might marry, but now at 27, she accepted her single status. God had other plans for her. She directed her energies into teaching and serving her church.

Tuesday and Thursday nights were now devoted to teaching adults to read. A few years into her stint as a teacher for this Kentucky mission, she discovered a large number of adults quit school to help their parents. When she sent home school papers and asked parents to read and sign them, she was surprised at first by some of the reactions. At church services on Sunday a few cornered her.

"We ain't be in yer classes, so don't ya be sendin' papers for us to read."

Or they came back with an "x" instead of a signature.

She talked it over with Sylvia one evening as they were hunting for wild berries.

"Many of the parents never learned to read. They're ashamed."

"Ashamed? Why?"

"I suspect they feel people will think they're too dull to learn."

"I wonder if a Moonlight school would help."

"A what?" Sylvia asked.

"It's a new Kentucky program for illiterate adults. I heard about it from area teachers. Books are printed specifically for adult beginning readers."

"Why the name?"

"They hold classes on nights when the moon is full enough so people can see to find the school. Do you think anyone is interested here?"

"I can think of several. But do you have the time?"

"It's a sacrifice, but would be a great improvement in their lives. Perhaps classes of simple arithmetic too." Cora's mind was racing with possibilities. "I think I have enough berries for jam. Let's head back," Cora said.

"I can't believe you still make jam too!"

"Farm girl, remember?"

After this, she approached the school board to ask permission to teach a class for adults two nights a week, using kerosene lamps for light.

Men from the community, including Pastor Martin Rehmann, and five others comprised the school board. Dickson Desjardin, the owner of the mechanic's shop, was now the school board president. His eyes pierced through her whenever they met, making her feel as if she should apologize for an unknown discretion.

The night of the meeting, they pulled chairs around her desk in the school room, and Cora explained her idea. She didn't request any additional pay but wanted them to know she'd be working with men as well as women, which they might see as a violation of the teacher's rules. Even after all these years, the teacher restrictions still applied to her. And funding was needed to purchase appropriate books.

Desjardin asked her to step outside after she made her plea so they could discuss the idea in private. However, because of the warm night, the windows were open, and she heard their deliberations with no effort.

"After all," Desjardin concluded, "Miss Cora's too plain to marry. There be little danger of her workin' closely with men." He snorted, and she heard others agreeing with him. Her eyes stung when she heard this, but Ma always said the same thing. She thought her heart had toughened against such words, but they still found a soft place to land.

The familiar voice of Pastor Rehmann cut through the crassness. "Cora is a good woman who can help improve the lives of these folks. That's the true issue at stake here." Thank goodness someone sifted through the nonsense, she thought.

The men called her back into the school and, to her surprise, they granted the request. She walked to her cabin happy for the victory but wounded by their hurtful words.

Sylvia helped her get the word out about the classes for adults, and the enterprise was now accepted in the community. Instead of waiting for moonlight, she set a schedule, so people knew when she was available. Not all were easy to teach. Four, or five attended most nights, but success wasn't just about numbers, she reminded herself regularly.

Tonight, as she ate her vegetable and bean soup supper, she dreaded seeing Frank Desjardin again. He'd been showing up randomly for a few months, and something about him made her skin crawl. Over the years she ran into him occasionally but tried to avoid a conversation. Now he was coming to her literacy classes, and she was forced to engage him.

Sure enough, Frank was waiting at the schoolhouse, wearing his fancy dress shirt and narrow tie with pleated pants. So, unlike the bib overalls most men wore. But Frank was a traveling musician. He still sported a thin auburn mustache and perpetual sneer.

Cora worked with each adult individually but felt herself tensing when she had to assist Frank. His cat eyes made her shrink. Instead of looking at her face, he focused on her modest bosom and slight figure. She felt compelled to be kind to all people, but his mannerisms put her on guard.

After class Frank waited until the others left and he was alone with Cora as she tidied up. She moved toward the door of the school.

"Good night, Frank. I think you're making good progress," she said keeping her tone light as she locked the school building.

"My band be playing in a bar ore yonder Friday night, ifen ya'd like to hear us," he said as he lit a cigarette.

"Oh, sorry, my contract won't allow me to go to a bar," she said.

"I cud ask my pa to be changin yer contract."

"No, that's not necessary."

He curled his top lips in a mocked smile. "Well, maybe ya'd like to hear me on the radio." He blew a lung full of smoke in her direction.

"Sorry, I don't have a wireless. But, thank you. Good night," she said coughing and sprinted toward her cottage.

"Sure ya don't wants some company?" He wasn't giving up.

"No, thank you. I have papers to grade. And men aren't allowed in my cottage." She stepped onto her porch, but he was right behind her.

"They has ya on a tight leash. Don't ya wants to break out a bit."

"I'm perfectly content with the rules of my contract. Good night, Frank!" She stepped inside and bolted the door. She stood in the dark for a few minutes, heart pounding. When she peeked out the window and saw he left, she lit a lamp and closed her windows and pulled the curtains shut. It was a warm June night, but she didn't feel safe leaving windows open.

"Something about him makes me nervous, and he keeps asking to spend more time with me. I don't dare complain about him because of his father," she confided to Sylvia as they ate dinner in Cora's cabin the next evening.

"Ironic, the president of the school board has a son who can't read or write," Sylvia said.

"That's what I think. I wonder what happened when he was a child," Cora said.

"I've heard his mother sheltered him. I suppose she was embarrassed he was so slow."

"And he has no steady job. Plays guitar with a band now and then which seems shiftless."

Sylvia gave her a withering look, "Aren't you judging?"

"I suppose. I give him credit for wanting to learn, I just wish he'd stop lurking around me. I'm judging his behavior and trying not to judge his heart."

"Do you think he's dangerous?"

"Probably just lonely. But I don't want to find out."

"If you feel uncomfortable, tell the Desjardins."

"I'd feel silly. They'd think I'm a weak female. I'll be more direct with Frank in the future." Cora stood and brought a plate of molasses cookies to their table.

"Do you ever think about marrying?" Sylvia asked. It was a subject they talked about from time to time. "I worry I've waited too long."

"I'd have to leave teaching if I married. Besides no one is asking," Cora said.

"Except Frank," Sylvia teased.

"Stop it. I'd never marry him. And he didn't ask. Sometimes it seems he hates me rather than likes me. He seems to resent me for some reason."

"Maybe he's embarrassed he doesn't know how to read."

"But I'm trying to help him. You'd think he'd appreciate it."

"But don't you want to be a mother someday? I see how great you are with children." Sylvia seemed determined to stay on this topic. "Tasty cookies, by the way."

"Thanks. I realized long ago God has other plans for me. I'm too plain to marry, and most men don't want a woman with an education. I'm with children all day, so why do I need more?"

"You're not too plain. I wish you'd stop saying that."

"Why are you asking about this now? Are you longing to marry?"

"I've been working as a missionary for over a decade. I love my work and the people, but I keep wondering if I'm missing out. What it'd be like to be close to a man? A good man. And to have a child?"

Cora shook her head. "I don't know, but perhaps it's time to find out. Are you thinking about going home to Minnesota?"

"I don't know what I'd do up North. I guess I'm just restless for a change."

"Uf dah!" Cora said, and they both burst out laughing.

At the next session of Moonlight readers, Frank was again among the group of adults.

As she worked with him on his words, he reached for her hand. She moved it away and pursed her lips.

"Please read the sentence again," she coached.

"Yeren such a skinny lil thing. Ya be needen to put some meat on yer bones." One of the other adults heard him and snickered.

"Read the page, Frank. Just the page in the book." She was determined not to lose control of the class.

He raised his eyebrows and looked her up and down, his thin lips disappearing into a smirk.

"I'll let you work by yourself," Cora said and moved on to another student. Frank was a slow learner, which made lessons all the more tedious.

At the end of the hour, she gathered her things and stayed close to the others as they left the building. Frank lagged behind so once again she was alone with him as she locked the school.

"So lil lady, my offer still stands to hear my band."

"And my answer is still no. Goodnight, Frank."

"I'm a great musician, ya know."

"Wonderful. Good night."

He hesitated for a few moments and then walked off as Cora scurried to her door and got safely inside.

In early July, as she was eating her supper, someone knocked at her door. She looked cautiously out the window and saw the school board president standing on her porch.

"I hope I didn't interrupt yer supper, Miss Cora," Dickson Desjardin said.

"What can I help you with?" She asked nervously, stepping out onto her porch. Was this going to be about his son, Frank?

"I wanted to let ya know my sister died. She never married, like ya, but we wants to have a proper wake and funeral for her in two days."

"I'm so sorry."

"Ya didn't know her cuz she done lived in another village, but she's to be buried here. The funeral will be at our community church. I wonder if ya could hep us with the food preparation."

"I'd be happy to. What's the plan?"

"The wake'll be Thursday evening in the church. Afterward, friends be invited to our home to share memories. Just some simple refreshments and we'll purchase what's necessary." He handed her money for ingredients.

"Certainly. And what about the funeral?"

"Most of the families who are attending the funeral Friday morning'll bring a dish to share for the luncheon. So, we only need your hep Thursday evening."

Thursday after school she prepared simple fare and brought them to the Desjardin home during the vigil. Mrs. Desjardin left trays and other food for her to set out and serve. She was working alone when Frank walked in so quietly she didn't hear the door open.

"Thought I'd hep with the food," he said, and she jumped.

"I can manage," she replied but wondered why he wasn't at the vigil.

Frank walked over to where she was standing and looked at the trays of fruits and vegetables. He helped himself to a few bites of fruit, and she felt the weight of the silence between them.

"Sorry about your aunt."

"Thanks," he said looking her way but avoiding her eyes.

She felt uncomfortable and tried to finish her work quickly. "Were you very close to her?"

"No, not really. Not as close as I'd be liken to be with ya." Frank took a step forward.

She stepped back and tried to make light of his statement. "Well, you know, I'm an old school marm, not allowed to be alone with a man."

"It was fine for ya to be teachin' me."

"Yes, but I got special permission to teach men." She kept her tone light. The hairs on her neck stood up. She wanted to run. But she didn't want to cause trouble. After all, he was the son of the school board president who controlled her livelihood. Frank took another step forward. Trapped her against a wall.

"I'm finished here. Let me pass."

Frank grabbed her. Pulled her toward him. Did he want to hug her? She wasn't insensitive to his grief. Then she smelled alcohol. She tried to pull away, but he became more forceful. She fought to escape.

"Stop this at once!" She hoped her school teacher voice would be a warning.

"Ya think ya be bettern me, little miss teacher. But yer not!" He squeezed her arms.

"I never said I was better than you. I was trying to help you. Let go, you're hurting me."   He squeezed harder.

"Stop!"

"Ya cain't fool me! I know ya likes it!"

"Help!" Cora shouted.

"No one out there to hep ya," he sneered. "Them's all at the church."

"Where you should be! Let go!"

"I see ya walkin' around all high and mighty. Everyone thinkin' yer so special." He was breathing down her neck.

"You have gifts too. Music is a gift." If she kept him talking, perhaps someone would barge in and put an end to his abuse.

"If ya thinks my music is such a gift, how comes yer too important to hear me?" His face contorted; his breath was sour.

"My contract won't allow it, I told you," Cora struggled and twisted to loosen his grip. She screamed as loud as she could. "Help!"

"Oh, come on. Ya cain't be tellin' me ya don't want a little fun!" He pulled her arms tight to her sides.

"This isn't fun. Stop it!" She tried to kick him. He moved to the side still keeping his grip on her. "Help, someone please help me," she screamed louder.

She tried to bite him.

"That's the way ya want it? Ya like the rough play?"

"No. Stop this. Help!" She screamed again.

Frank became more aggressive as if her protests gave him courage. When she tried to kick him, he knocked her feet out from under her and threw her onto the hard kitchen floor.

"No," she screamed. "Don't do this," she begged, terrified.

Chapter 6

Frank overpowered her, in spite of her pleas and screams.

When he rolled off, she scrambled to her feet and fled. She looked back over her shoulder as she ran. Would he follow? She was in shock. Like a wounded animal needing to hide she ran through the dark woods to find safety. Inside her cabin, she locked the door and pulled curtains shut. She heated a few pails of water she pumped earlier and then soaked in the small tub. And sobbed.

What just happened?

Did she encourage him? No! Never!

Why didn't she run when she first saw him? But that was silly. How was she to know he'd be violent? She'd been alone with him once while tutoring him and nothing like this happened.

How was she so naïve?

When the bath water turned cold, she dried herself and shakily pulled her nightgown on, then retreated to her bed. Her body trembled, in spite of the warm night, and as much as she wanted to escape into sleep, her brain gave her no release.

When she finally fell asleep, her screams woke her and she realized the nightmare was real.

Cora wanted to stay in bed the next day but had to attend the funeral. She ached all over.

She dressed in a simple black dress. When she pulled on her cloche, she noticed a tenderness on her skull. From hitting the hard floor. She remembered. Her stomach was queasy, and her nerves were raw, but she pushed past it to make an appearance.

Frank's mother approached her after the funeral.

"Miss Cora, thank you for helping set out the food last night. I was sorry you left so soon."

"Yes, well, I had to get back." She avoided looking Mrs. Desjardin in the eyes, afraid she might burst into tears. And even more afraid of the shame she'd endure if someone found out.   Frank sidled up to her while she was speaking with his mother.

"Hello, Miss Cora. It be nice to see ya," he sniggered.

Cora jumped and gasped. Her hand flew to her mouth, and she feared she might vomit. She turned to Mrs. Desjardin. "I'm sorry, I'm behind on lesson preparations."

As she rushed to the door, Sylvia stopped her.

"Cora, I've hardly said 'hi.' Can't you stay?"

"No, I'm behind in my work. I've got to go."

"But you'll have all day tomorrow! Come and sit with me."

"I'm sorry, Sylvia, I have to go." She pushed past her, tears pooling, and raced home to endure another sleepless night.

Cora avoided church for a few weeks, not wanting to see or talk to anyone. When she couldn't stand it any longer, she invited Sylvia to her cabin, needing the comfort of her friend, even if she wasn't ready to divulge her secret.

"How are you, Cora? Are you feeling better?" Sylvia took a sip of lemonade.

"Better?"

"When you raced out of the funeral, you looked pale, and I thought you must be ill. And it seems you've been avoiding me since then."

"That's why I invited you to lunch today."

"To tell me what's wrong?" Sylvia asked.

"No. I'm fine. I just thought it'd be good to see you."

After a moment of silence, Cora added, "The students are doing well, and I think all of them will pass their exams."

"You would tell me if something was wrong, wouldn't you?" Sylvia asked. "I mean, I tell you just about everything and I hope you trust me enough to tell me if something's bothering you."

Cora looked away instead of at Sylvia. "I'll be fine, Sylvia. Promise. Just this sweltering summer heat."

Silence followed as they sipped their lemonade.

"I understand you stopped teaching the adult classes?"

"Yes, it was taking too much time," Cora answered.

"Was Frank getting to you?" Sylvia asked.

"Somewhat," Cora's said. "More lemonade?"

They chatted about the weather and the people Sylvia was helping, but the conversation threads grew thin. Sylvia stood to leave.

"Thank you for... Will I see you at church Sunday?"

"Yes, of course," Cora answered.

But Cora now made it a habit of dashing into church services minutes before they began and left as soon as they ended to avoid conversations. Minnie was standing guard at the exit one Sunday in September and caught her arm as she tried to leave during the final hymn. "Cora dear, come for supper tonight?"

"Sorry, Minnie, too many papers to grade."

"But you look like you could use a good meal," Minnie urged. "I've made an apple pie with the apples from Jeremiah's aunt's cousin's orchard. The one down the hill and off to the southeast and around the creek. And I have a new quilt to show you. The Lady's Aide group is working on another benefit for..."

"I'm so sorry, Minnie. Thank you, but not tonight."
Cora didn't have the energy to listen to a rambling story. She
avoided church for the next few weeks.

On a brisk fall evening, Sylvia and Cora were walking
in the woods, and Sylvia was sharing a story about a new baby
born to a young couple. When she got no response from Cora,
Sylvia stopped talking and stood still.

"Cora?"

"Huh? Yes, what were you saying?" The thought of a
woman joyfully bringing a child into the world was like a kick
in the stomach. Her heart raced, and she had trouble breathing.

"Are you sick? Please tell me what's wrong?" Sylvia
pleaded.

"I need to sit," Cora looked for a tree stump and
collapsed.

"What happened to you Cora? For the past few
months, you've withdrawn from me. I know something's
bothering you. Why won't you tell me?"

Cora looked around to see if anyone was lurking
nearby as she worked to steady her breathing. They were
alone.

"If I tell you, you'll think less of me." But she was
exhausted from keeping her secret and on the verge of tears.

"I thought you had a higher opinion of me. No matter what you've done, you know I won't judge you."

"I suppose you'll find out soon enough anyway." She looked at friend's face and knew she needed to unburden her soul. Keeping her secret had isolated her from everyone she loved.

"Find out what?"

"I'm pregnant, Sylvia."

"What? How? Who is the father?"

"Frank Desjardin." And she started to cry. She twisted a handkerchief in her hands and blotted her tears as she poured out the details of that terrible night.

Sylvia listened in horror and then reached out and pulled her into a hug.

"Why did you carry your burden alone? Why didn't you tell me? We could have gone to the police!"

"I'd have lost my job for sure since I'm not allowed to be alone with a man unless I'm teaching him. I never thought I'd get pregnant, so I kept the incident to myself."

"You mean the rape! Let's not downplay what happened to you."

"OK, yes. I was …violated. And now I'm expecting. I'll lose my job and be driven out in shame."

"Wait a minute. You're not the one at fault here."

"But how can I prove it? And I don't want to marry Frank."

"Then what will you do with the baby?"

"I don't know. If I want to raise the baby on my own, I'd need the school board's approval, and that'll never happen. Can you imagine the scandal of having a single mother teaching at a Christian mission? They'd tar and feather me!"

"What if you give the baby up for adoption?"

"Yes, I've thought of adoption. How would I love a child and not think about its conception? But how can I hide my pregnancy? What kind of example will I set for my students?"

"We need to think about you and this baby, not your students."

"But I need my job to survive. I can't see a solution. I feel as if my world is closing in on me." She covered her face with her hands.

"Speak to Mr. Desjardin. When he finds out his son did this, he'll have some leniency and let you take a leave of absence before you deliver the baby. Then you can adopt it out."

"I can't imagine facing him."

"You did nothing wrong here. It was his son who was the monster which Desjardin should understand."

"I feel ashamed. I keep trying to think back on it to see if I led Frank on in some way."

"Do you think you did?"

"No! Never! I don't like Frank, and I've kept my distance, even when I was teaching him. I suppose I was more sympathetic because of the death of his aunt."

"Sympathy is fine, but it does not excuse his behavior. Let's go to the police."

"No, I'd be branded for life."

"Then you've got to talk to Mr. Desjardin and ask him to let you take a leave of absence. It's the only way out of this."

Cora nodded. "I think you're right. But how will I get the courage to tell him?"

"How did you get the courage to tell your mother you were leaving for Kentucky nine years ago?" Sylvia smiled as she looked into her eyes. "Tap into the same well."

Cora took a shaky breath. "OK, I'll, I'll go see him tomorrow," she whispered.

"Do you want me to come with you?"

"My heart would love it, but I need to face him alone. Besides, I don't want him to think other people know what his son did. I don't know how he'll react."

"Then I'll pray for you for strength and courage."

The next day she couldn't keep her mind on lessons. The students seemed to sense she was distracted and found every opportunity to try her patience.

After school, she walked into the village to see Frank's father, Dickson. Cora knocked timidly on the door of the tidy yellow cottage.

"What a surprise, Miss Cora! Please come in." Mrs. Desjardin said.

Just as she asked if Mr. Desjardin was at home, he entered their sitting room.

"Wantin' to get the adult learner program started again?"

She wished it were that simple. "No, I'm afraid… I have a problem involving…your son," she stammered.

"Please sit," Mrs. Desjardin said and motioned to straight-back chairs facing one another in their small sitting room.

"Now what be this about?" Mr. Desjardin bellowed.

"When Frank was coming to classes, he acted inappropriately towards me. I made it clear I didn't want to be alone with him, but he followed me to my cabin several times."

"Well, he musta liked ya!" Mr. Desjardin declared.

"My teaching contract forbids me to be alone with a man, and I have honored my contract."

"Then what be the problem here?" Mr. Desjardin asked.

"The night of your sister's wake, when I was alone in your home preparing food, Frank came in. He made several advances in spite of my objections. When I tried to leave, he grabbed me and knocked me to the ground." Her voice was a whisper. "He violated me."

"Why didn't ya call for help?" Mr. Desjardin asked.

"I did! Over and over I screamed for help, but no one heard me."

"Did ya tell Frank to stop?" Mr. Desjardin asked again.

"Yes of course! I begged him to stop and fought to push him away from me."

"Is that why ya left in such a hurry?" Mrs. Desjardin said.

"Yes! I was injured body and... soul!"

To her surprise, the Desjardins were silent for a moment. She saw them exchange looks, but couldn't interpret what it meant. The school board president spoke.

"Have ya told anyone about this?"

"A close friend."

"And do ya plan to go to the police now?"

"No!" Cora said.

"Then why do ya be bringin this to us now, months after the incident." Mr. Desjardin's forehead was creased, his face was flushed.

"Because I'm expecting a child. Frank's child."

"What?" Mrs. Desjardin's hand flew to her heart. "Are ya certain it be Frank's child?"

Cora's gasped. "Yes, very certain. I've never been with another man."

"And what exactly do ya be wantin us to do 'bout this?" Mr. Desjardin's ears were purple. Sweat was bubbling on his brow.

"I was hoping to take a leave of absence once I start showing. Then I plan to adopt the baby out to a couple who can't have a child. I'd be gone about five months and then I'd come back and resume classes."

Mr. Desjardin stood. His chest puffed out with erratic breaths.

"Miss Cora, I needs time to think 'bout this. Ya come back tomorrow after yer classes, and we'll settle things then." His face was tomato red.

"Settle things? But how?"

"We'll be talkin 'bout this tomorrow. I've heard quite enough for today."

Phyllis Desjardin had gone pasty white. She sat on her chair staring ahead as Cora stood to leave.

She gladly escaped from the Desjardins home, but couldn't imagine what they were thinking. Her knees shook as she made her way to Sylvia's.

"He said we'll 'settle things' tomorrow. I have to go back," she said.

"Settle what? What an odd response."

"That's what I thought. And they expelled me out of their house like a tub of dirty bath water. Just like that! He said he'd heard enough." Cora was pacing like a caged tiger.

"Do you think they believed you?"

"I can't figure it out." She stopped and looked at Sylvia. "At first Mrs. Desjardin asked if I was sure Frank was the father. What a slap in the face."

"I'm sure they're in shock. I was yesterday when you told me."

"I'm sorry, Sylvia. I was embarrassed and humiliated. I couldn't bring myself to tell even you, my dearest friend. Forgive me?"

"Of course, I forgive you. In some ways I'm relieved. I was afraid you had some terminal disease. What happened to you is horrific, but I know you're strong enough to get through this."

"I wish I had the same confidence." Cora continued pacing. "I don't know what the next step is. I thought I had it worked out, but I feel uncertain now."

"You told them the truth and truth has to be on your side, doesn't it?" Sylvia said.

"I hope so. But this is Kentucky, in a small mission school. Do you think he'll contact the other board members and have me fired?"

"And risk having everyone discover it's his son who's responsible? I don't think it's likely. Maybe he's trying to find someone to adopt the baby."

"I'm not convinced I want to give up the child. I feel so conflicted."

"But what other option do you have? An unmarried woman with a child wouldn't be allowed to teach. Especially at a mission school!"

"Yes, I know. But to give up my child seems impossibly painful. What if I never have another child? If this is my only opportunity to be a mother?"

"I thought you didn't want to experience motherhood?"

"As I've gotten older, I've wondered if I'm missing something. Caring for other people's children is rewarding, but imagine having a child of your own? Someone to love who'll love you back unconditionally."

"I admit I've thought about that as well. At first it was a curiosity and now I think I have a longing to experience motherhood."

"You admit it then."

"Yes, but that doesn't help you. I can't see a clear way out of this."

"Perhaps Mr. Desjardin has a plan that I haven't thought of. Either way, I'll find out tomorrow."

Waiting 24 hours seemed a cruel punishment. But what choice did she have?

Chapter 7

"Alright class, open your math books and work on the next set of problems. Grade one, will you please come to the recitation table?"

Twelve squirmy children made their way to her table, but not before pinching siblings or punching friends on the way. Why did they choose this day to be at their worst? She already broke up three fights during their lunch recess.

"Hands to yourself, Henny!" The youngest Rigsby was taunting the smaller children as they walked by him.

"Tulip, please work with the second-grade children while I work with the first graders." Cora was thankful the older children lent a hand.

Chaos broke out again a few minutes later. Henny was throwing spitballs.

"Henny, to the corner. Right now!" He reluctantly lumbered over to the corner and stood looking out.

"Turn around and face the wall. Jumping beans! It's as if you all swallowed jumping beans for lunch."

The children giggled at the image.

"Please be still and work on your arithmetic problems."

Cora put her hand on her stomach not sure if it was nerves or "morning sickness" that lasted all day. She tried to focus on the problems the first graders were working on, but it was impossible to stay calm when her life was spinning out of control. She paced the front of the room for a few moments as the younger children were completing a worksheet.

"Are you alright, Miss Cora?" Sara Rigsby asked.

"Yes, Sara. Now go back to your lessons." Sara was the only student in the eighth grade. She had repeated third grade when she couldn't attend class for several months due to a bout of scarlet fever. But she survived and was a favorite of Cora's. She'd be sad to see her graduate. Then Cora realized she'd be gone for graduation. Either fired or in her confinement.

As the afternoon wore on, Cora's cheeks blazed with heat and humiliation when she thought of that night. Throwing her to the ground as if he was wrestling with an animal. She tried to focus on the classes but was relieved when the day was over, and she fled to her cabin for a few minutes to collect herself.

She splashed water on her face and pinned her hair to look as neat as possible. Even though it was warm, she wore a blouse with a high neckline. She was a dignified woman and Frank couldn't rob her of that. Although her nerves were raw, she didn't want Mr. Desjardin to think she couldn't do her job. She set out walking and once again approached the Desjardin house with what she hoped was a confident knock.

The door was thrust open by the brash Mr. Desjardin who hurried her inside and closed the door. There stood Frank, along with Pastor and Minnie Rehmann.

She looked from one to the other confused and embarrassed to see Frank again. The first time since the morning after he attacked her. Were they expecting her to ask forgiveness for making this accusation?

"Why are they here?" She asked trying to keep her voice calm. "Didn't you believe me?"

"We believes ya, Miss Cora. Unfortunately, our son has a reckless side that's needin to be tamed. We've had enough of his shiftless life and think it's 'bout time for him to be a man and do the right thing?" Mr. Desjardin said.

"But I asked for a leave of absence."

"Yes, but we ain't goin' to see our grandchild adopted to a stranger. Frank wronged ya, and we want him to make it right. Pastor Rehmann will hear yer vows. Frank can move into the school cabin, and ya can live like a family." Mr. Desjardin said.

"My contract said I couldn't be married!"

"I can work around yer contract. After nine years, the other board members will be happy to keeps ya on, even if ya is married." Mr. Desjardin said.

"I…I don't think Frank and I'd be happy together."

"Well now, you spent time alone with him when ya weren't supposed to be alone with a man. Ya musta seen something in him. What about all the time ya spent teaching him?"

"Our relationship was never a…a personal one."

"Frank, what do ya say about all this?" Mr. Desjardin glowered at his son.

"I just thought she was lonely cuz she's an old maid."

"Well she's ain't goin' to be alone now, is she?" Mr. Desjardin said.

"But I can't marry him. We barely know each other, and we share no affection." She wanted to blurt out "I don't love him," but it seemed harsh.

"No affection! Come now. It's yer word against his. We understand how things got a little out a hand. Ya got ahead of yer vows. We kin take care of it now," Mr. Desjardin said.

"Ahead of our vows? I had no intention of marrying your son. I was asking for a leave of absence." She implored Pastor and Minnie Rehmann.

Pastor Rehmann walked over to Cora and put his hands on her shoulders.

"Let me explain things to you, Miss Cora. You're in the family way, which is a violation of your contract. If you don't marry the father of your child, you'll be dismissed without a reference. We can't allow you to be a bad example to your students and others in the mission, by letting you take a leave and then coming back with some fictional story to explain your absence. The only honorable way out of this situation is to have you marry Frank. And Frank has agreed to settle down with you."

"I haven't agreed to this." Cora looked to Minnie who came forward.

"Cora, dear, this is the best solution for all involved," Minnie said.

"Not for me. This is not what I asked for."

Minnie spoke quietly. "But my dear, when you lay with Frank, you must have known you might end up with one in the oven."

"But he forced himself on me."

"No one else was there, and Frank says he'd been courting you," Minnie said.

"Courting me! It's a lie."

"That's a pretty strong word, Miss Cora! Frank is the son of the school board president. If you were violated, as you said, why didn't you go to the police?" Pastor Rehmann said.

Her head was spinning. Why didn't they understand? "I didn't go to the police because I didn't want the public shame of being violated."

"Well, Cora, now you're going to be a mother, and you don't want your child to be brought up with the shame of being fatherless do you?" Minnie asked.

"I was going to adopt the child out, as I've said," Cora implored.

Pastor Rehmann spoke gently to Cora. "In time I think you'll agree this is the best solution. God saw fit to bring this little one into the world, so you need to do what's best for your child."

Mr. Desjardin had heard enough. "Pastor are ya ready?"

No time to make any plans. To pick a bouquet of flowers or sew a new dress, not that she wanted to celebrate with flowers or lace. No time to ask her parents to attend. And no pictures to remember the day of her "shotgun wedding." Her options were to leave in disgrace with no reference or to marry her rapist.

Pastor Rehmann spoke a few words thinking he was helping the situation. "Many women first meet their husbands on their wedding day with arranged marriages or as mail-order brides. You two know each other and have spent some time together, although it may not have been ideal in the eyes of God. But now you can set aside your differences and be bound to each other till death do you part."

Right, yes. She shouldn't feel bad about her situation because it might be worse. Somehow this didn't soothe her soul.

Numbly she repeated the vows she was being forced to say. She didn't look at Frank. How had her life careened off the path? Will people be counting the months of her pregnancy? She'd be the topic of idle gossip, instead of the teacher looked upon with respect.

An awkward pause followed the lightening quick ceremony. Her life was altered again in a flash. Both times against her will. Thankfully Pastor Rehmann had not ended with the suggestion, "You may now kiss the bride." She had never kissed Frank and doubted she ever would. Kisses are reserved for those we love.

She stood looking at the Desjardins and realized she was also bound to them now. To honor them as her father-in-law and mother-in-law.

"Well that be all settled now," Mr. Desjardin was saying. "Frank ya kin move yer things into the school cabin tonight." He said this with the smugness of someone who was unloading an unwanted piece of furniture.

"Yes, welcome to the family Cora," Mrs. Desjardin held out an icy cold hand. Cora looked into her pale blue eyes and wondered if she ever showed any emotion. "Care for some sweet tea?"

"No, thank you. I need to get back to my home."

A wave of nausea hit her. She looked at Frank in a panic. He'd be invading her little cabin tonight. He leered at her as she escaped the house. Frank followed her out, and she heard the door slam. She stiffened when he tried to come close to her. He leaned in and whispered, "Don't think you can tie me down."

"So, you don't intend to keep the vows you just spoke?"

"Oh, I'll move in with ya all right. But I don't plan to alter my life. Music is what I loves and I won't let ya stop me from playin' with my band on the radio and in bars."

"I have no intention of 'tying you down,' as you say. But this baby is as much yours as it is mine and I'm hoping you'll live up to your responsibilities to the…the child." She couldn't say "our" child. "Our" sounded as if they had planned, dreamed and loved it into existence. She hoped she could love this child, but doubted she'd ever love the man who was standing in front of her.

"I sure hope ya kin cook. From the looks of ya, I be havin'my doubts."

"I don't have much time for cooking. If you recall I teach school all day. You might want to continue to have your supper with your parents."

He snorted, and she turned to leave. He grabbed her elbow. "I'm yer husband now, and I spect ya to act like it." She pulled her arm away and took off walking and was relieved he didn't follow. She needed time to think and to cry. She headed to Sylvia's cottage and poured out the bizarre details of the afternoon, ending with Frank's declaration that he didn't intend to be tied to her.

"But now you have yourself, a baby and Frank to provide for?" Sylvia asked.

"Exactly. They've added to my burdens. I think the Desjardin's just wanted to force Frank to settle down. He can't bring in much income traveling with his band. How will I live with him?" Cora asked.

"Can't he live with his parents?"

She gave Sylvia a withering look. "How will anyone believe we're married? It'd add to the gossip, which is precisely what we're trying to avoid."

"I see only one way to ease this situation."

"Tell me. I'm desperate Sylvia."

"You have to find it in your heart to forgive him, Cora."

"I'd rather leave. Maybe go back to my parent's farm."

"From what you've told me about your mother, I can't imagine she'd welcome the idea."

"Ma! How will I explain this to my parents? She'll blame me, I'm sure. Or maybe she'll be happy her homely daughter is finally married."

"You're not homely, Cora. She was wrong. Frank must have been attracted to you all the time you were trying to teach him to read."

"I don't think so. I think he wanted to hurt me. To punish me for something. I wasn't very successful at teaching him to read or write, and maybe he was embarrassed. But now I have to call him my, my, my… husband!" she whispered. The word sounded foreign.

"You have your position, Cora. You won't have to worry about income."

"Yes, and I'm thankful. I do love teaching, and I'm happy I won't have to leave the children."

"And you'll be a wonderful mother." Sylvia reached for her and pulled her into a hug.

"Thank you. And I have you as a friend which helps. What would I do without you?"

"You won't have to find out."

Cora let go of the emotions she'd been holding in and sobbed.

Mr. Desjardin helped Frank move his bed into Cora's cabin. She insisted he place it just inside the door, far from her bed. She saw the two men exchange looks when she made the request. Her eyes were still red from crying, but she held her head high, determined to hold onto any measure of independence.

"There ya be, Frank. All set now," Mr. Desjardin said as he prepared to leave. "I guess this be yer honeymoon night," he said as he winked at Frank.

Cora stiffened. "Goodnight, Mr. Desjardin."

"Ya can call me Pa now, seein as how ya be my daughter-in-law."

She was pleased Frank ate supper at his folk's, so their evening together was shortened.

She crouched on her chair like a cat ready to spring. As she tried to read a novel, Frank sat on his bed and picked up his guitar. He shook out a cigarette and lit it. Within minutes the stuffy cabin was filled with the acrid smell of smoke. She didn't mind pipe smoke but found his cigarettes irritated her lungs. But she said nothing, afraid to anger him. She was determined to keep him at a distance and to show her disdain for the arrangement. His presence grated on her nerves, but she knew she couldn't lash out at him.

When it was dark, Cora took her nightgown and went outside to change in the outhouse. When she came back into the house, Frank looked surprised.

"Ya don't have to dress in the outhouse. We be married now, remember."

"This is what I prefer."

"Well now, I prefer we acts like married folks, ifin you know what I means," Frank said as he walked closer to her.

Cora folded her hands across her chest. She knew what he was capable of and didn't want to provoke him.

"I don't feel very well, so I'm heading to bed now. I have to get up early to teach, so goodnight." Cora headed to her bed and dove under the covers, heart pounding. She pretended to sleep and eventually heard Frank get into his bed. She fell into a fitful sleep.

When Cora awoke, Frank was still fast asleep. To her relief, he stayed asleep while she dressed and fixed her breakfast. Then slipped out unnoticed to begin the first day as Mrs. Frank Desjardin.

That evening, Frank came in after having supper with his parents again and Cora was thankful for a few quiet hours. But they didn't last.

"Hey there, Miss Cora. You been waitin on me?" He sneered and walked close to her.

Cora caught a whiff of alcohol and cigarettes.

Chapter 8

"No, I'm enjoying my book," Cora said and backed up when Frank came toward her.

"Well I has an idea of what we be enjoyin together," Frank said and moved to grab her.

"You've been drinking," Cora sidestepped him.

"Why is it your concern?"

"It's illegal. If you get arrested for drinking, it will reflect badly on me, since we are now joined."

"Is that all ya be worryin about? Your job? Ya should be worried bout pleasing yer husband." Frank reached for her, but Cora slipped out of his hands.

"I'm also worried about the safety of the baby. Please go to bed and sleep off the alcohol."

"Oh, I'll sleep it off. But not before we has us some fun."

"Fun! Is that what you call it? It certainly wasn't fun last time." Cora was inching her way toward the door, hoping to escape, but Frank grabbed her.

"Please don't do this," she begged, but he was determined.

"I has a right now, as yer husband," he said as he clawed at her clothes.

"Don't be an animal. And don't tear my blouse." Defeated she unbuttoned her blouse as he gripped her arms.

"Well now, that's better," Frank said.

"Maybe for you. I don't want to do this."

"Well now, ya said the vows."

"I was forced to. Please go to sleep." She hoped to reason with him.

"Ya think ya kin boss me around, teacher-lady. Well, I'm the boss now," he said as he pinned her on her bed.

He forced her to have sex, but this time thankfully she wasn't thrown to the floor. He fell asleep immediately on top of her, and she had to wake him to get him off. In his drunken stupor he wouldn't leave her bed, so she crept out and slept in his. Feeling dirty and humiliated, she lay awake wondering what she had done to deserve this horrendous turn of events. Exhausted, she left in the morning to face a room full of children and hoped she had the energy to teach them.

Frank wasn't around when she got home from school. She was jumpy waiting to see if he'd come in drunk and demand a repeat of the night before. But he didn't come home at all.

"He's been gone now for three nights! It's such a relief," Cora told Sylvia who stopped by nearly a week after the wedding.

"Do you think something's happened to him?" Sylvia asked.

"I don't know, and I don't care."

"So, things aren't any better?"

"Better? How can they be? I don't like him. I know I'm supposed to look for the good in everyone, but it's difficult to see it through his alcohol."

"Alcohol? But what about prohibition?"

"He apparently knows someone who's selling him moonshine."

"Do you know who it is?"

"No! I try to stay out of his way as much as possible."

"Do you think you should find out and go to the police?"

"I don't want any more trouble. Going to the police may backfire. They may be in on it!"

"You might be right."

"And if Frank is difficult now, imagine his rage if I turned him in for buying moonshine?"

"I see your point, "Sylvia said.

"How did this happen? Six months ago, I was happy, and now I'm living a nightmare."

Sylvia hugged her. "I can't think of anything to say to make this any better, except …"

"Try to see the good in him. I know. But what if there isn't any good in him?"

"Maybe fatherhood will change him."

Cora looked skeptical.

"It might happen. Maybe he's one of those men who have trouble showing affection, except to a child."

Cora smiled. "Sylvia. Always looking on the bright side. Let's hope I don't kill him before we get a chance to find out."

On a cool October evening several days later, Cora was just taking a loaf of bread out of her wood-burning oven when Frank walked back into the cabin. Cora kept quiet while she watched him put his guitar case on his bed.

"Smells good in here." He said.

"Fresh bread," Cora responded.

"You makes yer bread?"

"I was a farm girl. It's what we do."

Then he walked over to her with his hand outstretched.

"Here. Take it!"

"Take what?" Cora asked.

"Some money I earned whiles on tour."

"On tour?"

"Yah. I be with my band. I told ya I be a musician. So heres some money to hep with expenses – food and stuff."

"Oh! Yes, this will help." Cora accepted the money.

"What! Did ya think ya be the only one who can earn anything?"

"No, I didn't know where you were."

"Did ya miss me?"

Cora wasn't sure how to answer without lying. She just looked at him.

"I ain't a monster, ya know," Frank said.

Cora remained silent, afraid anything she said might send him into a rage.

"I ain't been drinkin, Cora. Not yet anyways," he said and started to laugh.

"Why don't you play me a song on your guitar? I've never heard you sing by yourself," Cora said trying to distract him.

"I kept inviting ya to come and hear us."

"I'm sorry. I couldn't go before, but I'm here now."

Frank took out his guitar and sang a simple folk song. To her surprise, he had a rich melodic voice.

"Very nice," she said when he finished, and he smiled and launched into another song.

They passed a pleasant evening together. When it was time for bed, Cora started to take her nightgown with her to the outhouse to change. Frank stopped her.

"I'll head outside sos ya can change in here."

"Thank you!" Cora said, amazed at the change in his personality. She was grateful for a glimpse of kindness.

The next evening, Frank came home drunk and insisted they have sex again. When Cora resisted, he barred his teeth at her and said, "Fine, I'll find someone who wants to be with me." He stormed out and didn't return for five days.

Like the ebb and flow of a turbulent ocean, the pattern repeated itself. When Frank was sober, life was manageable. When he drank, he was demanding and belligerent. As her belly grew, she convinced him the marital act might hurt the baby, so he stopped asking. She didn't know how long she could avoid him after the baby was born. Was she wrong in the eyes of God? Now and then she allowed herself to think about divorce but knew the Bible spoke against it. But did God want her to stay with a man she deplored?

Frank was away the day she went into labor. Sylvia and Cora were taking a quiet stroll in the woods enjoying a warm April day when she felt the first stabs of pain. Sylvia hurried Cora back to her cabin and set off to fetch Anna, the area's midwife. Sylvia stayed with her through the night and just before daylight, Cora delivered a little girl into the world.

"Dark hair like her ma," Anna said as she placed the baby, wrapped in a flannel blanket, in Cora's arms.

Cora looked at her tiny fingers and rosy mouth. "So, this is what I've been missing. I didn't realize I could love another the way I already love her."

Sylvia smiled at them. Was there a touch of sadness in her eyes? Cora wondered.

"I'm not certain I'm cut out for motherhood. But today my heart is full for you and your new daughter," Sylvia said.

"I'll check on you later in the morning. Try to get some rest." Anna gathered her medical bag and left.

Sylvia brushed the baby's cheek. "So soft and beautiful, Cora. Have you thought of a name?"

"I haven't settled on one. I was hoping Frank would want to share an opinion of what we call her. But I'm never certain what he thinks."

Sylvia nodded in understanding. She tidied the cabin and brought Cora a bowl of steaming oatmeal, which she devoured while Sylvia held the tiny bundle.

"I'm so happy to see her. Somehow I thought she might not be right after the way she was…conceived."

"She's perfect, Cora. Just the way God intended her to be."

"I thought I'd resent her, but I just feel this overwhelming urge to care for her."

"God's love is pouring through you," Sylvia said and then yawned from the long night.

"Sylvia, we'll be fine. Go home and get some sleep."

"If you're sure. I'll let you get to know each other."

Frank came home the next evening. When he walked into the cabin and saw Cora sitting on the bed holding a tiny one, he walked hesitantly toward them. "So, what'd ya have?"

"A girl." Cora pulled the blanket away from her face. "I thought we could name her Ruby Jane, after my grandmother. Unless you mind."

"I don't mind. She be yers."

"She's ours, Frank. And she is perfect."

Frank nodded and then bent near the bed to get a closer look.

"Want to hold her?"

"Not till she be older. I don't want to break her."

They endured an awkward silence looking at this new life that caused so much chaos. Frank walked out of the cabin without a word.

Was he was leaving for a few days or a few hours? He was so moody and unpredictable, she thought.

Within minutes, Frank came back, this time carrying a bouquet of wildflowers. He said nothing as he filled a jar with water and plunked the flowers into it. Then he looked at her. "Fer you."

"Thank you. They're beautiful. Very thoughtful."

"I don't want ya to think I be a monster. What I did wasn't right. We've got this 'en now, and I don't want ya to hate me."

She looked at Ruby, uncomfortable hearing Frank speak of the attack. It wasn't quite an apology, but it was a start. A change in their relationship? Maybe.

School was canceled for a week to allow her time to get her strength back. Cora asked the Desjardins if they would look after Ruby while she taught, but Mrs. Desjardin said, "A baby should be with her mother."

She brought Ruby to school in a small box each day and set her in a corner of the room.

"Whoever completes their assignments first can hold Ruby," she told the class. It became a competition to see who got the most time to hold the newborn. By the end of May, she was glad for the summer break but also knew who to call on to watch Ruby if she needed a sitter. Little Sara had grown into a responsible young lady and a trusted baby watcher.

"Daddy's home," Cora said one August night. Ruby brightened and turned to the door to see her father. Frank's band was in more demand during the summer, but when he was home, he began to pay more attention to Ruby.

He put out his hands and Ruby snuggled into his arms. "I've missed my little Ruby," he said as he looked into her wide eyes. "I dedicated a song to ya last night." Ruby rewarded him with a smile and a "coo," and Cora wondered if she had judged him too harshly. As Frank played with Ruby, Cora finished supper preparations. Ever since Ruby was born, he ate supper at the cabin with Cora on nights he was home.

"And what has our farm girl prepared tonight?"

"Ham and potato soup. An Iowa favorite."

Frank nodded approvingly, and they ate supper in peace. He was sober, which saved the evening. It did her heart good to see he was a loving father.

Later, Mr. Desjardin stopped by the cabin.

"We were wonderin if y'all would like to come for dinner Sunday noon. Ma wants to be seein more a her grandchild."

Cora and Frank looked at each other and then nodded.

"Sure Pa. That'd be great." Frank said.

Mr. Desjardin held Ruby for a few minutes before leaving in his carriage.

Frank attended church services Sunday morning with Cora and Ruby. First time since their wedding.

Together they passed Ruby back and forth to keep her quiet during the service. Sylvia sat on the other side of Cora and helped with the rocking and swaying.

"Let me hold my granddaughter," Mr. Desjardin said when they arrived for dinner. When Cora told stories of the school children, he changed the subject. The meal revolved around Ruby.

"We never had a daughter, so little Ruby be especially precious," Mrs. Desjardin said.

But still, they never volunteered to watch Ruby, which frustrated Cora.

As they were leaving, Mrs. Desjardin took Cora aside, "Y'all look so happy together. I hope ya has learned to perform yer wifely duties. Now come back and see us real soon."

Monday afternoon Sylvia popped in for a report on the dinner.

"It was as if I was the broodmare who gave them their first grandchild. And she said we look happy together. Is she blind?

"She sees what she wants to see."

"When she asked if I've learned to perform my wifely duties, I wanted to tell her I get beaten if I refuse her precious son."

"Is it true?"

"Yes, when Frank drinks. He's calmer now with Ruby around, but he still makes life miserable for me. I've never seen him be impatient with her, so I don't think she's in danger."

"A decent father, but a horrible husband. He hasn't changed."

"Pretty well sums it up. I'm never at ease when he's around. His moods change with the wind. I give in to his demands, so he doesn't hurt me. But I don't love him."

"How could you? Love is meant to be given freely, not demanded."

"You say as if you know something about love," Cora said studying Sylvia.

"You know me too well. A new missionary named Harry has asked to spend time with me."

"Sylvia! When were you going to tell me?"

"It's all very new. I've just started keeping company with him."

"I'm so pleased!"

"What a relief. I wasn't sure what your reaction would be, given your situation."

"Happiness is all I want for you. More than anyone, you deserve it."

"Thank you, Cora. It's all I want for you as well."

Cora wasn't sure she'd ever be completely happy again. But she said nothing.

Ruby's first year sped by and Cora wanted to celebrate the milestone with a special birthday dinner. Days before the big day, she reminded Frank of the birthday hoping they'd enjoy their daughter together without any alcohol or arguments.

Because Ruby's birthday fell on a school day, Cora asked her eighth-grader, Sara, to look after the tot while Cora baked a cake, roasted a chicken and made new potatoes with garden fresh green beans.

"You be havin company, Miss Cora?" Sara asked.

"No, just her Daddy and me."

But Frank never arrived. Cora and Ruby ate alone. The quiet was eventually broken by a knock.

"Hope I'm not interrupting," Sylvia said.

"Come in. It's just Ruby and me. Frank didn't come home."

"Da da?" Ruby looked at Cora quizzically.

"Sorry baby, no Daddy tonight. But Auntie Sylvia is here."

"Just a small gift for my favorite toddler." Sylvia handed Ruby a small package. With a bit of help, Ruby pulled the wrapping away to reveal a small brown teddy bear.

"Bear," Cora coached.

"Bear," Ruby repeated, and Sylvia swooped her into a hug.

"I'm so glad you're here to help us eat this cake," Cora said. "We took the rest of our chicken dinner to the Rigsby's when Frank didn't come home."

"Out with his band?"

"Who knows? Either playing in a bar or meeting with other women."

"You don't care?" Sylvia asked.

"I'm happy when he brings home a few dollars."

"But it doesn't bother you when he's with other women?" Sylvia whispered as if Ruby understood.

"Of course, it bothers me, but I have no say in his behavior. And if I voice my disgust, it's only worse for me. I'm just trying to survive this. For tonight, let's enjoy Ruby's birthday and be glad he's not here."

The pattern of their relationship continued with Frank disappearing for days and then coming home, often drunk.

When he'd been drinking, he demanded he and Cora have marital relations. If she refused, he either forced her or left in a furry claiming he had other women to satisfy his needs.

By late summer Cora realized she was expecting again.

Helen came into the world on a cold February morning in 1924. The first thing Cora noticed was the reddish hair, like her father's. Adding another tiny bed to their crowded cabin was a struggle, but Frank was often gone, which helped to ease the situation…in so many ways.

Soon after Ruby's second birthday, Cora and the girls were at Sunday services. Cora was sporting a purple bruise on her cheek but decided not to hide because of it. She needed the support of friends and hoped if the Desjardins saw her bruises, they'd help Frank get sober.

Sylvia noticed it and asked about it after the service as they stood outside in the warm spring air.

"I just have to endure him," She confided holding tiny Helen. Ruby was scampering around in the grass at her feet. "Somehow this is my cross to bear. He's not always violent. Just when he's been drinking and then he punishes me for being alive."

"But eventually he'll get caught buying alcohol."

Cora handed Helen to Sylvia and lifted Ruby. She motioned to Sylvia to follow her away from the listening ears of others.

"Frank thinks prohibition doesn't apply to him," She said, lowering her voice to a whisper.

"Have you found out where he gets it?" Sylvia whispered back.

"I still have no idea. He's on the road half the time with his band. I suppose they have access to bootleggers. When I ask him about it, he shuts me out. Says it's none of my business."

"Can't you get him to stop? What if he is arrested?"

"You know I don't control anything about him! And if he gets arrested, it serves him right! I don't want the girls to have a jailed father, but right now they have one with a drinking problem. He's usually patient around them, but how long will it last?"

As they stood talking at the edge of the woods, she noticed a few men standing nearby. Instead of talking to each other, she realized they were frozen like statues, listening to her conversation. She motioned to Sylvia with her eyes, changed the subject and together they scurried to Cora's cabin.

Chapter 9

"Were those men spying on us?" Sylvia asked once inside Cora's cabin.

"I have no idea. Frank has so many secrets I'm almost afraid to discover what's going on with him. It sets my nerves on edge."

"Well, you're safe now. But lock the door when I leave."

On a steamy July night, Cora decided to take a cool bath once her girls were asleep. It had been a long day taking care of the girls alone. She pumped several pails of water from the outside well, warmed it a bit in large pots on the cook stove and then poured it into her small metal tub. She felt her muscles relax a bit, in spite of the cramped space.

Footsteps? Just rustling leaves, she told herself. She sat still. Listened. Held her breath. She again heard movement outside. A fox? Or coyote?

She hurried out and dressed in her cotton nightshirt. She cracked open her door. "Frank?" She whispered. No answer. She took one step outside. "Frank?" Darkness.

The hair on the back of her neck prickled. She shivered. Then rushed inside and relocked the door.

"Be calm. All is secure," she told herself.

She read by candlelight for a few minutes trying to relax. Then glanced at her two sleeping daughters. So peaceful and beautiful. Overwhelming love and gratitude filled her, even if her marriage was flawed.

Occasionally she wished Frank was there for protection. But that made her feel weak and vulnerable, qualities she detested. She was strong and wouldn't let fear rule. Her eyes grew heavy when she was able to still her mind. She blew out the candle and fell asleep.

She soon dreamed she was roasting in an oven.

Smoke and heat filled her lungs and she bolted upright. Her head was fuzzy. Did she blow out the candle? Yes. Was there a fire in the cook stove? No. Shaking off sleep, she realized the cabin was ablaze and not from the kitchen. The wall next to their bed was smoking and flames were creeping near.

Cora snatched up her sleeping daughters and rushed outside in bare feet, carrying one on each hip.

She gasped for air. "Help!"

As she hurried across the dirt road, she called out and surveyed the landscape frantically.

Two men dressed in dark clothing ran up the hill behind her cabin. Why were they running away? The cabin was alive with flames. Were they going to bring water?

"Fire," she shouted. "Fire," She screamed again, and Ruby and Helen started wailing. That'll wake someone, she hoped. "Help! Bring water!" She kept a firm grip on both girls. This can't be happening!

Neighbors came running with pails of water, but not enough to create a bucket brigade.

Cora held her daughters and stared in horror as flames consumed their home. Ruby screamed as she watched the blaze flare. "Fire, Mama!"

"Yes, dear, but we are safe." Embers crackled and crashed as the roof caved in. Ashes floated away buoyed by wind and carried Cora's sense of security with them.

Cora wanted to shout, "Is this what hell looks like, Lord?" But didn't. She was shaking all over, in spite of the heat. She wanted to collapse but knew her girls needed comforting. And then in the dark, a shawl was thrown over Cora's shoulders, and Sylvia pulled them all into her arms. The dam of tears burst. Cora wordlessly handed Helen to Sylvia, and they moved a safer distance away. They sank to the ground and rocked Ruby and Helen in an instinctive act to calm all four of them.

Sylvia looked at her with questioning eyes. "What happened?"

"I awoke and the cabin was on fire – and not from the kitchen. I saw two men running away as we escaped."

Sylvia shuddered. "Thank God you're alive. That's what matters."

"Yes, but how did this happen? And why?" Cora felt exposed. And vulnerable. All those years as a single woman living alone, she felt safe. But no more.

By the time the volunteer fire force arrived with a small tanker truck, nothing was left but a few burning embers. They escaped with nothing more than their night clothes. Fire, smoke or water destroyed everything else. But, yes, they were alive. She repeated it over and over as she clung to Ruby and kissed her feverish cheeks. Helen quieted in Sylvia's arms.

A few neighbor women offered quilted blankets for the girls, which she gratefully accepted. But now what? As they sat on the clammy grass, wrapped in blankets from the shock, she realized nothing prepared her for this.

When firefighters extinguished the blaze, Harold Murphy, one of the volunteers, pointed to his horse and buggy.

"May I drive ya to yer in-laws, Miss Cora?" he offered.

She wanted to go to Sylvia's cabin but knew she didn't have room for three more.

"Yes, thank you." She hugged Sylvia, and they walked to his buggy.

Harold handed the girls to her one at a time after she climbed into the small buggy. Helen was wide awake now and howling. The gentle swaying in the short buggy ride helped quiet her. Cora couldn't stop kissing them. How close she came to losing them forever. Smoke and grit smudged their faces but didn't harm a hair on their heads. Was God looking out for them after all?

When the buggy stopped, Harold took Ruby as she climbed out with Helen.

Her father-in-law dragged open his front door after she pounded on it for several minutes.

"What the devil's goin' on?" He thundered. Cora was still too shaken to speak.

"Their cabin done burned to the ground tonight," Harold explained.

Mrs. Desjardin appeared in her nightgown behind her husband. "Oh, my! Did ya be leavin somethin on the stove?"

"No, I checked it before I slept."

"The fire was started outside of that there cabin. We be knowin more after an investigation in the light a day. For now, Miss Cora and these here girls needs a safe place to stay."

Ruby started to whimper again.

"Why yes, a course," Mrs. Desjardin said backing away from the door and letting them in. "But for how long?"

Cora's shoulders ached. "Mrs. Desjardin, may we speak about this in private? The girls and I got out safely, and I don't want to alarm them any further. Please let me put the girls to bed, and we can discuss this tomorrow?"

"But where be Frank?" she asked as she led them to Frank's old bedroom.

"On the road with his band. I have no idea when he'll return." Cora met her stare. Yes, this was the arrangement of their marriage. Frank came and went as he pleased. But Cora knew she didn't want to hear this. No one wants to believe the worst about their children, even if it's true. Cora was the main supporter, and now the little they owned was lost.

"I'll let ya get them settled. Would y'all like a cup a warm milk for my precious Ruby?"

"Yes, thank you. And a basin of water, so I can wash the soot off their faces. We'll all need baths tomorrow."

Ruby took a few swallows of milk. She was wide-eyed and looked at her mama with confusion. Cora couldn't answer the questions she saw in her sweet expression. Her cheeks were flaming with wispy curls plastered to her temple. She ran the warm washcloth over her face. Innocent brown eyes watched Cora intently.

Next Cora washed Helen's face and wondered at the differences in them. She never knew she could love anyone as much as she loved these two.

She smiled to reassure Ruby and sat her on the bed close to her, with one arm around her while she nursed Helen. Thank goodness Helen was too tiny to understand the danger they escaped. When Helen succumbed to sleep, she laid her on the bed.

Then she scooped up Ruby who was still staring ahead in a trance-like state. She pulled her close and took deep breaths not to give into the tears streaming down her cheeks. She almost lost her daughters tonight! The cruel chant played over and over in her brain. Ruby smelled like burning timbers, and when Cora realized how close they came to being burned alive, she shuddered. Ruby pulled back and looked into her eyes. "Fire, Mama?"

"Yes, my love. But it's all done now. No fire here. You're safe. All done." She swiped her tears and rocked her toddler back and forth trying to convince herself she spoke the truth. Was it all done? Were they safe? She prayed quietly aloud and then sang to Ruby until she felt her shoulders relax and her arms swing free. She laid her next to Helen and squeezed in beside them. She needed to hear their squeaky breaths and to sense the rhythm of sleep. Even if she didn't sleep. They both breathed in the acrid smoke. Were their tiny lungs damaged?

But they were safe now. Weren't they? Long after both girls were asleep beside her on Frank's childhood bed, the questions wouldn't let her rest. Did those men she saw running away try to kill them? If so, why? Was Frank the target? Were they the same men she saw spying on Sylvia and her after church? Was Frank involved in some sinister activity?

Sleep came in fits and starts, mixed with horrifying images of fire and babies crying for her and not being able to reach them. At dawn, she realized it was safer to stay awake. She sat on her bed stewing and praying until the girls awoke.

She needed to get word to Frank somehow. Maybe he'd hear of the fire.

When she went into the sitting area, her mother-in-law showed her several piles of clothes and even a few pairs of shoes brought over by area women. Their kindness touched her. Cora bathed the girls and then herself to rid them of the smoky aftermath and found lightweight dresses for the warm day.

They crowded around the table for oatmeal, although Cora's appetite was not yet awake. After grace, they ate in silence, none of them knowing what to say. She was almost relieved when a knock at the door put an end to the awkward quiet.

"Excuse me, folks," Sheriff Patterson said as he took off his hard-brimmed hat, "I needs to ask Miss Cora a few questions 'bout what she saw or heard last night."

They moved into their adjoining sitting room, and Sheriff Patterson folded his large frame onto a small wooden chair. Cora clutched Helen while Ruby played beside her on the floor.

Frank's parents stayed with her while she answered questions. Cora told him about what she heard before she went to sleep and what she saw when she escaped.

"They were shadows, really of two men who ran away as I called for help," Cora said.

"There be strong evidence that the fire were set." The sheriff's eyes pierced Cora's soul. A tremor went through her clear to her bones. No doubt now. Someone wanted them dead.

"Miss Cora, do ya have any enemies?"

"Enemies? As the school teacher at a Christian Mission, I try to keep relationships on an even course. I can't think of anyone who was angry with me."

"Was someone angry about a teaching method? Or a grade their child received?" He asked.

"Would a quarrel about a teaching method be enough to want me dead? No, that seems absurd. And I can't think of any parents who have been unhappy with me."

Mr. Desjardin spoke. "I be the school board president. Miss Cora's been a fine upstanding teacher for the better part a 12 years."

Cora smiled a bit, grateful for his support.

"Where be yer husband last night before the fire broke out?" Patterson's dark brown eyes seemed to burn into her as if he knew the shame of her marriage.

She met his stare. "My husband….Frank, plays in a band and he is out of town now performing."

"When did he leave town?"

"Three days ago."

"Where can he be reached?"

"I don't know," Cora replied.

"Ya don't know what town yer husband be playing in?"

"No, I'm sorry. Frank doesn't share information with me?"

"Don't share it? He be yer lawfully married husband, correct?"

"Yes, we were married by an ordained minister. But Frank is…independent."

"Did ya and yer husband be havin a fight before he left town?" His eyes seemed to search for a hidden truth. If she looked away, he'd think she was hiding something, but she feared what he might see in her eyes if she continued to hold his gaze.

"I don't remember." She looked at Helen playing on the floor.

"Does yer husband have a temper?" As he asked this question, the sheriff reached out and turned Cora's face to get a better look at the bruises on her cheek and neck.

"He's not perfect. Why are you asking about him? What does this have to do with the fire?"

"We be havin to look at all the possible suspects. Perhaps yer husband wanted outta his independent marriage?"

Mrs. Desjardin gasped, and Mr. Desjardin lumbered to his feet, crashing his china coffee cup to the ground.

"Now wait just a doggone minute. Our son ain't perfect, but he loves them daughters a his and never'd do nothin to hurt 'em."

"Alls we needs to do to clear yer son is to find his whereabouts last night, Mr. Desjardin. Now, does yer son have any enemies ya knows about?" The sheriff looked from one to the other. They shook their heads. "Let me know as soon as he returns. He be needin at least two peoples to swear to where he be last night. Let's hope he be comin home in a day or two. Abandoning his family would not be lookin good to a jury." He put his hat on and ducked out the front door.

"Outrageous. Frank'd never hurt anyone!" Mr. Desjardin was pacing in the small sitting room.

Although Cora had fresh proof that Frank did hurt her, in her heart, she couldn't imagine him starting a fire. She knew he loved his daughters. Especially Ruby now she was old enough to talk. But she knew little about his activities and associates.

"The Sheriff is doing his job, looking at every possibility. Let's hope Frank is home soon so we can clear him and they can move on with the investigation. I agree Frank would never hurt Ruby or Helen," Cora said.

"But who did this?" Mrs. Desjardin's eyes were wild.

"Who? And Why?" The questions rang in Cora's mind.

They sat in silence as Cora tried to figure out where Frank might be. All possible clues vanished in the fire. Her head was pounding, and a crushing sense of despair smothered her. She read worry on her in-law's faces.

"I wonder if you might watch the girls while I go for a short stretch. I didn't sleep much, and the fresh air might revive me."

"Ya won't be gone long, will ya? Almost time for Helen to nurse." Mrs. Desjardin said as she took the baby from Cora.

"No, just a short walk."

She strode to the end of their street and crossed to the wooded area to take shelter in the canopy of trees. The shade provided a respite from the unrelenting sun. She needed to think without seeing faces who wanted more from her than she was capable of giving. She didn't know what to do. How was she expected to produce a plan when her life had been zigzagging out of control? Where was God?

And more urgently – where was her husband?

When the girls napped in the afternoon, Cora asked for a carriage ride into town to send her parents a telegram in case they heard about the fire. She needed the comfort of her Pa and longed to see him.

Two endless days later Frank burst into his parent's home. "What happened to our place, Cora?" He snarled. "Ya be leavin candles burning?"

"No! Someone burned it to the ground. The girls and I barely escaped."

"Daddy," Ruby said as she rushed to his arms. He scooped her up and hugged and kissed her as Cora filled him in on the fire and the investigation. His shock and genuine concern was a relief. Perhaps he wasn't involved.

"I'll go see the sheriff and answer his questions. I need to clear my name sos they kin find them butchers who nearly killed my girls."

Cora was surprised and relieved to see him almost acting like a responsible adult, but then he had to know his lifestyle didn't put him in a favorable light to most people, especially law officers. She wondered what his alibi was.

Frank came back a few hours later and told them the sheriff cleared him, but asked him to stay in town until the investigation was complete.

"How long will it take?" Mrs. Desjardin gasped.

"I don't know Ma, but where ya expect us to go?" Frank asked.

The snug home had only two bedrooms.

"Can't you be findin a place to rent in town? We don't have enough to feed y'all."

"We just lost everything we have, Ma. Beds, clothes, furniture, pots. Everything!"

"Well, all that time ya be out playin with yer band, ya musta made some good money."

"Not much," Frank said.

"Cora, what about yer salary?"

"I don't get paid in the summer or the long winter break. I save a little bit from each of my eight teaching months to get me through."

"Well there now, tap into yer savins," Mrs. Desjardin said.

"We can help with the food expenses, but I don't have enough to pay rent anywhere or to buy furniture. My cabin came with my teaching position."

Mr. Desjardin stood. "Enough! No more of this. We just has to put up with things." He stormed out of the house, slamming the door, which woke Helen. Cora was thankful for a reason to end the discussion and take the girls outside.

Days stretched into a week as they waited for news of the investigation. Cora felt as if she was tiptoeing around trying not to step on raw nerves. Her only pleasure was playing with her daughters, but her suspicion that Frank was continuing to buy illegal whiskey dampened even that.

When Sylvia arrived at the door one morning, Cora was overjoyed. "Let's look for blackberries," Cora said, lifting Ruby. "Helen's napping."

"How are you surviving?" Sylvia whispered when they were out of earshot.

"Barely. The tension is thick. No one has any privacy. My mother-in-law is constantly worrying about money. And Frank is here most of the time since the sheriff said he couldn't leave town until the investigation is over."

"Do they suspect him?"

"Not of setting the fire, but I wonder if he's connected in some way to the men who did this."

"Has he stopped drinking?"

"Not completely. Of course, he doesn't want his parents to know, so he drinks after they turn in for the night. But at least he's keeping his temper in check – most of the time."

"Will the mission rebuild the cabin?"

"Not that I've heard. There isn't money. And without it, my salary won't provide enough to rent anywhere."

"Cora, what will you do? You can't stay with your in-laws!"

"No, not much longer if I want to keep what's left of my sanity." She stopped and took a deep breath. "Sylvia, I don't know how to tell you this."

Chapter 10

"Tell me what?" Sylvia asked.

"I've written to my parents and asked them if we might stay with them for a while. At least we have more room on the farm." She fought back the tears.

"Oh, Cora! What a difficult cross this has been." Sylvia struggled not to cry.

"But I don't want to leave you. You're the one person I trust."

"I don't want you to go, but you have to keep your family safe."

"And even without the threat of the arsonists, we have nowhere to live without the school cabin. I've gone over and over it, and I cannot see another way out."

"Mama cry?" Ruby said looking at Cora.

Cora quickly wiped away the tears. "Mama's fine baby.

"What do you think your Ma will say?"

"I'm hoping she's mellowed after all these years. She does write occasionally. And I miss my father. But I hate to leave you."

"Let's not worry about it until we have to," Sylvia said. "For now, you're here. Let's enjoy this time together."

"Always the optimist."

Sheriff Patterson arrived at the Desjardins' home one sweltering afternoon a few weeks later. Frank, Cora and the elder Desjardins sat in the stifling sitting room fanning themselves, cloaked in perspiration. Windows were open, and a small ceiling fan whirred like a cricket. The Sheriff lowered his voice to deliver the news as if spies might be circling outside. The wooden chair groaned under his weight as he leaned closer with the horrifying information.

"These two characters were makin moonshine, and we questioned them bout it a week before that fire at yer cabin. We didn't have enough evidence to get a search warrant, but they knew we'd be workin on it. In anger, they set fire to yer home, hoping to silence you, Miss Cora. Apparently, they thought ya had turned their names into the authorities."

"They were after me? I didn't know anything about them. Why me?"

"Ya have a reputation as the law-abiding Christian teacher. I don't know if they wanted to kill ya, Miss Cora, but they sure did want to scare ya."

"They succeeded, and they nearly killed my girls and me!"

"I told em yer not our informant, but I don't know if they believed me."

"How long will they be in jail now?" Cora was feeling less secure by the moment.

"It depends on many things. But they can bond outta jail while awaitin the trial."

"But what be their charges?" Mr. Desjardin asked.

"Probably arson, and moonshining. Attempted murder maybe."

"How long will they be in prison if they're convicted?" Cora asked.

"The punishment varies. I can't give ya a set answer. For now, yer safe. But I'll let ya know if they bond outta jail. I don't mean to frighten ya, Miss Cora, but ya need to know the facts."

"Thank you for telling me so quickly. I…I do appreciate knowing the truth of the situation, as shocking as it is." Cora's hand was over her heart and she could feel it beating wildly.

Sheriff Patterson stood and nodded. Job done. He held out a hand to shake Mr. Desjardin's and then turned to Frank.

"Yer all clear now, free to leave town." He popped his brimmed hat on and headed out.

Cora turned to face the other three. "I don't feel safe here. What if those men get out of jail and try to hurt us again?"

Mrs. Desjardin opened her hand-held fan. "Dear heaven, ya mean they might burn down my home too?"

"It's possible if they're set on killing me." It was extreme, but wasn't that what the sheriff just told them?

"They nearly killed my grandbabies," Mrs. Desjardin said fanning herself wildly.

"Let's not be gettin excited. For now, they be in jail. I kin get us a watchdog and keep him outside at night," Mr. Desjardin said.

"Frank?" Cora turned to him for his reaction. His silence was unnerving.

"We might hafta move somewhere. Me, you and the girls." Frank did seem to grasp the gravity of the situation.

"Yes, but my job is here, and we need my salary."

"Surely ya might find another teaching position…with a cabin," Mrs. Desjardin said.

"At a mission, perhaps. But I don't have proper teacher's training from a college." She knew of a solution, but not one that sat comfortably with her. She had been mulling it over for days. "I do have one idea," Cora said. "I've had a letter from my parents. They'd like us to come back to Iowa and stay with them until we get things sorted."

"Iowa?" Frank sounded as if it were a foreign country. "On a farm?"

"Yes, they live on a farm and are getting older and may appreciate help with the farm."

"I ain't no farmer." Frank crossed his arms.

"Now listen here, son. Ya need to do what be best for yer family. Farm work might toughen ya some." Mr. Desjardin was standing now, looming over them with his height and his will.

"Yes, but I don't want little Ruby and Helen to grow up far away. I'll never see em," Mrs. Desjardin said.

"This isn't easy for any of us, but we need to consider their offer," Cora said.

Later, after Cora put the girls to bed, she asked Frank to walk with her so they could speak in private.

"Tell me why you don't want to go to Iowa?"

"I told ya. I don't want to be stuck in the middle of a farm."

"But we're stuck here now in your parent's home. All crowded into one bedroom!"

"So, ya be wantin us crammed into your parents farm?"

"We'd have more room. They have two extra bedrooms and plenty of room for the girls to play outside. And they'd learn about animals."

"And what bout me? My band be here."

"But you hardly ever play together."

"What's that supposed to mean?"

"You leave for days but rarely bring home any money. If you're playing, where's the pay?"

"None of yer bizness."

"Not my business? How is it none of my business?" Cora was angry. Normally she held back, but they were at a crossroads.

"Jist stay outta my affairs."

"You admit it. You're having an affair." She turned to face him. He lit a cigarette and turned away from her.

"I ain't admitting nothin."

"I can't go on with this. I'll take the girls and go to Iowa, and you stay here with your band."

"Fine, go. But leave Ruby." Frank said.

An involuntary shiver went up her spine. "I'll never leave one of my girls. Never."

"Well, if ya want to get outta this marriage, you'll have to choose." He lit a cigarette.

Her cheeks flamed with rage she didn't dare express. Frank didn't know her if he thought he was going to lay claim to one of her daughters. Yes, he was legally their father, but she was the one who carried them in her womb, gave birth to them, nursed them and was a constant presence to them. Frank came and went randomly.

"Tell me this. Do you know the moonshiners who tried to kill me?"

"I know most everybody. So what?"

"Frank, are you buying whiskey from them?"

"I don't have to tell ya what I do."

"Well, your activities might have been the death of our girls."

"Don't go getting excited. Everyone is fine."

"Fine for now. But for how long? If these men get out of jail, how do you know they won't come after me again?"

Frank blew out a puff of smoke but said nothing.

"I am not going to risk my life. Or the girls' lives. We're all going to Iowa," Cora said. "I see no other option."

Cora's parents wired the money for the train fare from Kentucky to Iowa, and Cora quickly purchased tickets after Frank reluctantly agreed to the move.

The Sunday before they left, Cora, Frank and the girls attended church together. Minnie organized a breakfast reception in the church hall after the service. Former and current students lined up to say goodbye, along with their parents. Cora's heart broke as she realized she might never see them again, but held herself together through all the hugs and well wishes.

"Thank you, Minnie, for organizing this. It meant the world to me," Cora said as the crowd thinned.

"When we heard you were leaving, I called the Lady's Aide together. Cecelia, whose sister-in-law, Virginia is the one whose husband's brother-in-law sawed off his finger, well she thought we should make you a quilt, but I knew there wasn't time. Besides, I think those Iowa farm wives are big quilters. So then Betty Jo, Sara's mother, who lives on the northeast corner of the southern part of the hill, said we should…"

"Say goodbye Minnie," Pastor Rehmann said and gave Cora a knowing smile.

"Goodbye dear. God bless you on your way," Minnie said to Cora.

"The reception was a perfect gift. Thank you both for everything," Cora said. She realized they thought they had her best interests at heart when they pushed her into marrying Frank. They loved her, and for that she was grateful.

Sylvia stopped by for a final visit the night before they headed north. She and Cora went for a stroll in the woods one last time.

"I promise to write when we get settled," Cora said.

"Me too. I'll let you know if anything changes at the school. At least you can wear bright colors now that you're not under the teacher's rules. Get yourself a red blouse, Cora!"

"Ha! Like the Vermilion Flycatcher. He's a beautiful bird, but I'll stay in the background in my drab colors."

"I hope there are colorful days ahead for you."

"Not likely, but let me know if you and Harry decide to marry."

"It's too soon for talk of marriage," Sylvia laughed.

"Your laugh," Cora said. "How will I get through anything without it? Tell Harry to take care of you."

"And you take care of you and these precious little ones," Sylvia added. They clung to each other for a moment relishing the comfort of their long friendship. Tears streamed down their faces.

"Goodbye my friend," Cora whispered as she turned toward the house. Swallowed into an ill-fated marriage and uncertain future.

Chapter 11

Cora, Frank and the girls departed for their new life with one suitcase of clothes for the four of them. And a guitar. She felt as if they were running away, but couldn't see how else to resolve the conundrum. Her heart ached as the view of mountains faded. Quitting a job she loved and abandoning a village of families who had accepted her into their community was agonizing but the safety of her children was her priority. But her thoughts turned dark. Would Frank get along with her aging parents? Would he would stay out of trouble? There were no guarantees, but at least they'd be safe on the farm.

Ma and Pa met them at the dusty train station with the horse and buggy. Their faces were etched from years of working in the elements. Pa's once dark brown eyes now were lighter and milky around the edges. When he pulled her into a hug, she knew he was relieved to see them. She wanted to stay in his arms to feel secure again, but Ma was nodding unsmiling at her, expectantly.

"Hello Ma, it's good to see you." They embraced with stiff arms and then Ma held Cora's hands for a moment.

"No more callouses," Ma said. Her eyes were puffy and sunken with age.

"Haven't milked a cow in over a decade," Cora said and then introduced Frank, Ruby, and Helen.

"You've had quite the ordeal," Ma said.

"Yes." She held back tears, not wanting to upset Ruby who was always attuned to her emotions.

"Well, ain't ya just the spittin image of yer mama," Ma said to Ruby. Ruby hid behind Cora's dress. Too shy to respond to Ma's imposing ways.

"This little one seems to favor ya, Frank," Ma said.

"Yup, that's what everyone says," Frank responded dully.

They stood awkwardly in silence for a moment.

"We're grateful to you for sending the train fare and letting us stay with you." Cora looked from one to the other of her parents needing them to understand how much it meant. Frank looked away.

"We didn't like havin ya so far away, Cora. And now we'll get to know these two lil ones. Oh, and you too, Frank." Pa smiled at Frank.

Frank nodded, but his eyes searched the landscape.

They climbed into the squeaky buggy, and Cora's eagerness to reach the farm intensified as they grew closer. Pa drove the horses in their single-seat hitch. The late summer heat made the close quarters uncomfortable. Cora opened the window, even though she was inviting dust in from the dirt road. Frank held Ruby while she cuddled Helen. Cora reached over and untied the girls' bonnets and loosened the top buttons on their cotton dresses. Ma sat across from them and studied Frank. He shifted uneasily from the unwanted appraisal, then looked out the window and pointed to a field.

"Corn?" Frank guessed trying to redirect Ma's glance.

"No beans, soybeans," Ma responded. They rode awhile in silence then Ma pointed to another field.

"That there's corn. For the animals. Ya kin see the corn still on the stocks. Not yet ready for harvest."

Frank nodded. "Don't cha be eatin corn on the cob here?"

"Well yes! Sweet corn's all been picked, and what we don't eat, we put up in cans for the winter. That's field corn. And take a gander at them Black Angus cows," Ma said as if it was going to help Frank become a farmer. Cora smiled to herself. Ma seemed to be bragging. Hadn't she always complained about life on the farm?

They bumped along the rest of the 40 miles, juggling the girls, saying little.

It was nearly supper time when they reached the farm. Ma told Cora and Frank to get settled in the two small bedrooms upstairs, while she started cooking. Cora stood for a moment and looked around the room of her youth. It looked nearly the same, with faded green paint and yellowed curtains. A patchwork quilt, no doubt dusty with age, lay at the foot of the bed. She put her few clothes in the dresser.

A wooden crib was in the room next to hers. She grabbed it and started to drag it. "Frank, please help me move this into my old room."

"Why do ya want the crib in our room?"

She shut the door to the room so her parents wouldn't hear them downstairs and turned to face Frank.

"I think it's best if you sleep in the other room. I'll want to keep the girls close to me."

He glared at her. "Gettin' kinda bossy ain't you? Don't think ya kin shut me out."

Cora kept her tone light. "Ruby's been having nightmares since the fire. And I have to get up to nurse Helen. This way you get some rest while I tend to the girls."

Frank backed down. "Speaking of rest, where does yer Pa keep the whiskey? Ya know I needs a shot to sleep."

"My parents don't drink. You know it's illegal. While we're living in their home, I don't want you drinking."

"What is this, a prison?" Frank sneered.

"My parents are conservative, and if they catch you with strong drink, they'll throw you out. And then where will you go? Because I won't be supporting you any longer."

"Some support. Ya think yer better'n me?" He grabbed her arm, and she knew she had to calm him.

"I think you'll like it here if you give it a chance." She forced a smile, and he reluctantly let go of her.

The next day, after breakfast, Cora tried again to show Frank the beauty around them. "Let's take the girls outside, and I'll show you around the farm."

"I'd rather play my guitar," he said sullenly.

Cora took Ruby outside later while Helen napped. Ruby toddled after baby chicks. Cora caught one to let her caress the downy feathers. They waved at pigs in their pens, and Jersey and Hereford cows grazing in the pastures. They even managed to lure one of the tabby barn cats over to let her experience the vibration of a contented purr. The knot inside Cora loosened a bit. Maybe they'd be happy here. Perhaps this was just the change they needed. Baby animals were the best part of farm life, and she wanted Ruby and Helen to experience it all.

After supper, Frank brought his guitar and sat on the back steps. Soon they all dragged chairs outside, and Pa invited him to play something so they could sing along.

Simple songs and hymns to lightened the night and take their minds off the relentless humidity which bolstered the heat to oppressive levels. Peace reigned for a few blessed minutes.

The mood quickly changed when Ma saw an opportunity to spear them with questions.

"What's yer plan now, Frank?"

"Well, ma'am, I'm hoping to find me some places to play my music."

"Uh huh. And how will ya pay the bills?"

"Not now, Gertrude, this ain't the time." Pa frowned at Ma, but when Ma had a bee in her bonnet, there was no stopping her.

"John, we've got to git things settled. We can't be expected to take in four more mouths to feed with no extra money. I just want to know what the plan is. Frank? Cora?"

"Of course, we plan to help, Ma. Frank is going to look for some paying music gigs, and I'm going to see about teaching in the area," Cora said as she rocked Helen.

"Teaching?" Ma challenged.

"I do have 12 years' experience."

"Not in Iowa. Those mission schools don't count here where they require college. You ain't got that," Ma said.

"Yes, I'm painfully aware I didn't go to college. If it weren't for Pa, I wouldn't have gotten a high school diploma."

"What about you Frank? What kinda education you got?" Ma turned her beady eyes toward him.

"I play music. It's what I do." Frank picked up his guitar and plunked out a melody.

Subject closed.

The first few days sailed by with no further arguments. Cora took over the laundry for everyone and helped with cooking when Ma relinquished control. Frank watched the girls while Cora did the dishes, but it was the only assistance he offered. He wandered around the land at times, with no purpose or plan, smoking cigarettes. Cora was collecting eggs one morning as he strolled by headed for the far pasture.

"What the devil is he doin' prancin' about the back 40?" Ma asked when she saw Cora watching Frank.

"I suppose he's trying to get acquainted with the land."

"In his fancy dress shirt?"

"It's what he's used to Ma." She changed the subject.

Frank continued to keep to himself, wandering the fields or playing his guitar. He enjoyed playing with Ruby while Helen napped and Cora labored with farm chores.

It didn't take Ma long to push her plan at supper the fourth night.

"Now Frank, those Jersey cows need to be milked mornin and night. It's high time ya lend Pa a hand to earn yer keep round here. Right, Pa?"

Pa nodded at Frank and smiled. "Well Frank, that'd be a great help. Have ya ever milked a cow?"

"I don't milk cows."

Pa ignored Frank's response. "Why don't ya meet me in the barn at daybreak tomorrow and I'll show ya the ropes."

Later, as Cora was putting the girls to bed, Frank cornered her.

"What the hell was all that 'bout milking cows?"

"Watch your language and lower your voice. You know we have to help with the chores. Milking is just part of it."

"How am I spost to know when daybreak is?"

"If you listen, the roosters crow just before daybreak. In case you miss it, I'll come and wake you."

"I can't believe ya growd up here on this stinkin' farm. I don't know ifin I kin stands it."

"It's not like you have a lot of other options."

The next morning, at breakfast, Pa and Frank lumbered in from the barn. Frank's white button-down shirt and brown pleated trousers were covered in mud. He was rubbing his hands together in pain. Pa noticed and reached for his palm to examine them.

"Blisters. Don't worry none, Frank. They'll turn into calluses and won't hurt once they harden."

"Great," Frank muttered.

Cora looked at his clothes. "We'll have to get you some overalls."

"No thanks! These'll do me fine."

Cora let it drop. No point arguing in front of her parents. But two weeks later, when Cora was outside scrubbing clothes on the washboard, Ma brought more laundry for her to wash. She stood by her silently for a moment. Cora looked at her Ma who rarely stood still for more than a few moments. Ma's feet were planted on the ground in her thick-soled black shoes, hands on her wide hips. Her lightweight cotton dress fell midway down her meaty calves.

Cora wiped the perspiration from her brow and met her stare. "Is something wrong, Ma?"

"I'm just wonderin' what ya see in that fella. Ain't like any man I ever met."

"Give him a chance, Ma. This is all new to him."

"Yes, but even in Kentucky, it seems he didn't know how to hold a steady job. Ya been supportin' him all along?" Her beady eyes trained on Cora.

Cora stared back but said nothing.

"Don't seem right, Cora."

"I don't want to talk about it, Ma. I'm trying to hold things together."

"And where is he gittin money for cigarettes?"

"Leave it alone, Ma," Cora said.

"Humph." And she trudged off.

Cora wrote numerous letters to the school districts in the area hoping to find another teaching position. But her inquiries were all returned saying she didn't have the necessary credentials to teach in Iowa. Not even as a teacher's assistant.

When she lay in bed on sleepless nights she tried to imagine a workable plan to get out from under her parents. But came up empty every time. Life had taken another turn down a road she never intended to travel.

Sundays became the bright spot of the week. Cora was surprised when Frank agreed to come to services. The first time he went, he brought his guitar to their small assembly. He approached the choir leader and asked to play along with the piano. Cora was heartened to see how easily he worked with the choir. She had to admit he had a rich voice and played guitar with ease. The bit of Kentucky twang he added to chords seemed to delight the choir director.

Their church met for a service on Sunday mornings, and they came together again Sunday night for Bible studies. The few times Frank came to the Bible studies, Cora was encouraged. She prayed he'd have a change of heart about the farm and stop drinking. And they'd both find a clearer path. She didn't share much about their circumstances, but still appreciated the fellowship of the congregation. In spite of this, Cora longed for the friendship of Sylvia and wrote to her often, but it wasn't the same as a long talk to sort out problems and share confidences.

Now Ma looked at her with criticism written on her scowling face. As an adult living with her parents, Cora felt the need to balance pleasing them, while maintaining a modicum of independence. All while caring for a toddler, an infant, and skirting around Frank's moods. And his secretive side. In Kentucky, she never probed about his outside activities. Afraid of what was behind them. Like peeling back wallpaper and discovering that underneath the wall's been eaten by termites, she knew their marriage was rotten at its core. This was not the model she wanted the girls to emulate but felt powerless to end it.

The weeks were settling into a pattern. But not a smooth one. Frank was a river of resistance. One cool Saturday evening, Frank appeared on the back porch where Pa was smoking his pipe and Cora was reading to the girls. Frank was sporting a clean white shirt and one of his tiny string ties. His boots were polished, his hair slicked back. Even his mustache was waxed into a smile.

He approached Pa. "I'd like to borrow a horse sos I kin look for work tonight."

"Have ya found someplace to play some music, Frank?" Pa asked.

"Sometimes ya just haveta git there at the right time."

Pa looked at Cora. She shrugged as if to say, "Let him go."

"Are you wantin' to go inta town with him? I see the girls is 'bout ready for bed."

"No, Pa, I'll see to the children. It's fine." Pa nodded at Frank who vanished in a flash. Cora breathed a sigh of relief and sat back in her chair. She usually relished autumn but having Frank at loose ends stole the joy from each day. Pa studied her.

"Don't seem right to send yer husband out like that alone. All kinda loose women meet up in those bars."

"It'll be OK, Pa. He's hoping to play with some musicians." She set Ruby on the porch floor and gave her a tiny wooden top.

"She's sure a cute one. Looks like you with her dark hair."

"Thanks, Pa."

Pa nodded and took a drag on his pipe and blew it out. "Cora, ya know I've never pried inta yer bizness, but something ain't right here."

"I know Pa, but I don't want to talk about it. I'll try to figure something out soon so we can get our own place."

"Cora, ya know it's not what I mean. Stay here as long as you need to. But Frank ain't interested in farmin', and he dont seem to know how to make a living."

She couldn't deny it. "I'm sorry, Pa."

"Yer sorry? It pains me to see ya trying so hard while he doesn't seem to have a lick of ambition."

She shrugged. Helen started to fuss. Time to nurse. "I need to put the girls to bed, Pa."

"Tell me one thing. How'd ya meet him?"

"I was teaching some of the adults to read and write, and he was one of my pupils."

Pa looked thoughtful as she stood up. Subject closed, please. She took Ruby's hand, and they traipsed upstairs.

Cora heard Frank creeping up the stairs hours after she went to bed. He stopped, and she heard her bedroom door squeak open, but she kept her eyes shut. He stood by her bed, breathing heavily and the stench of whiskey wafted over her. She hardly dared breathe but pretended to be asleep. After a long moment, he closed her door and skulked to his room.

After he left, she lay awake wondering why he didn't stay in Kentucky. Their marriage was an empty shell, and she dreaded the scandal it would invariably cause when she ended it. Somehow, she would put an end to it. Watching her daughters grow was her only joy, but she had to find a way to provide for them.

Ma was eating breakfast alone when Cora brought the girls downstairs for breakfast.

"Pa had to do the milkin' alone this mornin. I thought Frank was supposed to help." Ma was spoiling for a fight.

"He went out looking for a music job last night. He must have come in late."

"We'll see what he went out lookin for!"

"Ma! Not in front of the girls."

She glared at her. "Did he bring home any money?"

"I don't know, I haven't spoken to him."

She snorted and picked up her oatmeal dish and brought it to the sink.

"Better get ready for church."

"We'll be ready Ma."

"Him too?"

"I expect so."

Frank joined them for church in the morning and seemed unusually light-hearted. He even smiled while he was playing his guitar along with the choir.

He must have some good news. After church when they were alone, she questioned him.

"Did you make any money last night?"

"Nah. There be no work out there last night."

"Then why were you out till all hours?"

"Ya don't need to know."

"I think as your wife, I'm entitled to know your whereabouts."

"Oh, now ya wants to be my wife! Ya never asked me before, so don't ya start tryin' to hem me in. Anyway, it don't matter no more."

"What do you mean it doesn't matter anymore?"

"Nothin, I don't mean nothin. And don't you be tryin to correct my talkin." His lip curled as he glared at her through squinty eyes.

Cora knew better than to pressure him, but he seemed more secretive than usual. Had he met someone special last night? She knew he'd been out with other women in Kentucky because he liked to brag about it as if he was trying to make her jealous. But you can only be jealous if you love someone. She didn't even like him.

After supper, Frank said he was too tired to join them for the evening Bible study.

"Leave the girls. I kin watch 'em tonight sos ya has a break. Then I'll just head to bed after I gets 'em settled."

She agreed. It'd be nice to have an evening of adult companionship and get a break from the constant demands of motherhood. He loved the girls, and she trusted him to care for them for a few hours.

When they arrived home after the Bible study, Cora ran upstairs to check on the girls. Helen was asleep, but she couldn't see Ruby's face. She pulled back the covers to peek at her. A rolled-up bedroll was placed where Ruby should have been. Cora froze!

Chapter 12

Cora bolted into Frank's room. When she couldn't see him, she ripped his blanket back. Another bedroll placed in an empty bed. He was gone.

Cora screamed and tore down the narrow staircase.

Pa jumped out of his easy chair, eyes wide. "What in tarnation!"

"Frank's gone! And he…he took Ruby."

"What? He was supposed to be watchin' the girls!" Ma growled. Pa stormed up the stairs to see for himself.

"He took Ruby! She's gone." Cora dashed outside, searching frantically in all directions. Was it possible they were outside?

The porch door squealed open, and Ma stuck her head out. "What are ya lookin' for out there?"

A cloud of mist rose when her words met the chilled night air. "Maybe he took her for a walk. We have to find her."

"Ya woke Helen with all the commotion. Git inside."

Cora searched the blackness but saw no movement. The leafless trees stood like skeletons with bare limbs. She shuddered. Was Frank capable of hurting Ruby? She didn't dare ask the question aloud. Reluctantly, she returned to the safety of the kitchen.

Pa brought Helen downstairs and passed her to Cora who clung to her.

"My poor baby. He left you all alone. But where is your sister?" She whispered into Helen's hair as she swayed back and forth. Her insides shook uncontrollably.

"Pa, do you think he's on the farm somewhere with Ruby?" She knew it was illogical.

"Cora, why'd he hide bedrolls under the blanket to go for a walk? I'll head into town and see what I kin find out."

"At this hour?" Ma said.

"If I go now, I might find 'em or at least someone who seen 'em." Pa grabbed his coat and hat. In minutes they heard his horse thunder by the house. They listened in silence until the pounding hooves faded into the night. Ma went into the kitchen and put a pot of coffee on the stove to boil.

Cora sat in a rocker, the uncontrollable shaking continued. Despair washed over her. It felt like the night of her cabin fire. She hadn't thought life could get any darker, but she was wrong. She nursed Helen for a few minutes to soothe her back to sleep. Then looked at her innocent face and wondered if Frank had hoped to take both girls. Had he left Helen because she still needed to nurse? What if something had happened to her while she was alone in the house? The rage she felt for Frank was stoked again and again as the reality sharpened. What an angry and evil sin he committed by stealing her child.

And now Ma saw her soul laid bare. Ma who never seemed to think much of her or expect much from her. Was she gloating? Cora remembered her prediction eons ago that she would marry a hillbilly.

Ma was rarely without words, but tonight she was eerily quiet, except for the cracking of her wooden rocker, groaning under her weight. Cora wished she could have had a mother who held her and comforted her as Sylvia would have? Ma stared at a spot on the worn green and brown rug on the floor of the sitting room for several minutes. Time ticked by. Then silently she trudged into the kitchen and brought back two steaming mugs of coffee and handed one to Cora.

After she sat back in her rocker, Ma broke the silence. "Who you cryin' for? Frank or Ruby?"

"Ruby, my baby." She teared up again. Where was she now? Was she in danger?

"How did the likes a you two end up married to each other?"

"You don't want to know, Ma."

"Were ya just lonely?"

"If I tell you, promise you won't blame me."

"Blame you?"

"Yes, Ma. You always try to make everything my fault. I need you on my side. For once."

"I'm on yer side. I just don't think much a yer marriage."

"I was forced."

"Forced? By who?"

"Frank was one of the adult students I was teaching. I didn't like him, but I had agreed to teach those who hadn't learned to read or write."

"Well if you didn't like him, why did ya end up with him?"

"I was helping to prepare food for a funeral, alone in his parent's home when he came in. He overpowered me."

"Ya shouldn't a let yerself be alone with a man."

"Ma, you said you wouldn't blame me. I'd been alone with him while teaching and although I didn't like him, I didn't think I had any reason to fear him."

"So, ya found yourself …in the family way."

"Yes, and I thought I could ask for a leave from teaching. I planned to go somewhere and stay until the baby was born and then adopt him or her out." Another wave of pain hit her at the thought she might never see Ruby again.

"So, hows it happen ya married him?"

"Frank's father was the school board president. I went to him and asked for a leave, but he refused. He told me to come back the next day, and when I did, he had a minister and Frank there. He said if I didn't marry Frank, I'd leave in disgrace without any reference. I figured I'd never be able to get another job. I was confused, and it all happened so fast."

"Why were his parents so keen on yer getting' married?"

"Frank was their only child. I was expecting their grandchild. I think they thought marriage would settle him down."

"I wondered. Yer letters didn't say much. After we met him, it just didn't fit."

"I thought we had to make it work for the sake of the girls. In spite of their father, I love my girls."

"Ya sure ya didn't want to marry?"

"Ma, believe it or not, I was happy being a single teacher in Kentucky."

"And yet, ya ended up married."

"Not anymore apparently."

They sat like two separate ships on a stormy sea as Ma absorbed the details of her marriage and Cora clung to Helen for comfort.

Finally, they heard the horse tromp up the road, and Pa scurried in with a rush of chilly air. She was almost afraid of what he'd say and yet desperately wanted to know where her Ruby was.

"Frank left tonight on a train for Kentucky and Ruby's with him. I found a guy at the station who says he seen them drive up in a pickup truck and git on the train. He musta met someone who agreed to take him to the station while we were gone." Pa sank onto the sagging couch.

"Who knows how long he's been a plannin' his escape." Ma shook her head bitterly.

Cora wanted to scream at Ma but knew she was right. He was miserable on the farm, and he must have been looking for someone to help him skip town. Why did Ma have to make her feel as if she imprisoned him? He trapped her. But the bond was broken. It was over.

"He had no right to take Ruby." She held Helen closer.

"Let's talk 'bout this in the mornin,' Cora." Pa's face was stamped with deep shadows, weariness overpowering him.

"Cows won't milk therselves," Ma grunted as she got up.

Cora climbed upstairs and put Helen back in her crib and crept into the room where Frank had been sleeping. She pulled open dresser drawers. Little was left. A few old socks and chipped guitar picks. Gone was their only suitcase. Looking around, she spotted his wastebasket. She frantically dug through it looking for clues. At the bottom, she found a small crumpled up piece of paper.

"Harold McClure. Sunday. 8 pm." What irony that she taught Frank to read and write.

In her room, she slumped to her knees. "Lord God, if you are there, please protect my Ruby." She alternated between yelling at God and pleading with him. How had he let this happen to her? The humiliation and horror of rape, the forced marriage, living with an abusive spouse and then the terror of the fire. Where was God in all of this? And what was the right thing for her to do now?

Finally, the cold chased her into bed. Alone without Ruby. For the first time, her brown-eyed toddler was not close. Tears spilled as she thought back to the last few years. She needed to talk to Sylvia to find peace. If peace was possible.

When she couldn't sleep, she got up and paced. When her feet grew cold, she sat on her bed, pulled her knees to her chin and looked out at the moon. Was Ruby crying for her? She tried to soothe herself by putting things in perspective. Ruby was alive. She was not sick. She was safe with a father who loved her. At least, she prayed this was true.

Helen's cries woke her in the morning and the agony of the situation struck her anew. She wanted to curl into a ball like a wounded dog but knew that wasn't an option. Life had to go on.

When Pa came in from morning chores, he turned to her.

"Do ya want me to go after them, Cora? I can take the train to Kentucky to find them."

She searched his eyes in gratitude. Yes, she wanted her daughter back, but not Frank. "No, I don't want you to have to fight with Frank."

"Are ya sure, Cora? Is it what ya want?"

"No Pa, it's not what I want. But Frank told me if I wanted a divorce, he'd take Ruby. I didn't think he'd act on it, but I underestimated how cruel he is. He's not going to give her back without a fight. And he has a terrible temper."

"Why would a single dad without a steady job want a child?" He asked.

"He was a good father, even if he wasn't much of a provider. And his parents wanted a grandchild."

"That's probably why they forced ya to marry him." Ma set three mugs of coffee on the table.

"Forced ya? Is that what happened?"

"Yes, Pa. First Frank forced himself on me, and when I found I was expecting, his parents tricked me into marrying him."

"That explains it. Ya deserved so much better than that fella."

Tears welled in her eyes. "Thank you, Pa. That means a lot to me. The problem is to have my Ruby, I have to take Frank back. And I can't bear a lifetime of his abuse, his temper and his philandering."

"I didn't realize it was as bad as that." Pa reached over and covered her hand with his leathered one.

"I didn't want you to know. I hoped he might straighten out here and see the beauty of life in the country."

"Well, it never happened. Him goin' about in his white shirts actin' like he was better n everyone." Ma said.

"I found the name of a man in Frank's wastebasket and I'd like to find him and talk to him so I can know for certain what Frank's plans were."

"Let's go," Pa said.

Pa got the buggy and Cora dressed Helen for the outing. They went into town and asked folks where they might find Harold McClure. Strangers directed them to a farm on the edge of the county. They found Harold outside working on an old pick-up truck.

"Please sir, I found a note with your name on it. Can you tell me where my husband, Frank, and my daughter might be?"

"I met Frank a few weeks back. He asked me if I'd take him to the train station and we agreed on a price. He said nothing 'bout bringin' a child with him. But that's what he did. On the way to the station, he says his wife don't want to live in Kentucky with him, and he don't like Iowa, so he was takin' one of the children with him. Made it sound as if his wife agreed. I stayed outta it. That's all I know."

He confirmed what they suspected. They rode back to the farm as Cora tried to line up the pieces of her life.

Later in the afternoon Cora and Pa went into town to speak with the sheriff.

"I want to report a kidnapping," Cora told him.

Sheriff Peterson led them to his office and got out his pen and paper. "Who was allegedly kidnapped?"

"My two-year-old daughter, Ruby Desjardin. Her father took her last night."

"She's with her father? Then this ain't a kidnapping."

"But he took her without my consent, and we believe he went back to Kentucky."

"Kentucky?"

"That's where we were living, and I think he brought Ruby back to his parent's."

"Sounds like a custody issue, not a kidnapping. You know who the child is with and where they are. Is she in any danger?"

"I, I don't think so."

"Sorry, Mrs. Desjardin. I can't pursue anything across state lines. Sounds as if you and your husband need to work this out with an attorney."

Back at the farm, Cora mulled over her next steps. She wrote to the Desjardins to be certain Ruby was with them and asked for a response.

And she desperately needed to speak to Sylvia. Cora wrote a letter to her and arranged a date and time to use public phones.

"Sylvia?" At the sound of her voice, Cora began to weep. Between sobs, she poured out the horror of Frank kidnapping Ruby.

"Ruby is with the Desjardins Cora. They brought her to services on Sunday and told everyone you gave up custody of her."

"That's a lie."

"I knew it was."

"How did she look?"

"She looked well. No signs of any…abuse."

"That's a relief. I don't know what to do next," Cora said.

"What are your options?"

"Stay in Iowa and lose Ruby or go back to Kentucky and take Frank back. Either way, I lose. I already resigned my job, and I don't want to live with him anymore."

"Can you divorce Frank and still get custody of Ruby?"

"I don't know. I'm wrestling with these questions. But how will I support myself and two tiny ones without my job? I keep going round and round. The only thing I'm clear about is I cannot live another day with Frank."

"That's a step."

At this point, the operator cut in and told them they had no more time.

"I have to go, Sylvia. I'll write soon. Thank you!" And the line went dead. Cora had no more money to continue the call.

At night Cora woke up certain she heard Ruby calling "Mama." Ruby must be confused, wondering where her mother was. But it didn't help to dwell on it. She reminded herself others had experienced the death of their child. Ruby was alive. And she was loved. But the little comfort it brought was a tiny patch on a gaping wound.

When the pain became unbearable, Cora clung to Helen.

She borrowed money from her parents to seek the counsel of an attorney.

"On what grounds do you seek a divorce?" He asked her.

"I never loved him. He was unfaithful, shiftless and disappeared for days at a time," Cora answered. "And he kidnapped our oldest child and left the state with her. I want my child back, but not my husband."

"This is a complicated case. You married in Kentucky and now are living in different states. Do you have proof of his infidelity?"

"No, but he used to brag about it," Cora said.

"I'm afraid it's not sufficient evidence. As for getting your child back, you'll have to work it out with your husband."

Another dead end.

Cora wrote to Frank and arranged a phone call.

"So, is ya comin to yer senses and comin back to Kentucky?" Frank's sneer was evident through the phone.

"No! Come back to what? I don't have a job."

"Well, ya has a husband and daughter here."

"A husband with no job who kidnapped my daughter."

"Our daughter. It ain't kidnappin' cuz I'm her dad."

"It was cruel. I'll never forgive you for this. Frank, I want a divorce."

"Fine, but I gets Ruby. Only fair. We each has one."

"I'm her mother. The one who has taken care of her night and day. You can't lay claim to her as if she were a baby goat. I want my daughter back."

"Then ya has to come back to Kentucky and live as a family."

"Live where? With your parents? No, I want a divorce. I don't want to live in Kentucky."

"Then that's it."

"No, wait. Let me talk to Ruby."

"We is done talkin," Frank said, and the line went dead.

Cora had asked him to bring Ruby to the phone, but Frank's cruelty denied even this small request.

She filed for divorce and planned to fight for custody of Ruby when she found another job.

Without Frank around her, the persistent mantle of fear lifted. She was determined to turn her life around and to find a way to win back Ruby.

Christmas without Ruby was more painful than she could have imagined. Cora made a few dresses and a small cloth doll and sent them to her in-laws home hoping Ruby would receive them. She made a matching doll for Helen. They celebrated the day with Alice and her husband, Ed, and their three children, but it was a subdued day. Cora was in too much pain to celebrate the birth of another child. Even if it was her Savior.

For several months Cora had been looking for a way to support herself and Helen. Her soul searching and research led her to a possible solution, but it would require help from her parents. She dreaded asking them. But couldn't wait much longer.

Pa stomped onto the porch and knocked the snow off his galoshes and overcoat. Once in the kitchen, he reached for the coffee and turned around to face Cora and Ma who were silently peeling potatoes at the kitchen table. Sun streaming in through the windows did little to chase the January chill.

"It's bitter out there. Them cows weren't happy to give up their milk," he said, leaning against a wall near the stove to warm himself.

"I spect not," Ma replied. "My chickens is hardly layin'. With few eggs and little milk to sell, how're we goin' to git through the winter?" She adjusted the knit shawl around her shoulders.

"We have plenty of vegetables in the root cellar and a few apples," Cora added. Her chafed hands were raw from washing and peeling vegetables, but she didn't dare complain.

"I kin butcher a few chickens, but then the egg count'll be even less," Pa said.

They were silent for a few moments as the weight of their situation hung like the icicles that dangled on the eaves of their farmhouse.

"Well now's as good a time as any to tell you my plans," Cora said looking from one parent to the other.

"What plans?" Ma challenged. She put down her paring knife.

"I'm going to college. I've found a way."

"College? What in tarnation for?" Ma asked.

"To become a nurse."

"Nurse? How long'll that take?" Ma questioned.

"Three years—"

"What! Yer a mother. That's ridiculous!" Ma said.

"Gertrude, let's hear her out," Pa said evenly.

"Thank you, Pa. Getting my nursing degree would help me contribute to the household income. And hopefully, I could save enough to fight Frank in court to get custody of Ruby and someday live on my own with my daughters."

"Why can't ya just work in a shop?" Ma asked.

"I don't want to work for low wages and uncertain hours. I'd earn a steady income as a nurse and would always have a job."

"That's a good point, Ma. Nurses are always in demand," Pa said.

"Just how do ya plan to pay for this?" Ma's eyes bore into her.

"I've already looked into it. There are scholarships and grants available. After the first year, I'll work part-time at Methodist hospital and start to earn while I attend classes."

"But what about Helen? Yer still nursin' her!" Ma said.

"Classes don't start until August, and I can wean her by then." Cora looked over at Helen who was pulling herself up to a table in the sitting room.

"Ya can't take her to classes," Ma said.

"No, I can't. And I can't afford to pay someone to watch her." She took a deep breath. "This is where I need your support, Ma. I was hoping you could watch her. I know it's a lot to ask—"

"Yer darn right it is. I raised my family, and I don't wanna raise more young uns," Ma said slamming her hands on the table.

"Gertrude, calm down. I can help with Helen. Cora needs a way to provide for herself and Helen and maybe Ruby someday. It won't be forever," Pa said as he bent down and corralled Helen.

"It'll be three years. Three long years of chasin' and feedin' and bathin' Helen," Ma said.

"I won't be gone the whole time. Classes are in Des Moines, and I'll stay in the dorm at the hospital during the week. I can come home weekends. In the summer, I'll work part-time at the hospital, but I'll be home when I'm not working. If all goes well, I'll be a nurse in three years."

"And then what?" Ma glared at her.

"And then we'll move out on our own."

"So just when ya start makin' money, you'll move out," Ma charged.

"Ma! You complain about having us here. I thought you'd be happy for a break. Besides, I'll start earning money after the first year, and I'll be able to contribute then."

"Helen won't be old enough for school when, or if, ya finish classes. Who'll take care a her?" Ma asked.

"I'll find someone else to watch her while I'm working."

"I don't like it. A mother needs to be with her children," Ma said shaking her head and looking down at the table.

"In a perfect world, yes. But we both know I don't have a perfect situation," Cora said. "We can't go on scraping by. I need to find a way to earn an income, and I believe this is it."

"It might come in handy to have a nurse in the family, Gertrude. We're not getting any younger," Pa injected.

"Speak for yerself!" Gertrude shot back and stood up defiantly.

"Cora, give us time to think about all this," Pa said. "Let's have a peaceful day and we kin talk more tomorrow."

"I won't change my mind," Ma grumbled but let the subject drop. She marched over to the counter where bread dough was rising and took her aggressions out kneading it.

Few words were spoken at dinner, their noon meal. The day dragged on with endless kitchen chores. Cora broke the silence at supper.

"I think Helen's about ready to walk," Cora said.

"I noticed that," Pa replied.

"I thought we could invite Alice and her family for supper next month for Helen's first birthday," Cora said. "I can bake a cake and prepare something simple."

"That'd be fine," Pa said.

Ma grunted but looked straight ahead as she plowed her way through her potatoes.

Long after her parents retired for the night, Cora could hear them arguing. Cora was trying to read but knew that the discussion downstairs was pivotal to her future. She felt guilty asking them for help, but she looked at her situation from every which way and felt this solution would help them all. Eventually. She would earn enough to fight for custody of Ruby. She ached from missing her for the past four months. And Cora longed to be independent again, with her own home. Ma would have her peace after Cora and Helen moved out, but she was a nose-to-the-grindstone sort who distrusted the notion of hope.

Cora vowed to find a path out of poverty, with or without her parent's help. But without them, it would be far more difficult. Even with their help, the hurtles were enormous. How would Ma treat Helen? Pa couldn't be around all the time, and Cora worried that Ma would be harsh with her little one. Weren't grandmothers supposed to be more patient and loving as they aged? She prayed her mother's temperament would move in that direction. But so far, she hadn't taken much interest in helping with Helen or any of Alice's children.

When Pa came in from milking cows the next morning, Cora was in the kitchen with her mother and Helen. She waited expectantly, her nerves firing.

They poured coffee and sat down at the kitchen table. Pa took the lead.

"Cora, this is difficult to say the least. But if going to school is a way for ya to get yer daughter back, we want ya to have the chance."

"So you'll watch Helen when I'm gone?" Cora asked.

"Yes. Yer Ma and I both'll help with her care," Pa said.

Cora exhaled and bit her lips to keep from crying. "Thank you! Thank you, both."

"We do expect ya to contribute some a yer earnings," Ma said, "once you're workin'."

"Yes, of course," Cora said.

Pastor Rehmann and their current pastor wrote letters of recommendation to the Methodist School of Nursing and Cora was accepted.

"I'll be back this weekend," Cora whispered to Helen before the first day of class. She nuzzled her neck and kissed her cheeks. "I'm so sorry I can't take you with me."

Helen smiled at her and Cora handed her toddler to Ma.

"Thank you, Ma. Please be gentle with her."

"Let's hope this works out for ya, Cora."

Chapter 13

1934 – Nine years later

*Helen

I'm starving, Helen thought as she and Grandpa stopped in front of the once-white farmhouse. Grandpa John reached a leathered hand behind him and helped Helen slide down Lady, their ginger-hued Belgian draft horse, and onto the ground. "Thanks, Grandpa," she said, smoothing her plaid jumper and hitching up her socks.

"Git your chores done, Ole Bean. See you after a bit." Grandpa nodded at her and rode to the faded red barn with the peeling paint.

What kinda mood was Grandma in today? She giggled as she watched chipmunks scatter into the wood pile on the side of the farmhouse porch. "Grandma's gonna git you with her broom," she whispered to them. *Wonder if there are any kittens around?* She looked toward the barn and thought about heading for it, but the gnawing in her stomach grew louder.

She hopped up the three steps on one foot. Maybe Mama was home today.

"Helen Jane!" Grandma bellowed through two doors.

Her shoulders tensed as she squeaked open the porch door, took off her faded blue sweater and hung it on the hook next to the wringer washer. She hesitated as she turned the cold knob, took a breath and shouldered the door into Grandma's kitchen. A stew pot was boiling on the cook-stove, and fresh bread was cooling on the wooden counter. But her nose caught the scent of cinnamon.

Her eyes lit up at the sight of oatmeal cookies lined up in orderly rows.

"Cookies," she breathed as if in the presence of something sacred.

"They're for supper, leave 'em alone," Grandma snapped as she turned around from the stove, her face a permanent snarl.

"But I'm hungry now," Helen said, although she knew Grandma was as uncompromising as a stone statue.

"And how many times do I haf to remind ya to take off them shoes!"

Helen untied her scuffed leather shoes with the dented toes.

"Eat a carrot and git yer chores done," came the reply. Grandma's bulky arms crossed over her considerable bosom. "And no lollygagging." Her dark eyes peered at Helen over the top of her spectacles.

"Yes, Ma'am." As usual, Helen found a carrot, cleaned it and chomped on it noisily. Her eyes stayed glued to the cookies. "Where's my Mama?"

"At the Watson place, delivering their fourth baby. And if ya ask me, Flossie Watson can barely manage the three she already has." Grandma's lips were pulled tight; her chin jutted out. Her grey hair was wrapped tightly in a bun.

I wonder why no hairs ever get free of her bun. They're prisoners, like me.

"Ya need to darn those socks, child!" Grandma barked.

Helen looked down at the toes peeking out of her knit socks.

"Yes, Ma'am." Helen swept the kitchen floor but kept one eye on Grandma who was putting the cookies in the jar shaped like a little Dutch girl with braids on the sides of her head. The braids stuck out like two smiles. *The only smiles I ever see in this kitchen.* She watched as Grandma pushed the happy face to the back of the countertop. *Ha, she thinks it's outta my reach.*

The screen door banged. Grandma headed outside to collect eggs, and Helen seized the moment. She moved the small stepstool over to the counter and tiptoed up two steps. With trembling hands, she lifted the smiling face off the top of the cookie jar. She inhaled the scent of cinnamon, then reached in. *She won't miss one cookie.* She plunked it into the front pocket of her dress. She picked up the lid to replace it and instead banged it onto the bottom of the jar, scraping glass on glass. *Oh no!* She held her breath and listened. No thundering footsteps. In spite of her nerves, she got the lid back on the waist of the plump girl who seemed to smile and wink at her. Helen hopped down and moved the step stool back to its home by the broom closet. She hightailed it upstairs past her and her mother's tiny bedrooms, her socks sliding on the hardwood floors and catching here and there on nails that were poking up. *No wonder my socks have holes in them.*

She climbed another set of even steeper stairs to her corner of the world. *Safe,* she thought, as her heart raced from the close call. The unfinished wood walls slanted sharply in the dark crawl space with only a bare lightbulb hanging from the ceiling and a single window for light.

She snuggled into a pillow on the floor of her attic alcove. Here she was away from Grandma Gertrude's prying eyes, orders, and chores. Adults had to stoop over if they visited, so they rarely bothered.

Her favorite library book of the moment, "Little Women," was right where she left it. She wanted to spend time with girls her age – even if they were imaginary. She reached into her dress pocket and pulled out the oatmeal cookie. She nibbled around the crisp edges, her favorite part. Slowly she bit off tiny bites of the cinnamon-sweet center, careful not to leave a crumb of evidence. She hoped there might be a raisin inside, but Grandma must have ruled them too pricey for their meager budget.

She grabbed her rag doll, Amy, named for the strong-willed sister in "Little Women." She looked into Amy's embroidered blue eyes and pug nose and smoothed the auburn yarn hair. *You're lucky you don't have my freckles.* She and Amy had been fast friends since Mama made her in time for Helen's last birthday.

As she devoured the adventures of the four March sisters in "Little Women," it sharpened her longing for a sister. She'd been living with mama's parents, Grandma Gertrude and Grandpa John, her whole life. Mama left her, sometimes for days delivering babies, and Helen had no one to talk to, play with, hug or hold.

Jo, Beth, Meg and Amy March also lived during difficult times but had each other to meet each challenge. Helen sat propped against her pillow and let the characters transport her to another time and place.

She was lost in her book when the clip clop of horses and the squeal of wagon wheels brought her back to the present. She sat up and listened. Voices. She saw nothing out of the attic window, so she checked her face for crumbs and crawled back downstairs. When she peered out her bedroom window, she spotted a covered wagon. She scrambled down another flight of rickety stairs to the kitchen where Grandma Gertrude's girth was blocking the porch door.

Peering around Grandma, Helen spotted two women standing on the porch, an open burlap bag in front of each. They wore long, billowing skirts with cheerfully colored, floral patterns. Helen's mouth stood open as she took in the sight of their ragged blouses with daring necklines and flowing sleeves. Layers of glass beads and seashells adorned the necks of the mysterious strangers.

Helen blinked as she noted the contrast from their flamboyant attire to her grandmother's drab appearance. She peered at the covered wagon parked on the gravel next to their farmhouse. A man with a full beard wearing a tall hat and smoking a corn cob pipe waited in the driver's seat. The younger of the two women had a baby strapped to her front, and Helen saw two more little faces peeking out of the wagon.

Helen smiled at the little ones and waved. She took a tentative step outside toward them, and her grandmother's rough hand caught the back of her dress and grabbed her back inside like a ragdoll. Grandma shot Helen a warning glare, and she slunk back into the kitchen to watch from a distance.

"Vould you like to zee za hand embroidered tablecloth?" The older woman said as she held up a white tablecloth emblazoned with giant sunflowers.

"Too bright," Grandma said.

"Vat about dis basket? For za bread?" The younger woman held up an intricately patterned hand-woven basket. Long dark braids peaked out from a scarlet scarf.

"Got enough baskets."

"Yarn for knitting?"

"Don't need any."

"Ah, zoh, a beautiful necklace for you, maybe?" The older woman held up a string of jewel-toned beads.

"Don't wear no jewelry," Gertrude snapped.

Helen looked longingly at the beads. What fun to have a necklace to wear to church. She noticed the women looked at each other and shrugged their shoulders. She enjoyed watching Grandma barter and was hoping the show wasn't over.

The older woman dug deep into her large bag and drew out a wine-colored cloth. "How 'bout dis velvet piano cover? Look at da delicate flowers embroidered on it?"

Grandma snatched it and studied the fabric and the handiwork. Her eyes narrowed. "How much ya want for it?"

"One dollar." The older woman pursed her lips.

"Don't have it. How 'bout I trade ya for a chicken?"

"Do you have za firewood? If you add za firewood, ve might make za trade," she licked her lips and waited.

Grandma hesitated as she considered the velvet, feeling its softness in her hands. "I could give ya one armful a firewood," she said, still clutching the piano cover.

The women looked at each other with raised eyebrows. The younger woman gave a little nod and blinked her eyes.

"One chicken and an armload of firewood for the piano cover. My best offer." The finality in Grandma's voice said she wasn't kidding. Helen knew she loved the thrill of a good bargain, but when she reached her limit, she left no doubt.

"Vee'll take it," the older woman nodded.

Grandma lay the piano cover on the counter and went out to the hen house to collect a chicken and then gathered an armload of firewood for the women. Helen reached for the velvet and held it to her face. *Soft as a newborn chick.* She clung to it, admiring the delicate stitches.

"Give that to me," Grandma snapped when she stomped back into the house.

Grandma Gertrude walked over to the old upright and removed the framed pictures sitting on top of the piano. Helen watched as she lifted off the faded green cover with indentations where every picture frame was placed. Grandma smoothed the new cover over the top of the piano and replaced the pictures in the same order. Helen wanted the old cover, but Grandma chucked it on the pile of clothes waiting for washing day.

*Cora

"Come on, Flossie. Push. The baby's head is crowning. You're almost there. Push!" Delivering babies never felt routine to Cora. She'd been working as a midwife ever since she finished her nurse's training five years before. No clinics had openings which would have allowed her to work predictable hours and hopefully move away from the farm. Instead the only available opening was the county midwife. She was grateful for the work, but needed someone to keep an eye on four-year-old Helen. Babies arrived after long and unpredictable hours. Staying with her parents was the practical solution then and now that they were in the middle of the great Depression, independence seemed a lofty dream.

"The head is out! One more big push, Flossie. That's it. Keep pushing!"

The baby was born, and Cora quickly cleaned her up.

"She's a girl! And she looks perfect. Another beautiful baby, Flossie."

She placed her in Flossie's waiting arms and watched as Flossie kissed her head and counted her fingers and toes.

"Thank you, Cora," Flossie said as she fell back against her headboard. "Such a relief."

"What will you call her?"

"Haven't got a name yet."

When Flossie was stable, Cora went downstairs to share the happy news with Flossie's husband, Arthur.

"Another perfect little girl!" Cora told him beaming.

"Thank God," Arthur exclaimed and took the stairs two at a time to see for himself.

Cora flopped down in a chair for a few minutes. She loved her work, but it was exhausting. And each delivery reminded her of the child she lost.

"I'll take you home then," Arthur said when he came downstairs.

The horse-drawn carriage seemed to hit every bump along the roads, adding to the pain in her shoulders and back. When it finally pulled up to the farmhouse, she stepped carefully out into the dark evening, avoiding mud and horse droppings.

"Thank you again for all your help Cora," Arthur Watson said. "We'll pay you somethin' as soon as we can. You done real good today. That new one looks right fine."

"I had little to do with it. I'm happy Flossie and the baby are doing well. I'll be by tomorrow to check on them." Arthur tipped his hat and was gone.

Cora hurried to the house, pulling her long black coat closed against the chill of the autumn night. When she reached the porch, she set her heavy leather bag down. She stretched upward to get the kink out of her back and rubbed her neck for a moment. She never relaxed while assisting with a birth, in case of complications. There was so much joy when everything went well, but the fear of losing a baby, or a mother, or both, kept her vigilant.

Exhaustion was descending on her. It was nearly time for supper, and she braced herself for Ma's temper. She was eager to see Helen and hoped they might have a peaceful evening.

The hubbub of supper preparations drew her into the kitchen.

"Mama," Helen raced to her and hugged her tight around the waist. Cora kissed the top of her head.

Ma looked up from her cooking and shook her head at Helen's outburst. "Quiet child. It's only yer mama. No need to make a fuss."

"When did you get so tall?" Cora held her little girl and stroked her hair.

"Hello, Ma," Cora smiled at her, not expecting it to be returned.

"So what was it? Boy or girl?"

"A healthy baby girl. She looks perfect."

"Humph. Well, better git outta yer uniform. Almost time for supper."

"Wait, Mama, I want to show you something," Helen pulled her by the hand into the living room and showed her the exquisite piano cover.

"Grandma bought this?" Cora whispered.

Helen nodded. "She traded a chicken and some wood for it."

"Traded who?"

"Gypsies!" Helen whispered.

"It is lovely. Look at the tiny stitches. It certainly brightens up this dark room." It was beautiful, but stood out from the dark floors, peeling olive drab wallpaper, dark brown furniture in the room with few embellishments. Not much had changed in over 30 years. And now this?

"There were children in the wagon, but Grandma wouldn't let me play with them," Helen sulked.

"She just wants to keep you safe. Was there any mail for me today?"

"But I have no one to play with," Helen's face was serious.

Cora sighed. This was a subject with no resolution. "Get washed up for supper, baby," she gave her another quick hug. Helen wasn't ready to be set aside.

"Why don't we have a normal family? Why don't I have a father?"

Cora looked at her thoughtfully and touched her face. "I'm sorry, Helen. Life didn't turn out the way I wanted it to." She went upstairs to put an end to the discussion.

When Ma gave the 'supper' command, the four of them sat on creaking benches in front of the splintered table. They bowed their heads and thanked God for their food.

Pa dipped a hunk of wheat bread in his stew and broke the silence as they ate. "Was in town today. Went by a full city block a folks waitin' in the bread line."

"Watson's told me they have to eat at the soup kitchen most days now. Arthur's been out of work for six months," Cora said.

"And now they got another mouth to feed. I s'pose ya didn't git paid for the delivery!" Ma said.

"They'll pay me when they can, Ma. It's not like it's Arthur's fault. Millions are out of work."

"Well it ain't for me to say, but I won't be holdin' my breath on ya ever seein' that money," Ma inserted.

"We're more fortunate than most. We have some income and this land to raise food. Let's be grateful," Cora reminded Ma.

"I'd like to agree with ya, Cora, but the price a corn has dipped again. It ain't worth sellin' this year." Pa's news hit like a bucket of ice water.

Ma scowled, "Why'd ya say such a thing? How we s'pposed to survive if we don't sell the crop?"

"The goin' price for corn's nine cents a bushel. Some are sayin' they're just gonna use it for fuel. It's cheaper than coal now."

"Burn the corn in the cook-stove? Well if that ain't the dumbest thang ya ever said, I don't know what is," Ma said.

Pa chomped off another bite of his crusty bread. He said nothing more as he stared into his stew. Cora hoped Helen knew to keep quiet. When Ma and Pa were arguing, as they often did, Ma hushed Helen with, "Children should be seen an not heard." Just like she said to Cora and her sister

Alice when they were younger. Cora tried to be positive. "The stew has great flavor, Ma."

Ma dismissed Cora's words with a wave of her hand.

"Turn that radio on, John. Let's see if President Roosevelt has anything to say 'bout the price a corn." Ma was still spoilin' for a fight.

Pa got up and snapped on the radio sitting on the kitchen counter in time for another Fireside Chat, as everyone called them.

Cora knew times were tough, but they were better off than many in the county. She prayed the Depression would end. Soon. What would it take to usher in prosperity? Then she looked at her father's leathered face and wondered how long he'd be able to work out in the elements to keep the farmland and animals?

After the Fireside Chat, Cora said goodnight and went upstairs for quiet. Her shoulders and neck were still aching, and she needed rest.

She took a small rag and washed in the water basin on her nightstand. Then traded her soiled nurse's uniform for a flannel nightgown and hung the uniform over the chair next to the chamber pot.

As she tugged open her top dresser drawer for a pair of warm socks, her hands felt around until they lit on it. A small

black and white photograph, faded with time. She pulled it out
and sat on the edge of her quilt-covered bed. Helen's questions
had opened the wound again. Her heart ached. She looked up
at the crucifix, the only decoration covering the green walls,
and wondered, "Why Lord? Why me? How did you let this
happen?" Then finally, as she reflected, her prayer changed.
"What could I have done differently?"

She was lost in thought when Helen knocked at her
door. Cora looked up with a start and wiped the back of her
hand over her cheeks.

Helen pushed the door open, rushed over and climbed
onto her bed. The metal springs squeaked under their weight.

"Why are you crying, Mama?" Helen stroked her dark
hair as if she were petting a kitten.

Cora said nothing at first but looked at the unframed
photograph. What should she tell Helen? Was she was old
enough to understand?

"Is this a baby you delivered, Mama?" Helen snuggled
up beside her and looked over her shoulder.

She looked at her, swept the bangs from Helen's blue
eyes and replied, "In a way."

"Did the baby die?" Helen's eyebrows narrowed.

Cora searched her face. Helen was too young to grasp the violence of the past. And yet she deserved to know the truth. Part of the truth.

"No, she's still alive," she whispered. "But I haven't seen her since she was a toddler."

"Who is she, Mama?"

She took a deep breath. It was time.

Chapter 14

*Cora

"This… is your sister…Ruby," Cora told Helen.

"Sister?" Helen exclaimed bright-eyed. "Where is she? Why doesn't she live with us?"

"A long time ago, I married a man named Frank."

"My father?"

"Yes, dear. Frank was, or rather, is, your father. You were born in Kentucky, but when you were tiny, we moved back to Iowa to live here with Grandma and Grandpa. Frank, er, your daddy, was unhappy here. He hated farm work and wanted to be a singer —"

A sudden movement in the room stopped her. Ma's frame darkened the doorway. "Why ya draggin' up the past, child?"

She jumped a bit and stiffened. "She has a right to know, Ma."

"Right? Ya don't need to fill her head with a lot a trouble," Ma was in her war stance — hands on sturdy hips, feet planted.

"We need to get this out into the open," Cora turned to her with pursed lips. She took a deep breath. "It's my life, my secret and I'll be the one to tell Helen. I don't want to wait until she overhears the local gossip."

"What secret! Tell me." Helen said.

"Well now's not the time. Hal Cooper's waitin' outside in his buggy. Adeline's in labor. Spect it's goin' to be a long night."

Cora sighed and looked away from Ma. Lord give her strength. She turned to Helen and ran her hand over the sweet face in front of her, cupping her cheek. "Sorry, dear one. I promise we'll talk more about this tomorrow after school." She got off the bed and set the picture on her dresser and changed into a clean uniform as Ma plodded down the stairs.

"If you're home then." Helen's lip quivered. "Tell me now, please."

"Yes, if I'm home by then. Pray I am. We all know babies arrive on their own schedules."

"How old is Ruby?"

"She's nearly twelve," Cora said as she re-braided her hair.

"If I have a dad, why doesn't he send me presents?" Helen asked looking confused.

"I know this is a lot for you to hear tonight. Please try to put it out of your mind for now, and we can talk tomorrow. Good night, Helen." She gave her a quick kiss and headed downstairs. Her back ached, and she wondered how she'd make it through another long night.

Helen ran down the stairs after her as Cora latched onto the handle of her medical bag. "But Mama, doesn't he love me?" Helen whispered.

Cora turned and bent to give her another quick kiss on the forehead. "We'll talk about this tomorrow. Now go to bed." She dashed out the kitchen door and disappeared into the brisk night.

* Helen

"Good-by, Mama," Helen whispered. She peered out the kitchen window as horses' hooves and wagon wheels carried Mama away. Tears sprang to her eyes, and she bit her lip to keep from spilling them. She turned around, and Grandma's eyes bore into her.

"Don't start fussin' 'bout yer Mama. I raised my children, and I don't like havin' to bother with the likes of ya."

"Yes, Ma'am." Helen looked down and swallowed the pain. Grandma's words stung, even though she heard them often.

"Get to bed!" Gertrude commanded. No hug or kiss. No nighttime prayers.

"Goodnight, Ole Bean," Grandpa called from the living room. Helen wanted to race in for a hug but knew Grandma called it lollygaggin.

"Goodnight, Grandpa," she called loud enough for him to hear. Then added softly, "Night Grandma."

She raced up the hardwood stairs to the small, cold room next to Mama's. She turned out her light and climbed into the icy bed, the metal springs squealing like hungry pigs. She pulled the thin blankets over her head, happy she kept her wool socks on. As she cocooned, waiting for her body to warm the nest, she worried over Mama's words. A sister! An answer to her prayers.

She pushed back the covers and slipped out of bed as quietly as the springs allowed. She pulled open her door and tiptoed the few steps to her mother's room. She didn't dare turn on a light. Her fingers moved over Mama's dresser top until they found the small photo. She stole back to her room and closed the door carefully, trying not to make a sound. For a moment, she turned the overhead light on and peered at Ruby's face as she stood by her bedroom door.

"Helen Jane! Turn that light off and get to bed!"

Caught. But she memorized Ruby's face. Back in bed, she carefully placed Ruby's picture on her nightstand. Her heart soared at the thought of a real-life sister. But then sadness shadowed the news as she wondered why her father never sent her a Christmas or birthday gift or wrote to her.

What would it be like to have a father and a sister, all living together in their own house without Grandma Gertrude? She and Ruby would play together. Read the same books. Tell each other their secrets at night in a shared room. Her brain see-sawed. First with a rush of excitement at having a sister and then her heart plummeted wondering why her father never contacted her. She soared at the thought of living apart from Grandma Gertrude, but spiraled down wondering if her father was angry or evil.

*Cora

"Good evening, Ma'am," Hal said as he helped her climb into the buggy. "Sorry to bother you tonight, but it looks like our little one's determined to make an entrance."

"It's no trouble, Hal. Let's hope Adeline has an easy time of it."

Hal shut the door of the buggy and then pulled his wool cap over his ears and leapt into his seat. Cora saw Helen's face in the kitchen window as they drove off.

The buggy made slow progress over dirt roads and gentle hills yet protected her from the swirling wind. As Hal Cooper's tall frame sat up top and steered the horses, she was happy for a bit of quiet for soul-searching.

Was it right to protect Helen from the truth all these years? Was she introducing more pain into her life now that she knew?

She longed to see Ruby and thought of her daily. After three long years in college, she had hoped to land a well-paying job that would help her launch a custody battle to win her back. Instead the country was embroiled in a Depression and the only position available didn't pay a consistent wage. Drudgery was now the drum beat of their lives. Months turned into years as she and her parents labored to keep their farm, the source of their survival.

Depression of another sort washed over Cora. When she brought up Ruby while she was alone with her mother, Ma always shot back the same way. "Forget her! It's over and done. She's with Frank and her grandparents and that's the end of it. Ya made yer bed and now ya have to lie in it."

But how could it ever be the end of it? Her heart ached to see Ruby and hold her. Over the years, she tried contacting Frank, even though the memory of him still made her cringe, but he never answered her letters. She sent gifts to Ruby at Christmas and her birthday for many years, but never knew if she received them. Frank's parents also refused to communicate with her. She finally gave up. Had she sacrificed her child to exorcise an alcoholic, abusive man from her life?

She had always intended to fight for custody of her, but life seem to beat her back at every turn.

And now that Helen knew about Frank and Ruby, she'd never stop asking to meet them.

The buggy ground to a stop. Cora shook her head to snap back to the present and took a deep breath. The Cooper's third child was about to be born. Stay focused. She snatched her bag and dashed inside the small farmhouse.

Two tow-headed little ones were waiting at the door. Four-year-old Kent and two-year-old Annie greeted her wide-eyed. "Mama's gonna have a baby," Kent declared.

"Yes, your baby brother or sister is on the way. Mama will be fine. You two stay with Daddy," She said smiling as she took off her coat. Then hurried upstairs where Adeline was moaning from a strong contraction.

"I'll keep the children downstairs," Hal called.

"Thank heaven you're here!" Adeline said when Cora appeared.

"Sounds like this one is determined to meet you," Cora said. She delivered Kent and Annie and knew she and Adeline worked well as a team. Adeline's pretty face was flushed; her hair was matted to her head.

"They're comin' pretty regular," Adeline said when the next contraction subsided.

"Let's see how close you are," Cora moved to examine her.

They spoke little, letting Adeline rest between contractions. Cora was tempted to rest too but didn't allow herself to nod off, afraid she wouldn't be able to awaken. How many days since her last full night's sleep? She shook her head. Best not to think about it.

Hal must have read her thoughts. He knocked on the door and handed her a strong cup of coffee, which she happily received.

"How's she doing?"

"It won't be long now," She reassured him, then shooed him back downstairs to wait. Men were little help in deliveries. Even farmers used to helping birth calves were likely to faint at the sight of their offspring coming into the world.

Finally, a baby girl was born. She tried out her lungs as Adeline and Cora breathed a collective sigh of relief.

"Thank you, Lord," Adeline murmured experiencing the emotional high of meeting her newborn. She kissed her tiny face and hands. "We're calling her Mary."

"Lovely! That was your mother's name, wasn't it?" She never tired of meeting a newborn or seeing the excitement on the mother's face. No matter the circumstances, greeting a new life always seemed to bring joy.

"Yes, you remembered. After Mother passed away last year, we decided to honor her by naming our next girl Mary."

"I'm sure she would have been very proud."

"Well, yes. She would also remind me this is one more mouth to feed when money is scarce. But for tonight I'm going to put worries aside and thank God for a healthy little one. The newest member of our family."

Cora crept downstairs and found Hal, still awake and anxious.

"Congratulations, you have a beautiful little girl." The relief on his face spoke volumes, and he vaulted up the stairs to meet Mary.

She was happy for them. But a twinge of something tugged at her heart. She shook her head. No point dredging up the agony of the past. Where was all this coming from? Perhaps telling Helen about Ruby and Frank cracked opened the floodgates of her past. But in truth, Ruby was never far from her thoughts.

Cora slept on their couch to be certain mother and baby were out of danger. At first light, Hal drove her home.

As he helped her out of the buggy, he handed her a few crumpled dollar bills. "I know we don't have the full amount to pay you, Cora. The price a corn seems to be falling daily and my hours were cut at the plant. But we'll pay you a bit at a time." She looked from his faded and worn overalls to the sincerity in his warm brown eyes.

"Send it to me when you can." Talking about money made her uncomfortable.

"Thank you for bringing our little Mary safely into the world. I know times are tough, but this new life is still a gift from God," he said. Hal and Adeline shared a strong faith. They were a few years younger than Cora, but mature beyond their years.

"You're right Hal. She's a glorious gift." She shook his massive hand and made her way to the porch.

Helen was sitting on the bench at the kitchen table, eating her porridge when the door creaked open.

"Mama!" She hopped up and clung to her waist.

"Child! Let yer Mama be. She hasn't had a proper night sleep in days. Don't hang on her." Ma was never chipper in the mornings.

"Hi, Baby!" Mama hugged her back. "Long night. Adeline had a baby girl – Mary." Cora set Helen aside and urged her to finish eating.

"I s'pose ya didn't get paid agin," Grandma challenged.

"Hal paid what he was able to. He's good for the rest, in time, Ma."

"Believe it when I sees it."

"Mama, when can we talk?" Helen asked.

"After school Helen. I'll be here when you get home."

Helen sighed.

"Better eat somethin' before ya collapse Cora. Keep up yer strength. Never know when another baby'll be wantin' to be born."

"Yes, Ma. I'll eat. I think we're going to have a break from new babies for a few weeks."

Grandpa burst in through the porch. "Lady's saddled up. Let's go, Ole Bean."

"Don't forget your lunch," Cora said as she handed Helen her lunch pail.

Cora followed Helen and Pa out the door to send Helen off to school.

As Pa helped her onto the saddle behind him, she sniffed the air and giggled. "Smells like corn Grandpa. Guess we won't be popping any this year."

"Don't worry none, Ole Bean. There's plenty a corn – for fuel, feed and poppin'."

Cora smiled. Pa won again in his quiet way.

She went inside to get some much-needed rest and slept fitfully, most of the morning. Now she had to sort through what to tell Helen. How much could a ten-year-old understand? Cora wanted to be honest, without burdening her young heart.

She pulled her hair into a long braid and dressed in a clean cotton dress for a walk in the hills around the farm. The kitchen was quiet, so she snagged a crust of bread and a small chunk of cheese. The changing of the leaves and fresh air beckoned her outside. After being cooped up for days, she wanted to clear her head. Cora walked past chickens scratching outside the hen house, horses sunning themselves in their pasture, and pigs laying in the mud. When she heard her parents arguing while harvesting the last vegetables in the enormous garden, she hurried by, hoping they wouldn't notice her. Yes, she'd help Ma can the last of the vegetables later that afternoon, but right now time alone was critical.

She hiked along the gently rolling lush fields where the cows grazed. Mothers and baby calves together, contentedly enjoying the afternoon. Their lives seemed so simple and predictable. Unlike hers.

She missed her dear friend Sylvia. Her letters, though relished, were a poor substitute for a long soul-emptying walk together. Arm-in-arm they shared their worries, fears, and successes when they were together in Kentucky.

Several years ago, Sylvia wrote to say Frank married again. It made no dent in Cora's emotions, but she wondered if Ruby was being treated well by her stepmother. Then Frank's new wife had another child. A playmate for Ruby or a rival for her father's affection? The uncertainty was torture.

But now her thoughts turned to Helen, who would be home soon full of questions that deserved suitable answers. The bright sunshine energized her and the thought of seeing Ruby again elated her. Maybe this time she would make it happen.

"Mama," Helen yelled as she burst through the kitchen door.

"No need to be so loud," Ma shushed her as she worked on vegetables, getting them ready to be canned.

Cora pulled Helen into a brief hug. "Let's go for a walk."

"Not till after her chores," Ma scowled.

"I'll help you," Cora said. They collected eggs from the chickens, fed the pigs and swept the kitchen floor. Finally, Cora took her hand, and they trekked out to a back pasture where she'd been "gathering wool" earlier. The dry leaves crackled and scattered under their feet. When they were far from the farmhouse and out of earshot of Ma, they sat on a pile of crimson and gold leaves.

"I'm sorry I haven't told you about your pa and sister," Cora started. "I never wanted to hurt you, but I felt some things would be difficult to understand. You're older now, and it's time you knew."

Helen's curious blue eyes sparkled in the sun as she waited eagerly.

Cora told her about teaching at the mission school, meeting Frank and the birth of Ruby.

"What does Ruby look like?"

"I don't know, Helen. I haven't seen her since she was two and a half. She had dark brown hair and brown eyes, like me, but they might have changed."

"What does my pa look like?" Helen wondered.

"You have his auburn hair. I don't know where you got your blue eyes. Maybe from Grandpa John."

"Why doesn't my pa ever write or come and see us?".

"Your father and I are not married any longer, and money is tight everywhere with this Depression. It's difficult to travel that far."

"But he traveled with Ruby?"

"Yes, he left while the rest of us were at church."

"Why didn't he take me?" Helen chewed on her bottom lip.

"I don't know for certain. Perhaps because you were so little. I was still nursing you. Or because you weren't a boy. He never left a note, so I never found out." Cora reached for her hand and held it. They were silent for a few moments. "Helen, I'm grateful to God he left you with me."

"But Mama, don't you miss Ruby?"

"With all my heart. I think of her every day."

"Why don't we go see Pa and Ruby? I want to meet them."

Cora nodded. It was time. "I'd love to see Ruby. Let's try to contact them."

"Do you think he'll hurt me?" Helen's eyes were like saucers.

"No, baby, I'd never let him hurt you."

"Do you know where he's living?"

"I believe he's in Kentucky near his parents. I sent letters and gifts to Ruby, but I never heard back, so I assumed they must have moved."

"That's what Grandpa told me this morning when I asked him. I looked at it on the map, and it's a long ways away."

She smiled at her bright little girl. "Let's find them. I think we've waited long enough."

Helen brightened and threw her arms around her. "Thank you, Mama."

The next evening, Cora was home for supper. After they all gave thanks, She turned to Helen. "I don't want you to get your hopes up, but I wrote a letter today to an old friend who might be able to help us."

"What old friend?"

"When I worked as a teacher in Kentucky, I made friends with a woman about my age named Sylvia. I hear from her now and then, and I've asked her to find out where Frank and Ruby are living."

"I don't know why yer stirrin' up all this. We've been just fine for ten years. Now yer just invitin' trouble into yer lives." Ma shook her fork.

"Ma, I'm not stirring things up. Helen has a right to know her kin. She has a father and sister, and I have a right to tell her about them."

"Well if they were keen on meetin' her, don't ya think he woulda contacted you? It's not like you've moved in ten years."

"I don't know the reason for his silence. But one of us has to make the first move, for the sake of the girls. It's not right for them to grow up not knowing both their parents."

"Ya better not be plannin' to bring Ruby back here to live. We've got enough mouths to feed." Ma's lips disappeared like they always did when she was mad.

"I want a chance to see my daughter. No one said anything about her moving in here. Don't you want to see your granddaughter, Ma?"

"I gave up on seein' her when he ran out on ya years ago. It's better to let sleepin' dogs lie."

"She's not a sleeping dog. She's my daughter, and I intend to see her." Cora stopped eating, and her face turned scarlet.

Finally, Pa weighed in. "Let's drop this. Cora has every right to look for her daughter. And I have every right to eat in peace."

They finished the meal in silence. The adults scattered to different corners when they left the table, while Helen cleared the dishes. She headed toward the kitchen door as soon as she finished.

"Helen Jane, ya'd better not be feeding those cats." Grandma caught her arm before she got through the door.

"No Ma'am. I just want to play with them." Grandma let her go. Maybe the fight was out of her for tonight.

Later, Helen brought the tiny black and white picture back into her mother's room. Cora was propped in bed reading. Helen climbed next to her and gave her the picture.

"I wanted to see Ruby again." She handed the picture to her mother.

"I want to see her too, Helen. Please don't worry about Grandma. This is our problem, and we're going to solve it without her."

"Why is Grandma so mean?"

"Life didn't turn out the way Grandma wanted it. I don't think she ever wanted to be a farmer's wife. It's hard work. But girls didn't have as many options when she was young. Try not to think of her harshly."

Helen nodded thoughtfully.

Cora wondered how to keep Helen engaged in her studies while they waited to hear from Sylvia. The thought of seeing Frank again unnerved her, but she had to face him if she wanted to see Ruby. After she heard he married again, Cora stayed away, even though she wanted to know how Ruby was doing. Did Frank learn a trade or find a steady job? Was Ruby living in poverty? Perhaps she was friends with younger siblings of the students Cora taught when she was in Kentucky. A warm thought.

Cora tried not to be bitter about the painful things Ma said to her. Cora fought to hang on to shards of hope. Wasn't that the essence of faith? Now a new bud of hope stirred within her and a new prayer. "Please God let me see my Ruby and have some part in her life."

But Ma carried a perpetual anger toward God and everyone around her. She attended church regularly, but the gospel never seemed to penetrate her soul. Joy was not an emotion she accepted or experienced.

Over the next few weeks, Helen burst through the door daily asking if there was any news from Kentucky. And every day Cora reminded her to have hope.

The autumn leaves abandoned their posts as the night air grew crisp and the harvest moon was a golden spotlight. Fall in Southern Iowa. Life was routine, except she and Helen both had a heightened sense of anticipation.

Finally, one evening, she pulled Helen aside after dinner and whispered, "I have some news."

Chapter 15

*Cora

"News? From my Pa?" Helen asked as the two dashed upstairs to talk without interruptions.

"Well, no, not yet. My friend Sylvia has written. She did some digging and found your Pa's address. Shall we write a letter together to your sister?"

Helen threw her arms around Cora. "What should we say? I don't want her to think I'm a baby." They debated what to write. At last Helen put pen to paper, shaping each letter with care, stopping to think about the correct spelling of each word.

"Dear Ruby,

Mama said I could write to you. I want to know you and to meet you. What do you look like? What do you like to do?

I like to read and to play with my doll, Amy.

We live on a farm in Iowa. I love animals. My favorite is Grandpa's horse, Lady. We have lots of kittens, and I wish I could make one my pet.

Please write back to me. Your sister, Helen

PS – I'm ten years old. I have red hair, blue eyes, and freckles!"

"Very good! I'll post this letter tomorrow," Mama said.

"Mama, why didn't anyone tell me I had a pa?"

"I didn't want to burden you. When he ran out on us, I assumed he didn't want any part of our lives."

"I thought he was dead," Helen whispered.

"Which was worse? To know he was alive but didn't want anything to do with us? Or to believe he died?"

"Don't know. But will he be glad to meet me?"

"It's impossible to predict, but I hope he'll be excited to meet you again. He was a good father, and I'll bet he's been missing you just like I've been missing Ruby."

"But Mama, you won't leave me in Kentucky, will you?"

"Helen! Where do you get these ideas?"

"Well Grandma says she can't have more mouths to feed, so I thought maybe you were going to bring Ruby here and leave me in Kentucky."

"I will never leave you. Promise. We may try to find a way to bring Ruby home with us, but I won't be leaving you. Ever."

*Helen

As winter bore down, Helen spent more time inside. One evening, Helen stood next to her grandma watching her embroider a cloth.

"Git outta my light, child."

Helen moved to the other side but kept watching as Grandma used different colored threads to create designs.

"What are you making, Grandma?"

"Tablecloth for a weddin gift." Grandma almost smiled as she showed Helen her work. Helen watched as Grandma deftly brought multi-colored birds and flowers to life on the white Irish linen cloth. And was Grandma humming?

"Grandma, will you teach me?"

Grandma Gertrude peered at Helen for a moment over her bifocals. Then sighed.

"I guess yer old enuf. It'll keep ya outta trouble." She gathered a needle and different colored threads and an old flour sack for Helen to use as practice.

"We'll start with something simple. This is a running stitch." And suddenly, the door to a different grandma cracked open. An almost patient side emerged.

Helen practiced the stitch over and over. "But how do I make a bird Grandma?"

"Outline yer design with the stitch I showd ya and then fill in with a satin stitch."

Helen held her breath as Grandma showed her how to make a stitch that lived up to its' name.

Over the next few weeks, as Helen waited impatiently for news of her sister and father, embroidering helped keep her mind settled.

Ma took notice of her handiwork one evening. "Helen, you'll soon be able to make a piano cover as fine as the one Grandma purchased."

"Now, don't go gittin her all pumped up," Grandma said.

Helen was thrilled with the praise and wanted to learn more.

"Grandma, will you teach me to sew? I'd like to make something for my doll, Amy."

"We'll see," was all the response she got. But days later Helen found some fabric scraps left over from their kitchen curtains sitting by her embroidery.

"Grandma, is this for my doll clothes?"

"If ya finish yer chores without fussin, we'll work on it after supper."

Helen completed her chores without complaining and worked hard not to fidget at the supper table. When Mama came home from delivering another baby, she didn't yell out her name. Instead, she hugged her and whispered, "Grandma's going to teach me to sew tonight if I'm good."

"Well come over here child if ya want to learn," Grandma said to Helen after supper.

Together they cut out a simple dress, using Amy's measurements as their guide.

"Put right sides together and use the running stitch with this lightweight thread," Grandma said as she and Helen worked under the dim light in the sitting room. "You'll have to thread the needle. My eyes ain't too good in this light."

If Helen made a stitch that was out of place, Grandma made her rip it out and do it over. By the end of the evening, Amy was sporting a new cotton chintz dress, and Helen was beaming.

"Now leave me in peace child," Grandma said, but Helen noticed a bit of a smile when she saw their finished work.

A few weeks later, Helen was looking for fabric scraps in her grandmother's room when she came across the old faded green piano cover in Grandma's sewing pile. *What's this doing here?* She wondered. *Surely Grandma meant to throw this away.*

Helen took the cover to her niche in the attic, along with scissors, needle, and thread. She cut the old fabric and made a cape with a hood out of the piano cover for her doll, Amy. She even lined it. She put the cape on her doll. *It fits! And Amy looks so pretty in it.*

After Helen finished her chores the next afternoon, she ran to the attic to play with her doll. But the cape was gone and so was the fabric. Her heart raced to think her grandmother came into her playroom and took them. *She was here! I wonder what she'll do to me?*

Helen hid until supper time, and when Grandma finally called, she went downstairs with dread. She expected a paddling for taking the piano cover, but Grandma said nothing. The stress of wondering and waiting made Helen jumpy for days. Every time Grandma said her name, she was sure she'd get the strap. But no punishment ever came.

Almost every Sunday, they went to the country church where they all referred to themselves as Christians. It was a wooden building with a steeple and a bell tower. The heavy oak communion table stood in front with a large cross on it. Helen was always happy to be at church. It was the one place where Grandma didn't scold her, although she complained the hard wooden seats hurt her arthritis. Mama came with them when she wasn't delivering a baby.

Grandma's friend, Myrtle played the piano. They sang their favorites, "Faith of our Fathers," "Amazing Grace," and "The Old Rugged Cross," Songs they knew by heart, so no choir books were necessary. Helen loved to sing. After church when someone said her singing was "real pretty," it made her heart soar.

Shortly after Helen wrote to her sister, she was singing in church, lost in the words of the hymns. She daydreamed about the words to Amazing Grace. *"Saved a wretch like me," seems a bit harsh. Sure, I disobeyed sometimes, but am I a wretch?* Then she remembered taking the old piano cover.

The other line that bothered her was, "I once was lost, but now am found." She did feel lost, adrift. But not found. She kept waiting to hear from her sister or her pa. Somehow it would tell her if she was found. But no letter came. *Perhaps I am a wretch after all, and that's why Pa doesn't want to meet me.*

"You have a lovely clear voice," a woman who sat in front of her exclaimed.

"My pa is a singer," she thought. How she wanted to hear him sing.

*Cora

When Helen got home from school one day in November, Cora pulled her into a hug. She was happy no babies were due now, so they spent more time together.

"You smell like spices, Mama," Helen said. "I'm so hungry."

"I've been putting up the last of the pickles."

"I can hardly wait to try one."

"And I can hardly wait to tell you my news," Cora said and smiled mysteriously. She handed her a small apple and sat down at the kitchen table. She reached into her pocket and held out an envelope. "A letter's come from your sister."

Helen shrieked with delight. Grandma was working in the kitchen. "Land a mercy child!" she scolded.

When Helen finished her apple, she and Cora went upstairs to read the letter together.

"Dear Helen,

I got yer letter the other day an I was so serprized. I knew 'bout ya but I didn't think I'd git to meet ya. I be havin dark brown hair and brown eyes. I likes to cook and to look after the neighbor's lil uns.

Do ya think ya could come for a vizit? Pa says it'd be OK ifin yer ma comes to.

Love, yer sister, Ruby."

PS – please say Hi to our Ma for me. I reely want to meet her.

They read it over again, and Cora tried to imagine this was her child. The girl she hadn't seen in over ten years.

The teacher in her was disappointed to see Ruby's spelling and grammar. By 12, she hoped Ruby had a better grasp of the English language.

"They want us to visit. When can we go, Mama?"

"This will take some planning, and I have to save money for the train. But I think we should go down to Kentucky when school lets out in May."

"May? I was hoping we'd go for Christmas. I want to sew something for Ruby as a gift," Helen said.

"Why don't you still plan to sew something and we'll send it through the post." Cora hoped this gift would finally get to Ruby.

Days later, Cora walked in one afternoon as her parents were arguing about their financial situation. Helen was sitting quietly at the table with workbooks in front of her.

"We can't afford to feed that many heads a cattle," Pa said.

"Well John, ya didn't sell the corn crop, so what do ya propose to do?" Grandma stood with her hands on her hips.

"We'll have to sell the cattle."

"Prices are rock bottom. It'll be like given 'em away!"

"Gertrude, what do YOU propose? It's not like the Depression's my fault."

"If we keep sellin' cattle and hogs, what'll we have left?"

"We got chickens and whatever vegetables we put up last fall," Cora inserted.

"We didn't git the rain we needed for the garden. Our supplies are gitten' low already," Ma said.

"We have oats, and we have potatoes. Need be, we'll survive on those till I can find a job. I'll go into town tomorra." Pa hurried into his hat and coat and charged outside to the barn.

Cora soaked in the anxiety of the conversation. "I'll contact my patients who still owe me and see if I can bring in enough to help."

"Fat lot that will help," Ma said.

"It won't hurt to try," Cora said.

"When will the Depression end, Mama?" Helen asked.

"No one knows, but it will end. Until things get better, you'll have only a potato in your lunch."

"I don't mind. Lots of kids bring a potato, and we line em up on the big stove to cook. By lunch, my mouth is watering from the smell."

"Thanks for not complaining, my sweet," Cora said.

"But some kids don't have any lunch," Helen said.

"I can't stand to see children go hungry. Maybe we could send a few extra in your lunch to share, Helen," Cora said.

"Don't go givin our food away or it won't last through the winter," Ma said.

Cora tried to shelter Helen from the harsh realities of the Depression, but it cloaked all of them like a heavy wet blanket. Many of her patients were living on far less and stood in long bread lines daily. As she tried to save a little each month for the trip to Kentucky, Cora struggled with guilt. If she had extra, shouldn't she help the poor instead of putting the money aside? In spite of the guilt, she stuck to her savings plan. She needed to see her child and was determined to go even if it meant skipping a few meals or new shoes.

In desperation, Cora paid visits to each of the families that still owed her money for a delivery. Collecting money was the part of her job she detested, even if her rates were fair. In home-after-home she heard the same story about unemployment, low crop prices and a difficult growing season. Gardens didn't produce as much as usual, adding to the panic. A few clients offered chickens or a few eggs as payment, which she accepted. She came home defeated and guilty for pestering honest people caught in terrible circumstances.

Cora was fixing supper late one afternoon when her father walked in with a smile on his weary face. Helen was in her reading alcove.

"President Roosevelt has saved us," Pa said as he slumped onto the kitchen bench.

"What are ya talkin' bout now, John?" Gertrude asked.

"I've taken a job with the WPA. One of Roosevelt's programs."

"The Works Project Administration Pa?" Cora asked.

"Yes, I just filled out all the paperwork and got my assignment."

"What do they think yer fit for?" Ma asked.

"I'll be helpin' to build roads from rural areas into the towns. Guess they're gettin' ready for more traffic on them roads."

"Don't know who they think'll be buyin' them cars."

"Now Mother, this Depression can't last forever!" Pa said.

"When will you start Pa?" Cora asked.

"Monday after Thanksgiving."

As wonderful as the news was, Cora realized it would be another gut punch for Helen. She and her mother looked at each other as the reality set in.

Chapter 16

*Cora

"I'm afraid I have to start early of a mornin, so I won't be able to take Helen to school."

Cora slumped next to her Pa. "It's too far for her to walk. I'm not sure what to do."

"Don't look at me. I ain't goin to drive the carriage," Ma said.

"No one is asking you to Ma. But I need a bit of time to think about this."

*Helen

At school, the chatter was all about Thanksgiving and the feast they'd enjoy. Helen wondered if they'd have a turkey this year. Some of the students said their families were planning to roast a chicken or two; others couldn't afford any meat. Helen knew Grandma saved a pumpkin and she looked forward to the pie.

She asked Grandpa about it on their ride home one day. "Will we have a turkey this year?"

"I seen wild turkeys around our farm, but not for a while. Don't know if poachers picked 'em off. Want to help me hunt for one, Ole Bean?"

"Sure!" Wow, Grandpa never asked her to hunt before. The thought of helping Grandpa bag a wild bird left her giddy.

Two days before Thanksgiving, she bundled into her warmest snow pants, jacket, hat, and gloves. Grandpa got his gun, and the pair went to the ravine on their property in the late afternoon. They waited quietly in the cold, listening for the sound of a turkey. Grandpa knew a few turkey calls and sent one out now and then hoping to attract a bird. Helen stifled a giggle. Grandpa sounded so silly. Suddenly he hushed her. He spotted a tom, focused his gun and shot. But they watched as the bird scurried back into the woods. Cold and frustrated, they showed up at supper empty-handed.

"We'll butcher a few chickens in the mornin'," he told Grandma.

Grandma sighed. "We're lucky to have meat. And lucky ya didn't hurt this child. What was ya thinkin' bringin' a little girl with ya out huntin'?"

"I think she's a big girl now." He winked at Helen, and she winked back.

The next morning, Grandpa woke her early, before daybreak. "Hey, Ole Bean, wanna try 'n get a bird?" he whispered.

Helen bolted out of bed, dressed and scooted down the stairs.

An adventure with Grandpa! She couldn't believe it. Grandpa must have his heart set on turkey. They went back to the same ravine and climbed into a low tree, waiting for the fog to roll off the hills. Grandpa said this was the most likely place for success, but it was cold and dark. Helen tried not to make a sound, and to quiet her grumbling tummy.

Grandpa said, "Don't worry, Ole Bean, we just need one bird." One large bird to feed the crowd set to gather at their home the next day. Aunt Alice, Uncle James, and her four cousins would squeeze into their home for the celebration. Hopefully, Mama would be able to join them, as long as no babies surprised them with an early delivery.

Grandpa's patience paid off. He saw movement in the brush, shot and bolted after it. He came out holding the biggest turkey Helen ever saw.

"Its' wing was hit. I think maybe it's the same bird we took aim at last night."

"Nice job, Grandpa! I can't wait to eat it."

Grandpa carried the bird by its' feet in one large hand, his shotgun in the other. Together they walked into the barn and hung it upside down.

They headed for the house and surprised Grandma when they walked in from the porch.

"There's a gift for ya in the barn, Mother," Grandpa said to Grandma.

"Gift? What are ya talkin about old man?"

"A turkey for our table," Grandpa said, obviously proud to have delivered such a bird in time for the feast.

"Oh, and I s'ppose ya think I have time to dress a bird with everythin' else I need to fix!" Grandma Gertrude said.

"Cora's home today, she'll help ya," Grandpa said, and he headed out to feed the too-thin cattle and milk the Jersey cows.

"With this small oven, we'll have to make everythin' else today."

"I can help, Grandma!" Helen felt especially grown up after helping hunt the turkey.

"Oh, you'll be helpin' all right! Ya helped Grandpa get that bird, now ya can help me pluck the feathers! But first, you'd better git ready for school."

Helen couldn't wait to tell the others about hunting for a turkey, but before she left for school, Grandma warned her.

"Don't ya go tellin' others bout that wild bird or we'll have every Tom, Dick, and Harry in the county pokin' around our land." Helen nodded and took off with Grandpa on Lady.

*Cora

Cora and Ma set about making pumpkin pies, stuffing, candied sweet potatoes and getting dinner rolls started the day before the feast.

"Alice's bringin' apple pie, green beans, and spiced cranberry jelly." Ma was going over her menu. "Now the whole durn oven'll be needed tomorrow for that bird."

"Come on, Ma, the turkey will be the star of the feast. What a gift Pa shot one today!"

"I hope ya still think it's a gift after ya spend a few hours plucking out them feathers."

"Many hands make light work. We'll get it done, Ma." Secretly Cora was thrilled her dad asked Helen to hunt with him. She rarely had much time alone with him when she was young, and it warmed her heart to see him take an interest in Helen. He was like a father to her in many ways. He worked endless hours on the farm, with the land, animals and equipment repairs. Time was in short supply, just like money. So when he spent a bit of time on Helen, Cora was grateful.

"Mama, did you get our turkey dressed?" Helen asked when she raced in after school.

"I certainly did. All dressed and ready for the big day," Cora said.

"And I have four days off school. I can't wait!"

"Me too. I hope this will be a wonderful Thanksgiving."

How would she tell Helen? The timing seemed almost cruel.

"Is something wrong, Mama? Why aren't you more excited?"

"I'm very excited about your turkey and Thanksgiving and a long weekend together. But something has changed which will affect you."

"What, Mama?" Helen looked at her wide-eyed. "We're still going to Kentucky, right?"

"Yes, we'll go in May. I promise. But let's sit down for a moment." Cora led her to the living room. "We have a situation that will affect you. Not forever. But I need you to live with Aunt Alice and your cousins for the rest of the school year."

"Live with my cousins?" Helen asked. "Will you come with me?"

"I'm sorry, Helen, there isn't room for both of us. Grandpa has gotten a job helping build roads. He won't be able to bring you to school, and it's too far to walk. Your cousins live closer so you can all walk together."

"When will I see you?" Helen was biting her bottom lip, tears spilling over dark lashes.

"I'll visit when I can on the weekends. And we can see each other at church on Sunday." Mama tucked a runaway curl behind Helen's ear and then held her hand.

"When you're not delivering a baby, you mean."

"Yes, of course. Please be a big girl and try to understand. As soon as the school year is over, you can move back to the farm every summer."

"Every summer? Will I live with them every school year?"

"At least for the next few years," Mama said. "Hopefully things will improve in our country, and we can be together again."

Tears spilled freely down Helen's cheeks.

"You've always wanted brothers and sisters. Now you can see what it's like living with other children."

Helen nodded resolutely. "But I don't belong to them."

"They're family. You do belong, and I'm sure you'll be fine," Cora said trying to be brave for Helen. Her heart was heavy. Once again life was out of her control, and her children suffered the consequences. Alice would be good to Helen, but Cora would miss her. Weren't mothers supposed to be with their children? The constant longing for Ruby stoked her guilt.

*Helen

Thanksgiving Day dawned crisp and clear. Helen smelled the turkey roasting as soon as she awoke. She ate a small bowl of oatmeal for breakfast. Grandma said to save their appetites for the early afternoon feast.

"I need ya to whip the cream today. Hurry and git dressed. No lollygagging around, missy," Grandma Gertrude was in fine form, barking orders and assigning chores.

"Yes, Grandma," Helen said cheerfully. It made her feel grown up to have a job for the big feast. She dressed and found the cream chilling on the porch by the pies they baked yesterday. She used a whisk and whipped it until her arms ached.

"Don't whip it into butter," Grandma hollered on her way outside to collect eggs. Grandma was a whirlwind of activity.

Helen finished the cream, set tables and dragged in extra chairs from the barn. She pumped water from the well to fill the glasses and extra buckets to be heated later for the endless pile of dirty dishes. She was excited about the feast, but a sense of sadness clung to her, knowing she'd soon be moving away from her mother.

"They're here," Helen said when she looked out the window and saw her cousins walking up the path. She ran to the door and called to them.

"Hush child, no need to be so loud," Grandma said.

Aunt Alice, Uncle Ed and her cousins, Harriet, Celia, Robert, and Danny crowded in.

"Smells wonderful in here, Ma," Alice said. The fragrance of warm rolls baking and turkey roasting perfumed the air.

"Well, it should. I been workin on this for two days," she said. "Helen, take their coats," Grandma barked. Her face was red, and she used her arm to wipe away the sweat from her brow. In spite of the cold temperature outside, the house was warm from the cookstove.

There were subdued greetings. They knew not to agitate Grandma more than she already was.

Helen took a few of their coats and headed to Grandma and Grandpa's room to lay them on the bed. Aunt Alice followed Helen with another armload. Aunt Alice sat on the bed, gently reached for Helen's hand and held it. She smiled as she looked into her freckled face. "I told your cousins you'll be stayin' with us this winter. You can sleep with Harriet and Celia in their room."

"Yes, ma'am," was all Helen could manage.

"I know you'll be missing your mama, but I want you to feel at home with us." Aunt Alice gave her a quick kiss on the forehead, and they walked into the warm kitchen to rejoin the others.

"Outta the kitchen," Grandma hollered, and everyone, except Cora and Alice, obediently squeezed into the living room. The three women finished preparing dishes and carving the turkey. At last the feast was ready.

Helen and the other children went through the serving line first and helped themselves on small plates. Sitting in the living room, crammed around the tiny table, they were out of sight from their parents.

Harriet, the oldest spoke first. "So, you're goin' to live with us now. Mama says you'll have to share a room with Celia and me. We're going to push our beds together so the three of us can sleep together."

"I hope you're not a bed hog," Celia chimed in.

"I hope you don't have bedbugs," Robert teased as he took another mouthful of turkey.

"Hey, we don't have bedbugs," Helen shot back.

"Do you snore?" Celia asked swallowing a bite of her roll.

"I don't think so." She always slept alone, so she didn't know. "Do YOU snore?"

Celia shook her head.

"Well, I hope you don't have too much stuff. We only have one drawer in the dresser for you." Harriet tossed her dark curls.

Sharing a bed with two cousins and one dresser drawer for her things didn't sound promising. No more reading nook where she kept her sewing supplies and her doll. Would she ever find time alone? "I plan to bring my doll, Amy."

"Oh great. Big baby," Robert said, although he was only a year older than Helen.

Aunt Alice appeared at their table. "Enough teasing! I'm sure you'll all get along just fine." She gave the children a stern look. Before she left the living room, she spotted the wine colored velvet on the piano. "Ma, where did you get this fine piano cover? It must have cost a fortune."

Grandma Gertrude crowed, "I traded it for a chicken and a bit of firewood. Some gypsy ladies came by, and we bartered."

"Seems a bit frivolous when money is so tight," Alice said.

"Sometimes we need somethin to brighten up this bleak house," Grandma said.

Helen looked into the kitchen and saw the adults looked at each other and shrug their shoulders. Nothing more was said.

The children finished their feast, cleared dishes and went outside to play Hide and Seek. The cool air was refreshing as they looked for places to hide. No place was off limits. They hid in the barn, the chicken coop and even the outhouse. Little Danny had trouble finding them when it was his turn to seek. After a few turns, he decided to chase kittens instead, and Helen ditched the game to play with Danny. She caught her favorite black and white kitten and showed him to Danny. "I'm calling this one "Mittens."

"Can you bring it with you when you come to live with us?"

Before she answered, Grandma's imposing frame appeared at the porch door.

"Pie," came the call from the farmhouse. When Grandma spoke, everyone came running. The adults lingered over their meal by waiting an hour or more to serve dessert. But when Grandma was ready for pie, no one argued. The five children huddled around the table in the living room licking the pumpkin pie and whipped cream from their spoons.

Aunt Alice played the piano after dessert, and they joined in singing hymns and patriotic choices they all knew.

"No Christmas songs," Grandma instructed. "Too early for all that."

After she went to bed, Helen cried silently into her pillow. What would life be like at her cousin's? How would she ever see mama? She didn't belong there, but she didn't belong with Grandma either.

Chapter 17

*Cora

"It'll be a relief not to hafta look after that youngun' all the time." Ma and Cora were enjoying a cup of coffee before it was time to move Helen to Alice and Ed's home, the Saturday after Thanksgiving.

"I appreciate all you've done for Helen, Ma. But she's pretty good help now that she's ten."

"She eats more, and I can't afford to feed another mouth." Ma rubbed a spot on her leg, and Cora glimpsed her prominent varicose veins.

"I've contributed all these years, Ma. And now I'll have to split my wages between this household and Alice's."

"Yer goin' to have to be sure those ladies pay ya. No more charity deliveries."

"I can't turn someone down just because they don't have the funds. That would be unthinkable."

"Well, ya ain't running a charity program. Yer supposed to git paid for yer services."

"Let's hope the country gets on better footing, and that'll help all of us. For now, I've got to set aside money each week for the train fare to Kentucky."

"I don't know why ya had to bring up all that bizness. Helen was just fine not knowing about her pa and sis."

"She has a right to know and to meet them. And let's not forget, I need to see my other child. You have no idea how difficult it's been not to have watched Ruby grow up." Cora pressed her lips together to hold back the tears.

"Lots a people has it worse than ya. Don't go feelin' sorry for yerself." Ma stood and plunked her cup in the sink. Conversation over.

Cora climbed the stairs and sat on her bed for a few minutes. She didn't allow herself much time to focus on the past, but the magnitude of the day weighed on her. Once again, she felt like a failure. First, she lost Ruby, and now she was sending Helen away. Only for the school year, she reminded herself, but time with a small child was precious, and she'd be missing out of Helen's daily hugs and stories of school adventures. This was the only option that made sense. Perhaps if she had married again, life would have been kinder to her and Helen. A man to share her life. A husband she could respect and someone to be a father to Helen. But it never happened, so no point dwelling on it. Best to move ahead, not back.

*Helen

Mama helped Helen wash her few clothes, and they
hung them on the line to dry in the morning sun. Later, they
packed them in a small cloth suitcase. Helen added a few
favorite books, an embroidery hoop, and her doll. She looked
around her room wistfully and headed downstairs. Grandpa
got the carriage ready. As Helen and Mama climbed into the
carriage, Grandma shouted from the doorway. "Don't cause
no trouble over there."

"Bye, Grandma," Helen said and gave a little wave.
Stay out of trouble at Aunt Alice's house? What sort of trouble
did she mean? She hoped living with her cousins would be
fun, but was unsure what it would be like. At least with
Grandma, she knew what to expect. She would miss their
evening embroidery lessons. And she would miss Mama.
Achingly so.

When they drove up the long gravel driveway,
chickens, cats, and kids scattered to get out of the way. Danny
was outside chasing kittens. Helen jumped out of the carriage
to join him and ran after an orange tabby kitten. She held it to
her cheek and listened to its' soothing motor. Mama waited
patiently for a moment and then handed Helen her suitcase.

Helen visited their farmhouse in the past, but never to
stay overnight. Like her house, there were two small bedrooms

upstairs and a larger one downstairs where Aunt Alice and Uncle Ed slept. But unlike Grandma Gertrude's dreary home, Aunt Alice's walls were painted in the hues of spring flowers. Large windows were framed with crisp floral curtains coordinated to the wall colors. Helen took it in with fresh appreciation.

Mama and Aunt Alice went into the living room to talk, while Harriet and Celia showed Helen the room they would all share. White lace curtains adorned the window. Lavender walls were a background for the girls' own artwork.

"Your room is so pretty! I'm not allowed to put anything up on my walls," Helen said.

"Our mom likes us to display our art. She thinks we should be proud of it," Celia said.

"Helen, we need to get going," Grandpa broke into the conversation. "Grandma expects us to get back home for supper."

Celia and Harriet glanced at Helen, but she bit her lip and raced downstairs to say good-bye.

Mama pulled Helen into a hug. "Be good, and I'll see you very soon."

She clung to her mother and held her breath. "I'll try," was all she could manage.

"Harriet and Celia, help Helen put her things away," Aunt Alice said. And just like that, she was swallowed into their family and their routines.

Although she didn't get to see her mother every week, she stayed at her grandparent's farm during the Christmas break. While she was alone with her mother, Mama told her the news she was waiting to hear.

"I've heard from my friend, Sylvia, in Kentucky. She said we could stay with her this spring when we visit."

"We're really going, Mama!"

"Yes, Helen. Just be patient. And I have another letter here for you."

Helen tore open the envelope, and a small black and white photo of a little girl who looked like Mama stared back at her.

"Ruby sent me a little picture of herself. Is this what you looked like as a little girl?"

Mama took the picture and studied it. Her hand flew up to her mouth.

"Mama?"

"Sorry, dear. Yes, Ruby looks like I did, but she's prettier. How wonderful to see her. She must have gotten your picture as well." Mama's eyes were damp.

"Do you miss her?"

"Every day."

"But you still love me, don't you?"

"Helen! I love you both. But I get to see you often, so I don't have to miss you. But Ruby is also my daughter and I long to see her."

"Can we bring her back with us?"

"Let's not get ahead of ourselves. We still have to go visit."

"And I have to meet them both. I'm nervous about meeting my pa. He doesn't sound like a nice man. I've heard you and Grandma talk about him."

"I'm sorry you overheard. He wasn't very nice to me, but I believe he was a good father to Ruby. And he'll be happy to see you again."

Spring chased away the last of winter. Snow crocus asserted themselves first, then daffodils and tulips followed. May arrived, and Helen moved back to her grandparent's farm for the summer. Within days they would be heading to Kentucky. Helen could think of nothing else.

*Cora

Questions swirled in her head like leaves in a tornado, the night before the train ride. Cora tried not to let the questions drill fear into her soul, but she was afraid. Afraid

Ruby would resent her for letting her go. Afraid Frank would be ugly to them – especially to Helen. She was even afraid the girls would not see each other as sisters. So much anxiety.

In spite of little rest, she awoke feeling electricity running through her veins.

"Hurry up and finish yer breakfast or you'll miss yer train!" Ma too was a bundle of nerves as she hollered at Helen.

Helen was clutching Amy as she ate her oatmeal. Cora gave her a quick kiss on the forehead and sat on the bench to eat a bit. Her stomach was so tight, she couldn't manage much.

"Are you bringing Amy on the train?"

"No, Mama, I don't want Ruby to think I'm a baby."

"I don't think Ruby would think that, but I wouldn't want you to lose Amy."

They finished eating and gathered their suitcases. Ma stood at the kitchen door with arms crossed as they left. "I'm lookin forward to some peace and quiet," she said.

Cora stopped and gave her mother a piercing look, but said nothing.

"Cora, don't go gittin any wild ideas 'bout bringin' Ruby back here now. We have enough trouble feedin' the mouths we have. She's used to livin' in Kentucky, so let's just leave it."

Cora studied her bitter unsmiling face. She forced herself to take a breath, so she didn't respond in anger. "Good-bye, Mother," she said as she walked past her.

"Good-bye Grandma," Helen added.

They headed into the bright May sunshine where Pa was waiting in his new car.

"Stay outta trouble," said Ma. Always had to have the last word.

Pa drove them to the train station in the used Ford he purchased with money from his new WPA job.

Little was said as each was lost in their thoughts and expectations.

"Say hi to that little girl for me," Pa said when they reached the brick train station. He couldn't wait with them because Ma expected him back for dinner, their noonday meal. "Stay safe, Cora," he said with a quick hug.

"Goodbye, Ole Bean." He kissed Helen's cheek, and with a wave, he was gone. Cora dearly loved her Pa. She longed to hear more of what he was thinking, but he rarely shared thoughts or feelings. In spite of this, his steady presence made living with Ma bearable.

They waited outside for the train to arrive. Cora sat on a metal bench while Helen danced and hopscotched around the platform. Helen was 11 now. The trip was the only thing she wanted for her birthday. Cora hoped this trip turned out to be a gift and not another heartache.

When the train arrived, they settled into comfy leather seats across from each other.

Their senses took in the earthy aroma of the seats, the whistle of the steam engine, the etchings in the wood table between them. Cora enjoyed studying Helen's face as she watched the world whoosh by from the window next to them. Helen pressed her nose to the cold glass window and watched as her breathing left little puffs.

Cora couldn't help but remember her last train ride. From Kentucky back to Iowa with a part-time husband, a toddler and an infant. It was more of an escape from the men who burned their cabin. She fled to Iowa full of the same uncertainty she felt now heading back to Kentucky.

And yet it was different. The years blunted the sharp edge of her pain. She hoped this trip would help her restore her relationship with Ruby. Even more, she prayed for a path to regain custody of her. Certainly, a 13-year-old girl needed to be with her mother.

The rhythm of the train calmed her nerves. Helen, too, settled down and released the stream of questions brewing in her soul.

"Mama, why didn't you leave with Daddy when he went back to Kentucky?"

Cora searched her daughter's face as she sought the right words to explain the thorny situation.

"Your father and I married by mistake. Sometimes people get pushed into situations that aren't right for them. I tried to make the best of it, but neither of us was happy."

"So that's why he didn't take you with him?"

"Yes. And I suppose it's why I wasn't surprised when he left. But I never imagined he'd take Ruby."

"But why didn't you try to find my sister?" Helen solemn eyes searched Cora's face.

"Believe me, Helen, I did. But because she was with her father and he was in another state, the officials said it was a domestic situation that we had to work out. But the only way your father would let me have Ruby was if I would go back to Kentucky and be his wife. I was miserable with him, and he often hurt me. I was also miserable without Ruby. It was a terrible predicament. In the end, I made a choice to divorce him, and I planned to find a way to regain custody of your sister. But life kept getting in the way and here we are ten years later." Cora knew this was a complicated answer, but she hoped Helen understood.

Helen nodded and turned toward the window again, her brow creased. The train swayed back and forth as the landscape outside the window changed.

"I'm glad no one can ask you to deliver a baby this week."

"Me too. This is our time together, and I'm looking forward to more time with you."

"Did Ruby grow up without a Mama?"

"Your father married again. A woman from Kentucky, I believe. So, Ruby has a stepmother. Someone who has stepped into the role of mother. I believe she is a good woman."

Helen scrunched her face. "But, how do you know this Mama?"

"My good friend, Sylvia wrote to me and told me about the marriage."

She was relieved when the rocking of the train back and forth relaxed Helen and she fell asleep. Cora read her book, napped and stretched her legs by walking up and down the train's car.

While Helen napped, Cora faced her fears. She wondered if Ruby would resent her for not fighting for her. As much as Helen questioned why her father never contacted her, Ruby must have done the same, wondering where she was.

None of her letters to Ruby were answered. There was no acknowledgment of gifts. Cora doubted she received them, so she eventually gave up. But she never stopped praying for her. And longing to see her.

Cora braced herself emotionally to see Frank again. Would he be polite or rude? Would he gloat that he stole and then raised Ruby? Would he make lewd advances? She wished she didn't have to see him, but there was no way she'd leave Helen alone with him.

It was nearly dark when they reached Kentucky. Cora eagerly searched for Sylvia, wondering if she would recognize her after ten long years.

"Cora!" Sylvia called when she saw her get off the train and ran to embrace her.

"Sylvia! Don't you look elegant with your finger waves! This is my Helen. Helen, Sylvia was there on the night you were born."

Helen smiled shyly.

It was Sylvia's turn to introduce her family. "Cora you remember Harry," she said, and the smile on her face conveyed contentment. Harry shook Cora's hand vigorously and introduced their boys. Six-year-old Richard looked like his Mama with blond hair and blue eyes, and eight-year-old Jimmy sported darker hair and features like his father.

They all piled into the bulky black Buick and drove to their home in a small Kentucky town. The children caught the last of the evening outside while Sylvia and Cora picked up the conversation where they left off. Ten years sliced into nothing. George soon took refuge in another room to give them privacy to shed the secrets of their souls over a cup of tea.

Tomorrow Cora would face her attacker and finally hold her daughter again. She needed time with Sylvia to sort out the conflicting emotions stirring in her soul.

Chapter 18

*Cora

Cora awoke not to the sound of rooster's crowing, but to the sounds of a city coming to life. Doors slamming, cars starting, horns honking. She peered out the window and saw people riding bicycles and driving boxy black cars. No horses. She squinted against the bright sunshine and spied a few restless dogs.

This is the day the Lord has made. Let us rejoice and be glad in it. She would be reunited with Ruby today. Her heart swelled with anticipation. To look at her, hold her, speak to her as she dreamt so many times. The thought propelled her downstairs where she found Helen already up and dressed.

"When do we leave, Mama?"

"Right after breakfast. We're meeting them at a park nearby."

Sylvia handed Cora a picnic basket. "Lunch for four. I knew you wouldn't have time to get to a store, so I made a few sandwiches."

"So thoughtful. Thank you."

The intensity of the early morning heat took them by surprise as they walked to the park. Cora spotted a girl with dark hair sitting on a swing. Standing near her was a tall, thin man with reddish hair, smoking a cigarette. Frank. No doubt about it.

"Is it them?" Helen whispered.

Cora nodded as they quickened their steps.

"Ruby?" Cora called. She couldn't hold in her excitement a moment longer. Ruby looked their way, sprang off the swing and ran toward them.

Cora's heart fluttered. What a lovely young girl she was. Cora pulled her into an embrace. Then held her at arm's length and studied her face. "I'm your Mama, Ruby," she said as tears spilled from her eyes. "Do you remember me?" Cora brushed a kiss on her cheek.

Ruby shook her head. "No. But it be nice to finally meet ya."

Cora wanted to tell her how much she missed her, and how sorry she was not to have been with her, but she wasn't able to get the words out. "And this is your sister, Helen."

Helen looked at Ruby but said nothing at first.

"Hello, sister!" Ruby said. They smiled and hugged stiffly.

Frank hung back, still smoking.

Cora broke the ice. "Hello, Frank. This is Helen."

Helen turned toward Frank. She held out her hand to shake his.

"Hello, Helen," he said and dropped his cigarette on the ground. He took her small hand in his. "Can I hugs ya?" She nodded, and he pulled her into a gentle hug.

"Should I call you papa?" Helen asked, searching his face.

"Na, just call me Frank. It's what Ruby does."

Ruby nodded.

An awkward moment of silence ensued.

"I thought y'all would never git here," Ruby said. "Seems liken we been waitin' all winter to meet y'all."

Helen giggled. "You have a funny accent."

"She's from Kentucky. They pronounce things differently," Mama interjected. "Ruby, tell us what you like to do?"

"Wells, I likes to play wid my brothers and cook."

"Cook! How wonderful Ruby. What do you like to make?"

"Grits and collard greens mostly."

"Do you like to read? What are your favorite books?"

"Oh, I'm not real interested in books n stuff. But I do likes my teacher."

Frank snorted. "I'll say she do." Frank lit another cigarette.

"What's her name?" Cora asked.

"Oh, it's not her. He's called Mr. Filmore, and he's pert near perfect."

"I never had a man for a teacher," Helen said.

"Frank, why don't you and I go for a little walk to let the girls get to know each other," Cora said. "I'll leave the basket here on this picnic table."

Cora and Frank walked away from the girls to let them talk without adults present.

"Ruby looks so mature," Cora started.

"Yep, she's all growd up. Helen's bout there too," Frank said.

"She has your coloring."

"Yep, I seen it."

"So, you married again?" Cora asked.

"Yep. Names Audrey. You?"

"No. We still live on the farm with my folks."

"Oh yah, the farm. Yer Ma still the same?"

"She's well if that's what you mean."

"It's not what I mean."

They walked along for a few minutes both looking around, but not at each other. Finally, Cora found the courage to ask what she needed to know. "Why did you leave like that, Frank?" Cora tried to keep her voice even, but anger was just below the surface.

"I couldn't live on that farm with yer parents. Ya knew I hated it."

"Why did you take my Ruby?"

"She be mine too. I left ya Helen. It's fair." He shrugged.

"Children aren't bartering chips."

"Look, it's not like the marriage was ever goin' to last. And it weren't fair for ya to have both girls, so I takes Ruby. She does fine. Gets along with her stepmom and brothers."

"Half-brothers."

"OK, yah, half-brothers. Ya always had to correct me on everthang."

"Your taking Ruby was the most painful thing I've ever had to endure," she said.

"I didn't see ya running back to git her."

She winced. "Running back to what exactly? As you've said, our marriage was over, and I had no job after the fire. It took me years to get back on my feet."

"Sos, ya stayed wid yer parents."

"I went to college for three years and became a midwife," Cora said.

"College eh? Well, aren't ya the smart one?" Frank blew his smoke in her direction, and she could hear the sarcasm dripping from his words.

She tried to keep things friendly. "How's Ruby doing in school?"

"She does okay. Has a crush on her teacher. She be talkin' 'bout quittin' school. Knows enough."

"Enough? Don't let her drop out of school. Education is important."

"She don't need more schoolin' to marry and have babies."

"What are you talking about? She's 13!" Cora was aghast.

"She wants to marry her teacher."

"What? How old is he?"

"He be 24. They has a special bond."

"You said it was a crush. Girls this age don't know anything about love?"

"Ya wants her to be an old maid like ya was?"

Her face burned. "I was proud to be a teacher at the mission. Doing important work."

"Well, not all women folk wants to waste years sleepin' alone."

Cora took a breath and tried to refocus the discussion.

"Frank, look. This is just wrong. Ruby's still a child."

"I'm just goin' along wid what she wants."

"But she's too young to know what she wants."

"She's all growd up now. I is her parent, and I knows her." Frank's voice was rising.

"I'm still her mother, and I want what's best for her." Cora struggled not to scream at him.

"Well now, ya ain't the one what lives wid her," Frank sneered and punctuated words with his cigarette.

"And whose fault is it? You stole her from me and robbed me of raising her." Cora barely contained her rage. "My daughter."

"Look, the past be past? No point gitin all worked up, cuz if that's all ya want, we is done."

They were in an endless loop of disagreement. Echoes of their few years together went through her head. Perhaps having some time alone with Ruby, outside of Kentucky, would help Ruby see more possibilities. But Cora needed to act quickly.

"Let's go see how the girls are doing," Cora said and turned around. They walked back in silence.

*Helen

Helen was glad for the chance to be alone with Ruby. She kept looking at her face. "You look just like the picture you sent. Sorta like my mama."

Ruby smiled. "And ya got Frank's red hair."

"Everyone teases me about my red hair and freckles. Now I see where they came from."

"So y'all lives on a farm? With animals and everthang?"

"Yes, in Iowa. Mama says your pa, er our pa, er Frank wasn't happy and took off with you."

"Frank said Mama didn't like Kentucky so they decided to each have one of us."

Helen looked confused. "Ma said he just took you and it broke her heart."

"I cain't remember none of it. Used to done live with my grandparents, but then Frank got hisself a new wife, Audrey and we moved in with her."

"And you have a brother now?"

"Two of 'em, Henry and Frank, Jr."

"I always wanted a brother or sister. I was so happy when I heard about you. I can't believe we're finally here." Helen smiled at Ruby. She was happy to meet her sister, but seeing Mama with Ruby made her a little jealous. Did she want to share Mama all the time?

"Do you have any pets?" Helen asked.

"We has a Golden Retriever dog. Name of Sport. How bout you?"

"We have lots of cats, but Grandma Gertrude won't let me bring any in the house."

Helen filled Ruby in on life on the farm and the grandparents Ruby didn't remember. "Mama's hoping you can come for a visit." No need to mention Grandma was against it.

"Sure. Do ya think I could ride a horse?"

"Yes, I can teach you how to saddle Lady."

*Cora

Frank and Cora rejoined the girls who were lounging on the swings giggling.

"You two have the same giggles," she said.

"Helen's been tellin me bout all the animals y'all have."

"Spring is the most fun when baby animals are born. And summer too. We still have calves, goats, chicks, and piglets," Cora said to Ruby. "Have you ever visited a farm? I mean, one you can remember?"

"No ma'am."

"Please call me Mama."

"OK, Mama. I'd like to see them farm animals. Helen said she could teach me to ride a horse."

"What a great idea Helen! We have a gentle mare called Lady."

"Plenty a horses here in Kentucky. No need to go to a farm," Frank said.

"But I'd like to go for a visit, Frank," Ruby responded.

"Smells real bad," Frank said.

"We'd love to have you visit, Ruby," Cora said.

"Well I ain't payin for it," Frank said.

"No one asked you to," Cora said trying not to let her irritation show.

Silence.

"Ruby, are you musical like your, er Frank?" Cora asked.

"I likes to sing."

"Me too," Helen said.

Silence.

"Let's see what Sylvia packed for us, shall we?" Cora said.

"Ya two still thick as thieves?" Frank asked Cora.

"We're still friends, yes," Cora said and handed out sandwiches and apples.

The next day Helen and Cora were invited to Frank's parent's home so Helen could meet her other grandparents.

"Well, Helen, ain't ya just the spittin image a yer pa," Mrs. Desjardin said as she poured her a glass of lemonade. Cora was startled by her pallid skin and snowy hair.

"Yes, Ma'am. I guess so."

"Call me Grandma. It's good to finally meet ya. And to see yer ma." She offered a weak smile in Cora's direction.

"So, Cora, we heard ya got more education after… after ya left," Mr. Desjardin inserted. The years weren't kind to him. He was nearly bald with a protruding potbelly and a sausage shaped nose.

"Yes, I went to college for three years to become a nurse and then became the county midwife."

"Mama delivers babies," Helen broke in.

"Oh, my!" Mrs. Desjardin's hand fluttered to her heart.

"Still live with yer folks?" Mr. Desjardin asked.

"Yes, we live on the farm. When I have to be gone long hours delivering a baby, Helen is safe with my parents."

"So never remarried?" Mr. Desjardin asked.

"No."

"Our Frank married again." Mrs. Desjardin said.

"Yes, I heard," Cora said.

"Real nice lady. Names Audrey."

"Good."

"So, Helen, maybe ya cud stay for the summer. Give us a chance to git to know ya," Mrs. Desjardin said.

Helen looked at her mother aghast. "Um…It's pretty hot here and …I'd miss my mom."

"Thank you, but no," Cora said.

*Helen

Mama and Helen met Frank and Ruby one more time before they left for Iowa. Frank asked to go for a walk with Helen. She was hesitant to be alone with him but knew this was her last opportunity to ask him what was on her mind.

"Are you going to visit us in Iowa?" she started.

"Don't think so," he said. "I has another family here. Keeps me busy in Kentucky. But Ruby's almost growd, so she might go for a visit."

"Will you write to me?"

"Oh sure, yeah, maybe someday," he said, and she understood the answer meant probably not.

When they said goodbye for the final time, Ruby and Helen hugged and promised to write.

"Nice to meet you, Frank," Helen said.

"You too, kid. See ya," Frank patted her on the head as if she was a dog. No hug.

"Well, bye agin," Frank said to Mama as he blew cigarette smoke in her face and then turned around and left.

Helen watched Mama hug Ruby and kiss her forehead. Mama had tears in her eyes. Did Mama love Ruby more because she lived far away? She never had to share her before, and it felt odd.

On the train home, Helen tried to understand the ache she felt. After all, she and Mama had a great train adventure, and she got to meet her sister and Frank, just liked she wanted. But she wondered if she'd ever see Frank again. Something else was bothering her and she had to break through Mama's fog.

"Mama, can I ask you something?"

"Yes, of course."

"Ruby told me she's quitting school!"

"Yes, Frank told me. I'm sick about it. We need to urge her to stay in school. Some folks just don't see the importance of educating girls."

"But you do, don't you Mama?"

"Of course, Helen. I'm the first in my family to earn a college degree. Even though I don't make a lot of money, I'm proud to have a job that helps people. I hope you'll find the same someday."

"There's something else, Mama. I don't know if I should tell you this, but Ruby says she's going to marry her teacher." Helen scrunched her face as if she'd eaten a sour pickle.

"Yes, I heard it too, although I am hoping it isn't true. Helen, if we can get Ruby to visit us on the farm this summer, let's try to change her mind. She's far too young to be thinking about marriage."

*Cora

Cora broke into what little savings she had and sent money for train fare to Ruby. A month later she was due on the train and Cora hoped to convince her to stay in school. In her wildest dreams she also hoped she could find a way to keep her in Iowa to guide her into adulthood. Ma fought against the visit, but Cora stood firm and won the argument.

Pa drove Helen and Cora to the train station to collect Ruby.

"Ruby!" Helen and Cora both exclaimed. Helen raced to her sister as she got off the train. Cora's heart swelled to see the girls' excitement at seeing each other again.

Pa bent down and hugged her. Then looked into her dark brown eyes. "It's been quite a little while, young lady. I spose ya don't remember me, but I never forgot ya."

Ruby hugged him back. "Can I calls ya Grandpa?"

"Yes, of course."

Grandma Gertrude surprised them all with a plate of decorated sugar cookies when they arrived at the farm. Cora detected a smile in her Ma.

"Nice to meet ya agin, Ruby," she said.

"Is all this land yers?" Ruby asked. "Where be all the peoples?" They all laughed.

"Wait till you see the animals!" Helen said. As soon as they put Ruby's suitcase away, the two girls headed outside to play with the menagerie of critters.

Cora was thrilled to see how well the girls got on together. Even Ma was on her best behavior. But her true feelings came out days later.

"Watching the girls together makes me so happy," Cora told her Ma as they lingered over coffee after breakfast

"This ain't permanent, Cora. Just a visit. Don't be fillin' the girl's head with thoughts 'bout stayin' here."

"Ma, I'm going to do what's best for my daughter. With or without your permission."

"Well, then ya can't be stayin' on the farm."

"Oh, really, Ma? And who's going to help with the garden and all the animals? You know you and Pa can't manage this farm alone anymore. Having an extra pair of hands may be just what we need."

"We manage just fine!"

"I see you limping around. Don't kid yourself. And Pa's taking heart medication. This farm is a lot of work, and without Helen and me you couldn't stay here."

Ma pursed her lips. "Ya can't ask Alice to take both girls during the school year. She don't have room, and ya ain't got a way to get them to school."

"One step at a time. If she can stay, I'll do whatever it takes to have her here. Anything to keep her from marrying her teacher,"

"What?" Ma exclaimed.

"Both Ruby and Frank told me her 24-year-old teacher wants her to marry him and leave school."

"That ain't right!" Ma said.

"It makes me sick to think about it. Now you see why I am pushing for her to move here with us. What kind of life would she have married so young?"

"I wonder what her life's like, bein raised by a pa who tells her to call him Frank."

"I can't do anything about the past, but if I can help her now, I have to," Cora said.

Cora went outside to look for Ruby. She asked her to gather eggs and feed the chickens with her. Helen went inside to help her grandma make jam.

"I can't tell you how wonderful it is to have you here, Ruby. I've missed you terribly. I hope you believe me."

"Why didn't ya wants me to be livin with y'all?"

"I wanted it with all my heart, but I couldn't find a way to make it happen."

"But Frank says ya told him to take me. That ya each got one child."

"It's not true! Is that what you thought all these years?"

Ruby nodded.

"The truth is your father left one night without telling me, and he took you! No note, nothing. I was devastated. Ruby, you have to believe me."

"But why didn't ya come and get me?"

"I contacted the sheriff and an attorney, but they said I had to work it out with your Pa."

"I never heard from ya. Even on Christmas and my birthday."

"Ruby, I sent letters and gifts. Frank didn't give them to you?"

"No," she said and shook her head.

"Please, believe me, I tried to get you back. Frank said the only way I'd see you was if I went back to Kentucky and lived with him. This may be hard to understand, but we weren't happy married to each other. I couldn't go back to him."

"He be difficult to live with. Frank and Audrey fights all the time. I think he be seein other ladies while he's gone. She gots a job an all, but Frank, he only works now and agin. And he tells lies to her."

"I'm so sorry you're living with tension. But, Ruby, its' one reason I wanted to talk to you. Please don't think about getting married now. Wait until you're older."

"How old were ya when ya married Pa?"

"In my late twenties. But I wasn't looking to get married. I got trapped into it," Cora said.

"Were ya in the family way?" Ruby asked

Cora's cheeks grew warm. "I'm afraid so. I never loved your Pa. But I always loved you, and I still do. I want the best for you. I'm asking you to please stay in school."

Ruby studied her face. "I'm not sure I be the learnin kind, but I really likes my teacher."

"Ruby, think about it. If you'd like to move to Iowa to be with us, I'll find a way."

"I'll think on it, Mama."

At supper that night, Ruby was serious. "Grandma, can I ask ya bout something?"

"What's on yer mind child?"

"Were ya here the night Frank left?"

"I surely was and so was Grandpa John."

"Frank told me he and Mama decided they each got one child and she chose Helen. He said she knew he was leavin.'"

Cora gasped, but her mother put her hand out to silence her.

"Ruby, I'm sorry to say it, but yer father told ya a bald-faced lie. It bout killed yer mama. Grandpa John went out looking for ya, but Frank had already jumped on a train with ya. None of us knew anything about it."

"Yer Mama did everything she could to get ya back Ruby," Grandpa said.

"Except for move back to Kentucky," Ruby said.

"I couldn't go back to Frank. And I had no job. Some hooligans burned my cabin down and nearly killed you girls and me. I was in danger."

As she heard the girls' prayers before bed, Cora tried again to help Ruby understand.

"After Frank left with you, I decided to go back to college. I hoped if I earned enough, I could fight for custody of you. I even left Helen with my folks during the week, so I could get a degree. I didn't want to, but I thought it was the only way the three of us could live as a family. I hoped my plan would work."

"Did ya have trouble gittin a job?"

"No, I got a job right away as a midwife. My hours and pay were never consistent, but I started saving money when I could. Then, within a year, the country was plunged into a Depression. Many of my patients couldn't pay me. Times were tough. Still are. But I never go a day without thinking of you and wanting to find a way to have you live with us."

"Like this? All a us together on the farm?" Ruby asked.

"Yes, we'd love to have you live with us here, wouldn't we Helen?"

"I've always wanted a sister. I didn't know about you until last year," Helen said.

"I am havin a good time. I loves being with y'all," Ruby said. "Grandpa John's real nice, but I don't think Grandma Gertrude's keen on me."

"Oh, she doesn't like anyone," Helen said.

"Helen! She does. Grandma just has a difficult time showing love," Cora said.

"Ifin I come back to live with ya, would I be expected to go to school?"

"Yes, Ruby, you and Helen could go to school together. And your cousins would be there too. They have a wonderful teacher, and I think you'd enjoy it."

"I'm not real smart," Ruby said. "I don't get good grades."

"I can work with you. Remember, I was a teacher once. Please don't be discouraged," Cora told her.

Days later they were on the train platform again saying goodbye. Hugs all around and tears.

"Promise you'll think about coming back to live with us," Cora said to Ruby.

"I will, Mama," and she was gone on the train – again.

But this time Cora had hope. Two weeks together with her girls had convinced her she could win Ruby back.

A month later Cora came home and found a letter waiting for her.

"Read it, Mama! It's from Ruby," Helen said.

"Deer Mama and Helen,

I had fun at the farm, but my teechur wants to merry me. I'm quittin skool and we be gitting married fore Cristmas. Frank an Audrey is breakin up, and he don't have no where to live. Guess he'll stay with his folks. I'll live wid my teechur. It was reel nice meetin y'all. I'll right agin soon.

Love, Ruby"

Cora sat on the kitchen bench stunned, staring ahead into space. Her stomach twisted into knots at the news.

"So, she's not coming back, Mama?"

"No baby, we lost her. Again. I'm so sorry." Tears filled her eyes.

"I'm sorry too, Mama." Helen reached over and put her arm around her mother's shoulders which were shaking from her grief.

After Helen went to bed, Cora and Ma told Pa about the letter.

"It's shocking to me a teacher would be allowed to court an impressionable young girl, but that's exactly what he did," Cora said.

"It don't seem right, that's for sure," Pa said.

"I wanted so much more for her. Now I'm angry, and once again I feel powerless."

"Ya has to let it go. Nothin ya can do for her now." Ma said.

"I know. You're right Ma."

"For once ya admit it," Ma crowed.

Cora was devastated. For days she felt as if she was underwater and couldn't find her way to the surface. Her head was fuzzy. She couldn't concentrate. When she was alone, she let the tears fall and poured out her anger to God. Was He listening? As she walked around the farm, she cried and prayed to find the strength to let go of the anger and hurt. She was powerless over this.

Eventually, she realized she entered Ruby's life too late to have a lasting effect on her. Ruby's childhood was now cut short. At a time in her life when most girls were just starting to think about their futures, Ruby would now have grown-up responsibilities without ever learning about her unique gifts.

Chapter 19

1942 – Six years later

*Cora

"You ready for this, Ma?" Cora and her mother lingered over coffee.

"Don't matter. We made the decision."

"You must have thoughts about the move. Aren't you happy the farm sold so quickly?"

"Hmmph. I spect we didn't ask enuf for it. But the deed is done. It'll be Rob and Bessie Peterson's place soon enuf."

"Ma, you know it's getting nearly impossible for Pa to keep up with the animals, crops and his job. It's time to face it."

"No need to lecture me! We sold it. We're movin on."

"Helen's excited to walk to high school now, and I'll have less driving to see my patients."

"Yes, yes. Ya made yer point. Let's git on with the sale."

The decision was a logical one for Cora. Fewer women needed a midwife as hospital deliveries gradually became the norm. Cora now served as a private nurse to families who had loved ones in need of home medical help. The government was rationing gasoline and tires for the war effort, so Cora needed to be closer to her patients. She prayed her tires would hold out a few more years. She purchased a used Buick several years before but couldn't afford to replace the tires. Too late now. Thankfully because of her status in the medical profession, she received a "C" gas ration sticker, which allowed her to purchase more gasoline than the average person. But she used her ration sparingly. Always frugal. A lifetime of scrimping would benefit her during wartime. They prayed nightly for a swift end to the war but knew in their hearts it might take years.

Over the winter they sorted through their belongings and decided what to take and what to sell. An auction company was hired to assist. They arrived a few days earlier to direct the setup. Now long fold-up tables sagged under the weight of small household and farm items. Bits and pieces of their life both sentimental and practical. A tractor and large equipment rested on the lush green lawn waiting for folks to examine them. Everything wore an identification tag.

Excitement mounted and sentiments bubbled to the surface as Sale Day approached. Ma and Cora were up earlier than usual. Pa was already in the barn.

"I got another letter from Ruby," Cora said. "She's expecting again."

"Lord a mercy! What's this? Her third youngin?"

"Yes, and Ruby writes that Frank married again. His third wife." The thought of him still made her cringe.

"He's like a bad penny that keeps poppin' up. How on earth do these women git fooled by him?"

"I suspect this marriage won't last long when she realizes he can't keep a job and he won't keep his hands off other women."

"I don't know how ya got mixed up with the likes of him!" Ma's eyes pierced hers.

"Yes, you do Ma. I've told you. Let's not rehash this today." She held her gaze and Ma backed down.

"Well, we'd better git crackin' before folks shows up for the auction." Ma rose from the bench with some difficulty.

"Your knee bothering you Ma?"

"Nothin more than usual. Don't ya think ya should wake Helen before she sleeps the mornin' away? It's nearly 7."

A creaking on the steps announced Helen's presence. Her long untamed curls bounced as she traipsed downstairs in her flannel nightgown.

"Morning Helen. It's going to be an exciting day." Cora smiled at her.

"Mama, did you say Frank got married again?"

Ma turned from the kitchen sink, "Eaves droppin' agin young lady?"

"I wasn't trying to Grandma, but your voices carry. Besides, why shouldn't I know?"

Ma went outside to check on the chickens.

"It's OK. Helen, you have a right to know. Ruby wrote and said Frank found himself another wife. Oh, and your sister is expecting again. That's the news."

"Whoa, I can't imagine having a baby so young. And now she'll have three!" Helen said. "I'm not going to get tied down like that."

"They do things differently in the hills of Kentucky. But I agree with you. Too, too young. I'm happy to hear you want to wait."

"But I hope you're okay if I start dating," Helen said.

"Anyone in particular?"

"Maybe. I like a guy in my history class."

"Has he asked you out yet?"

"Well no, but a gal can hope."

"We'll cross that bridge when he does." Cora kissed her cheek. "I'm going to take a quick stroll around the farm." Her emotions were in high gear, and she needed to tame them before she saw her life displayed on sale tables.

A light sweater was all she needed, warm for April. Iris and daffodils peeked out. As she strolled past the barn, Pa was brushing Lady. His head was close to his horse of nearly 20 years as he stroked her mane and said farewell. Cora stopped for a moment unseen. At one point, he put both hands on her head and stood forehead to muzzle. The heartbreaking image propelled Cora forward, not wanting to intrude on Pa's private emotions.

Painful yes, but the money from the sale would give Ma and Pa a bit more security for their future. Still, the process of getting ready for the sale had been tedious.

Helen was the one most excited about the move which pleased Cora greatly. In spite of being raised without a father, she was proud of the young lady she was becoming. It seemed like a lifetime ago Frank was there on the farm. She was still angry at his memory but didn't want to dwell on it. Especially today. This day was about the future.

She had no regrets about years spent walking peaceful hills, helping with the animals, gardening and giving Helen a healthy appreciation for farm life. Yes, they were difficult years, but rich in other ways. And yet, today they'd sell their animals and equipment and begin again. ***Helen**

We're moving into the 20th Century, Helen thought as she surveyed the farm staged for "Sale Day." She was relieved to see sunshine. Grandma said people attended a rainy auction, but they didn't stay long meaning sales would be less.

Grandma had insisted they empty every cupboard and closet, so each item was examined and marked – pack, or sell. Rarely was anything thrown away.

She walked along the long tables of items and wondered how so many things fit into the small house and barn. She picked up threadbare tea towels that should have been put into a rag bag. Grandma thought everything was valuable – even chipped crockery. She spotted the candy dish she was hoping to win at the auction.

Helen discovered the dish in the back of a cupboard one Saturday morning as she emptied it. Delicate crystal etched with flowers that sparkled in the light. Helen was astonished to find such an elegant item among the aging brown stoneware.

Grandma grabbed it from her hands. "This was given to me by my mama for our weddin.' Be careful with it. Put it in the sale." She turned and hobbled toward the living room in search of a chair.

Helen gingerly picked it up again. "I'd love to have it, Grandma. For my hope chest."

Grandma hollered over her shoulder, "Well then bid on it when it comes up for sale. Yer not the only grandchild. Can't play favorites."

As Helen surveyed the farm, she peeked into the barn.

"You ready for this, Grandpa?"

"Yes, Ole Bean. It's time to sell. But that don't make it any easier. How 'bout you?"

"I'm excited to live closer to my friends, but I'll miss the farm." Grandpa nodded and went back to brushing Lady. The Petersons agreed to retire her and let her live out her days in a familiar pasture. No room for a horse in town.

Helen was astonished to see crowds of neighbors and strangers who came to snoop and to bid even before the auction opened. Several of Grandma's friends came early bearing casseroles and Jell-O salads, offering to assist with last minute sorting.

Grandma whispered to Helen, "They're just hopin' to git first dibs on items they might fancy." But she accepted the food with a nod of thanks and crooked smile.

It had been a dry spring so the cars and trucks lining the long driveway and both sides of the road for a quarter of a mile were dusty, but not muddy.

Aunt Alice and Uncle Ed showed up along with Helen's three youngest cousins, Celia, Robert, and Danny.

Harriet arrived with her new husband, Kenny, who said he was interested in the farm equipment.

The household items were auctioned in quick order: a butter churner, lamps, dishes, tea towels and Grandma's pie safe.

Helen got a paddle with a number so she could bid on the candy dish. The auctioneer held it up and started the bidding at 25 cents. She raised her paddle, yes. But Aunt Alice bid higher. Then a stranger added her bid. Helen again said yes to a bid of $1.00, but Aunt Alice looked at her with eyebrows raised and pursed lips. The bidding war was quickly over when the stranger shouted, "Three dollars."

"Too rich for my blood," Aunt Alice said, and she and Helen shook their heads in defeat. The family memento went to a stranger.

*Cora

Cora watched Helen bid on the prized dish, but didn't jump into the fray. Her practical nature wouldn't allow her to outbid the stranger, even if she could. Small farm items were next including the larger garden tiller and milking pails. Anything made of metal was snatched up eagerly as rumors of more rationing spread faster than the flu. Pa insisted they hold onto their small tiller and garden tools. But their acre-sized vegetable garden was now a thing of the past.

The Farmall General Purpose Tractor, Pa's prized possession, was the last item sold. After a flurry of interest, Kenny won the bid and Harriet hugged him as if he'd just made the winning score in a baseball tournament.

Auction over. They finished packing and within a few weeks were ready to move. Farm friends showed up with pickup trucks to help move their furniture to Greenberg.

"Can I bring a kitten with us, Grandma?" Helen asked.

"No. Cats and kittens belong outside. The Petersons'll need 'em as mousers," Grandma said.

Pa gave the Petersons a few chickens in exchange for letting Ma relocate a bit of the farm: peony bushes, a heritage rose bush, and bulbs for her favorite spring flowers. Helen and Ma packed a bit of rich dark soil around the bushes. Transplanting a bit of the farm to the city made the transition more manageable for Ma, even if May wasn't an ideal time to transfer bulbs.

Their city house was a three-bedroom, two-story home built at the turn of the 20th century and then modernized years later. The color of a newborn chick, it sat on the corner of Broad Street and Fourth Avenue, just blocks from the town square.

"I'm gonna git me two rockin' chairs for that there porch," Ma bragged on moving day. "Pa and I can sit and watch the world go by."

Cora smiled to herself, thinking about Ma reigning over their corner of the world from the generous wrap-around porch. Shooing away stray cats and dogs and keeping tabs on neighbors.

Like their farmhouse, it had one bedroom on the main floor and two upstairs, but unlike the farmhouse, it had indoor plumbing and running water. For the first time in any of their lives, they had an indoor bathroom. That alone was exciting enough.

The day they moved, Helen turned on the faucet in the bathroom just to see the water pour out. "I can't wait to soak in that tub Mama. And no more chamber pots. What a relief to say goodbye to the outhouse."

"I agree. I still can't quite believe it. But I hope you're not too disappointed we don't have a home for just the two of us."

"No, Mama, I'm used to living with Grandma and Grandpa. And I'm excited to be able to see my friends anytime I want."

"As long as you don't ignore your studies, young lady!"

They were both warming to the idea of city life.

"I can't wait to bake a pie in the oven. It won't heat up the house in the summer because we have a separate furnace just for heat we can turn off in the summer," Cora said.

"But without much sugar, now that it's rationed."

"I'll use extra sweet apples."

"And, Mama, maybe we can get a telephone!"

"Whoa, girl. We're not ready for that yet. Besides, who would we call? We don't know anyone who owns one. And the government is halting production to save all the materials for the war effort."

"Will we have enough room for a garden in town?"

"We'll make room. Even if we have to dig up the whole backyard. With other foods rationed, we need to keep growing our own vegetables."

"My friend, Emily, says her Mom calls theirs a Victory Garden," Helen said.

"I think lots of town folks are learning to garden. You can thank me for keeping us on the farm all those years. Skills you learned will be handy forever, but especially now."

Cora smiled to herself as she drove to a patient's home. She loved the way Helen embraced the future and their move to town. But Cora's thoughts turned dark while listening to the radio news. The US was now involved in World War II.

Everyone was asked to make sacrifices. In England, citizens had ration cards for meat, bacon and other items. If this happened in the US, they might regret moving off the farm. Already there were rations for sugar, tires, and gasoline. What would the future bring?

Chapter 20

*Cora

"I need your help for my wife, Lillian," Warren said, reaching across his desk to shake Cora's hand.

"What sort of help, Mr. Frantz?" She sat stiffly on the leather chair across from him. Always a bit on edge in a law office.

"She's been diagnosed with cancer... stomach cancer." He drummed a thumb on the edge of his expansive oak desk.

"I'm sorry. How is she doing?"

"Not well, but she's having surgery next week to remove part of her stomach and then she'll be in the hospital for, a week or two, I presume. However, I'd like her to be able to come home as soon as possible. To do this, she'll need a private nurse to visit daily to change her dressings and administer whatever drugs she requires." He grabbed his pipe and filled it with tobacco. "Mind if I smoke? Nervous habit."

Cora shook her head. "Are these her wishes too?" She glanced at his office walls, covered with framed family photos.

"She doesn't want me to go to the expense of hiring a private nurse, but I want her to have the best care. To give her a fighting chance to beat this. You come highly recommended by her doctor." He took another puff on his pipe.

"Thank you. Did her doctor give a prognosis of how advanced the cancer might be?"

"He hedged when I asked. Said he'll know more after the surgery. Lillian hasn't felt well for some time, and it took far too long to get a proper diagnosis." He rubbed his free hand along his forehead. "I can't lose her."

"I understand. I'll do my best to help her recover from surgery. But even excellent care can't guarantee she'll be restored to health." Cora looked beyond the well-dressed man in the suit and saw a husband whose world was threatened.

"Yes, but you'll try your best?"

"Of course. When may I meet her?"

"We live just a short walk away. Would you like to go now?"

"Shall I get my medical bag?"

"No, let's just let you two get acquainted. Of course, you should bill me for your time." He straightened a pile of papers on his desk and led her out of his office.

Cora had trouble keeping up with Warren, but they soon stopped in front of a stucco and brick home with a steep gabled roof. "Tudor?"

"Yes, we built it about 20 years ago when the children were growing up."

"It's beautiful!"

"Thank you." He gripped the black iron handle and pulled open the heavy oak door. "Lillian?"

"In here, dear."

"I've brought you a visitor." Warren reached her chair in a few long strides. "This is Cora Harper, a nurse."

"Nurse eh? Oh Warren, is this necessary?" Lillian was sitting in an overstuffed chair knitting. Classical music was playing on the record player nearby.

"Not today, but it will be after surgery. Please sit, Mrs. Harper," Warren said.

"Please just call me Cora."

"Yes, please sit, Cora. May I get you some iced tea?" Lillian asked.

"I'll get it," Warren said and headed into the nearby kitchen.

"Warren tells me you're having surgery next week."

"Yes. If all goes well, they'll remove the cancer, and I'll be fit as a fiddle."

"Have you been sick for long?"

"Not sick. Just not well. For months. But some days are better than others."

"How about today? Is this a good day?"

Lillian shrugged. "I'm up and dressed, so I guess it is." Her chair sat near a window making her pure white hair sparkle in the May sunshine.

A still life painting hung on the wall next to the window. "Beautiful painting."

"Thank you. My wife is the artist," Warren said bursting in with a tray of glasses.

"What a gift you have," Cora said to Lillian. "Do you paint often?"

"Not much lately. But it keeps me out of trouble." Lillian's smile brightened her pale pink and white complexion.

"Trouble indeed! How many times will I have to bail you out of jail," Warren teased.

Lillian laughed. "Tell me, Cora, how long have you been a nurse?"

"About twelve years. I was a county midwife first, but I've expanded my practice to private care patients."

"I used a midwife when my three were born, but I guess most babies are born in hospitals these days."

"That is the trend, yes. So, you have three children," Cora prompted.

"Yes, all grown and gone," Warren said.

"Do they live nearby?"

"No, that's the problem," Warren said.

"Our oldest, Matthew, is an attorney like his father. He, his wife and two children live in Chicago. Our second child, Andrew is an accountant. Married with one child. They live in Kansas City. The youngest, Mary, is a high school music teacher in Davenport, IA. She's still single."

"It's difficult having children so far away," Cora said.

"How about you?" Lillian asked.

"My Helen is in high school. We've just moved to Greenberg, and she's excited to be so near to her friends." Cora finished her tea and stood. "It was lovely meeting you both, but I'm afraid I have another appointment."

"You seem like a very nice lady, but I doubt I'll be needing a nurse."

"Let's pray you're right," Cora said.

Several weeks later, Warren called Cora. "I think Lillian is strong enough to go home, with help. The surgery knocked the stuffing out of her, but she's longing for her own bed. Are you still available to help us?"

For the next few weeks, Cora tended to Lillian whose strength was slow to return.

"Feel like a short walk today?" Cora asked Lillian on a warm July day. Although they lived in Springfield, a smaller town about ten miles from Greenberg, Cora made regular visits.

"Yes, I'm feeling stronger today."

Cora handed Lillian her cane, and the two gingerly stepped out into the sunshine.

"My last summer," Lillian said wistfully.

"You can't know for sure. You're responding well to the medications."

"It's okay, Cora. I've made my peace with this disease. My doctor says although he removed the stomach tumor, cancer has spread to other organs."

"I'm so sorry, Lillian. I'll look for his report."

"Tell me, how are you and your family enjoying life in Greenberg?"

"Helen adjusted the fastest. She adores being close to her friends. My mother is relieved not to have the huge garden to take care of – and the chickens. Pa is having the hardest time. He loved tending all the cows, pigs, goats, and his beloved horse."

"Oh yes, leaving a horse is difficult. I had a horse as a child. Named her Ginger and I loved her more than I loved most people."

"You lived on a farm as well?"

"Yes, until I went away to school. But what about you? Are you missing the farm?" Lillian asked as they slowly walked to the park a block away.

"Not as much as I feared I might. And I am delighted to have indoor plumbing! And a modern stove." The heat was making Cora warm, and she dabbed at the perspiration on her brow with a handkerchief.

"I remember how excited I was when we got indoor plumbing when I was a youngster. Changes your life in so many ways." Lillian laughed quietly. "Do you cook much?"

"My mother rules the kitchen. But I do enjoy baking and cooking when I have time."

"I used to love baking treats for my children. But now they're grown and gone. I don't spend much time in the kitchen. Poor Warren has been stuck with most of the cooking lately."

"Is he a good cook?" Cora asked.

"Not really," Lillian laughed. "But I don't have much appetite, so it doesn't matter."

"Are you feeling warm?" Cora asked her as they sat on a park bench under an oak tree.

"No, the sun feels wonderful. But if you are, we can head back."

"I'm fine. You mentioned going away to school. Was it for college?" Cora noticed how white and transparent Lillian's skin looked.

"Yes, I went to a teacher's college. Taught school for several years until we started a family. I left to raise the children. But I loved teaching."

"I did too! Love teaching that is."

"Cora, I didn't know you were a teacher. You are a woman of many talents. When was this?"

"For over ten years I taught at a Kentucky mission school."

"Gave it up to raise Helen?"

"Something like that. How are you feeling? Do we need to head back?"

"Yes, but this was wonderful. Thank you for getting me outside. Warren is busy during the day with his practice and often brings work home at night, so I hate to bother him. But I feel alive when I can walk outside and see a bit of nature."

"Me too. Being in nature always soothes me."

"You always seem so calm, Cora. When do you need to be soothed?"

"Everyone has difficult moments, and I'm no different. Now let's get you back home."

Cora helped Lillian back home and into her favorite chair with a promise to check on her the next day.

When she did, Warren answered the door. "Cora, wonderful to see you. We're having a good day."

"I'm happy to hear it." She checked Lillian's vitals. "I think the walk did you some good yesterday."

"Care to stay for lunch? Grilled cheese and tomato soup," Warren asked. "I was just about to dish it up." Warren had his suit jacket off and was wearing Lillian's frilly lavender apron over his suit pants and crisp white button-down shirt.

"I don't want to intrude." Cora smothered a smile at the sight of Warren.

"Please stay," Lillian said. "And we can walk after lunch."

"Well in that case, grilled cheese is my favorite. Thank you."

The three of them sat at the kitchen table and laughed like old school chums.

"Remember when we took the family out for dinner, and as we were leaving, Andrew told everyone around us that he didn't have to wash the dishes," Warren laughed. "He was six at the time. I wondered if folks would think we were making a six-year-old do dishes or if they thought we couldn't pay for our meal."

"Either way it was embarrassing," Lillian said. "As if we made him do dishes!"

"When Helen was about that age, she became obsessed with barn cats, especially kittens. She would sneak food to them. One time I found one of the kittens in the attic alcove like a stowaway on a ship. Poor little thing was howling. Helen was at school. Luckily I found and freed him before my mother discovered there was an animal in the house."

"Our Matthew loved animals. He brought home a dead squirrel one day. Carried it by the tail and when he got to the door, I spotted him before he brought it inside. He wanted me to explain why it died," Warren said. "What could I tell him? Why does anything die?"

"Or anyone," Lillian said.

They all focused on their food for a few long moments.

"Let's not get morbid. It's part of life," Lillian said.

"The worst part," Warren said. He reached over and covered Lillian's hand with his.

"Ready for a walk?" Cora asked Lillian. "This warm weather won't last forever."

"Yes, and Warren, don't forget to take that apron off before you go back to your office," Lillian said with a giggle. He kissed her forehead.

Cora felt comfortable with both Lillian and Warren, but was surprised and awed by their open affection.

As Lillian's energy flagged, and the weather got chilly, she was less interested in being out in the cold.

"Do you play Gin Rummy, Cora?" "It's too cold outside, but I don't want you to leave yet. Warren, why don't you stay for a bit and play cards with us? It is Saturday."

"Hmm let's see. Go to the stuffy office and do paperwork all afternoon alone or play cards with two lovely ladies. Not a difficult choice."

"You'll have to remind me how to play. We were never ones to play games, but I do enjoy learning."

The three of them drank coffee and played cards for several hours.

"Gin! I won," Warren said.

"Again. Really, Warren, you should let someone else win now and then," Lillian teased.

"Sorry, my competitive nature gets the better of me."

"Well I didn't expect to win, but I enjoyed playing," Cora said. "Thank you for a fun afternoon." Cora drove back to Greensburg.

"Where've ya been all afternoon," Ma said to Cora as she sat on a rocker on the porch.

"With Lillian. My patient. You remember, Ma."

"That was hours ago."

"They invited me to play cards, so I did. I had a fun afternoon."

"They?"

"Warren played too."

"Ya charge for that time?'

"No, Ma. We just played cards for fun. People do have fun you know."

"Getting awful chummy with them."

"There is no law against playing a few card games."

"Well Miss Fun and Games, I thought ya was goin to put up the last of the tomatoes from the garden."

"I didn't forget. Still time."

In October, Lillian's doctor told Cora there was little more he could do for Lillian. Cora must try to make Lillian comfortable in the last weeks or months.

From the doctor's office, Cora went straight to the Frantz home.

"Cora! I can't stand it. Just sit by and watch her suffer. The doctor says there's nothing more that can be done. There must be something!"

"I'm sorry, Warren. That's what the doctor told me too. We do have medication to help with the pain. Is Lillian in bed?"

"Yes, trying to rest. How long has she got?"

"No one can tell. Weeks. Or a few months."

Warren rubbed his hand over his face and smoothed his hair back. "I don't know what to tell our children."

"The truth. Let them spend as much time with Lillian as they can."

"She doesn't like having visitors when she's in pain."

"I understand. But I think they'll want to know her time is short. May I see her?"

"Yes, of course. Please help her." Warren led her into their bedroom and then backed out of the room.

Cora sat by her bed for a few minutes studying her breathing.

"Cora?" Lillian came to, and her eyes brightened at the sight of her friend and nurse.

"How are you doing today?"

"Not great. I'm ready to go."

"Sorry, Lillian, not today." Cora smiled gently. "Let's see if we can make you more comfortable."

She gave her a shot and waited until she fell asleep. Tears came to Cora's eyes. This friendship had nearly reached its' end.

"She's resting. Her breathing is still strong and regular. Good signs," Cora told Warren.

"Sorry I was so agitated earlier."

"It's understandable. Call me if there's any change. Otherwise, I'll be back tomorrow."

"Please stay for a few minutes. I'll make some coffee," Warren said.

They sat silently in the living room. The heavy cloud cover outside seemed to settle on their shoulders. As the howling winds stripped the trees of their fall grandeur, a raw feeling of helplessness descended. Cora broke the silence.

"How are you doing – with your practice and all Lillian's care?"

"My clients will have to wait. Every day I wonder if this is the last time I'll see her alive."

"I think she still has time left, but I encourage you to let your children know we're just making her comfortable."

"I thought we'd have another 20 or 30 years together. I feel robbed."

"I do understand the feeling."

"Are you a widow, Cora?"

"No, but I know what it's like to lose someone."

"Who have you lost?"

"I don't want to burden you now, Warren. Let's focus on getting you through whatever the future holds."

Cora was surprised to see Lillian sitting up in a comfy chair, a crocheted blanket tucked around her lap, the next time she visited. A small table was at her side where the remains of her lunch sat. Her hazel eyes looked as if a nap was in sight. She brightened when she spotted Cora and offered a frail hand, which was icy cold, in spite of the sunny day.

"How are you today, Lillian?"

"Do you want the long version or the short version?"

"Tell me whatever you think is important."

As she listened to her, she couldn't help but notice the prominent lines in her face, exaggerated for a woman in her early 50's. Cancer robbed her energy and was stomping on what was left of her life.

"Are you finished with this?" Warren pointed to the plate of food.

"Yes, dear. Thank you." Warren cleared the dish away and set about efficiently making coffee.

Cora admired the quiet love they displayed for each other. She felt almost as if she was intruding on their private moments. Over the past many months her routine visits had endeared them to her. Perhaps because they were nearly the same age, they found many things to discuss beyond Lillian's health needs. Most of Cora's other patients were decades older than she was.

Warren always insisted she stay for a cup of coffee and she found herself looking forward to her time with them. Both. Normally she didn't reveal any of her private life to patients, but she felt comfortable with these two.

"Helen was chosen to sing a solo in her high school talent show," she said after blowing on her hot coffee.

"How wonderful! Do you sing too?" Lillian shifted in her chair as if to relieve an ache.

"No, she didn't get her musical talent from me. Her father was, er, is a singer." Cora looked down not wanting to see their reaction.

There was an awkward moment of silence. She always regretted mentioning Helen's father.

"Where is Helen's father?"

"Warren! Sorry, Cora. In his legal practice, Warren is used to asking very direct questions."

"Yes, sorry. Please disregard the question."

"It's fine. He lives in Kentucky." She looked at Lillian, not certain what to add. Then she decided to brave a bit of the hideous truth. "He left me years ago."

"Cora, why would a man ever leave you?"

"That's very kind of you Warren, but it's not a very interesting story." Her cheeks were flaming from the attention. "Lillian, is the medication helping?"

When she saw Lillian's eyes flutter shut, she took her cue to let her rest. Warren walked outside with her. "How is her appetite, Warren?"

"She eats very little. I'm not much of a cook, but I try to make things she might like."

"I'm sure you're doing all you can. But don't forget to take care of yourself."

"Easy to say. Every day I wonder how many more we'll have together."

His dark brown eyes were earnest. How fortunate they were to have each other. Cora noticed what a handsome face he had with a prominent cleft in his chin. Then berated herself for such silliness.

"I need to head to my office and get some work done while she's napping," Warren said.

"Yes, of course." But neither of them moved.

"Cora?" Warren took her hand in both of his. "I can't tell you how much we've appreciated all you've done for Lillian over the months."

"I just wish I had a magic potion to make her well."

"Me too." He kept ahold of her hand and held her gaze. "Thank you."

Cora's cheeks flushed as she turned to walk away. She never felt comfortable with men. Especially handsome men.

As the weeks went by, Cora found Lillian in bed more often than not. She perked up when Cora visited, but Cora was careful not to stay too long. There was little medically to do for her.

Warren was often at Lillian's side. How did he manage to maintain his practice with the demands of caretaking? Occasionally one of their children visited, but none stayed more than a few days.

Cora looked forward to her visits with Lillian and Warren, but coming to know them as friends also made Lillian's decline more painful. She dreaded the day when she'd have to say goodbye to her. And to him.

One late January day Lillian rallied. The sun seared through open curtains in her bedroom window and allowed her a view of freshly fallen snow. Tree branches looked as if they were sifted in powdered sugar. The energy from it seemed to revive her spirits. She was propped in bed by a sea of pillows which Warren adjusted from time-to-time. Once again, Cora watched his large hands as they wiped Lillian's brow and offered her a sip of water. A twinge of what? Jealousy? Ran through Cora. Why hadn't she found anyone to love? And to be loved like this. What would life have been like?

"Are you too warm with the curtains open?" Warren asked Lillian.

"Stop fussing Warren. Why don't you go back to your office and let us have some girl talk?"

"I guess I can take a hint." He kissed her on the forehead and left.

"Sit by me, Cora."

Chapter 21

*Cora

Cora sat in the small bedside chair, happy for a few moments together when Lillian's pain seemed to have ebbed.

"I know my time is short."

"No one knows for sure, Lillian."

"Cora, I feel it in my bones. I'm tired of fighting. And I'm worried about Warren. Our children don't live near us, and I'm hoping you'll help Warren through his … through this…time."

"I'm never very comfortable alone with men, but I'll try to be a support."

"But you were married once."

"Yes, but it was a terrible situation. We were never meant to be married."

Lillian searched her face. "Do you want to talk about it?"

"No, we have more important things to dwell on now. Like making you comfortable."

"It'd give me great comfort to know if you and Warren will be friends after I'm gone. In fact, I pray Warren will marry again. Some men cannot live alone, and he is one of them."

"I'll try to be a support to him, and if I find a suitable woman, I'll introduce them, I promise. But for now, I wish you wouldn't talk about the end. Warren isn't the only one who'll miss you, Lillian." She had to stop before tears started.

As she thought back on her conversation with Lillian as she drove home, she let the full weight of it settle on her. Lillian was releasing her husband to love again. A final generous act. Cora thought for a few moments about any single women she knew and decided not to worry about it until after Lillian was gone. How she dreaded that day.

In so many ways Lillian reminded her of Sylvia, who she left in Kentucky. They still wrote now and then, but it wasn't the same as having her near to sip tea, walk with and share secrets. She missed Sylvia's friendship, and now she was losing Lillian. Cora was always sad when one of her patients died, but Lillian was special. Of course, Lillian knew little about Cora's sordid past. Perhaps she would have kept her at arm's length if she knew she had abandoned her oldest daughter to get away from her husband.

Cora wouldn't be comfortable seeking Warren out after Lillian was gone. Or any man. It would be too forward. And she didn't want to explain the pain of past decisions. For Lillian's sake, she might try to find someone who'd keep him company after she was gone. Someone worthy of the handsome attorney with the devoted nature.

Lillian's energy surge didn't last long. Warren called days later and asked Cora to come and check on her. He was noticeably upset when he opened the door. A blast of fresh snow followed her inside.

"Lillian's been asleep all day. I can't wake her to eat or drink anything."

Cora shook off her heavy wool coat and boots and followed Warren into their bedroom where Lillian slept. After a quick examination, she took a deep breath and faced Warren.

"I think the end is near. I'm so sorry. Her breathing is labored, and I believe she's in a coma."

Warren's knees buckled. He dropped onto the chair by their bed. "Can you stay with me? I can't face it alone."

"Yes, of course." Even when death was expected, the end was always a painful jolt. Warren was losing his partner – and love - of 30 years.

"Should we call your children?"

"No, Lillian said she doesn't want them to see her die. She wants them to remember her as a happy, vibrant woman."

Throughout the long evening, Warren and Cora offered Lillian sips of water, but she was lost to them. As she slipped deeper and deeper beyond their reach, they sat close together in two overstuffed chairs in their living room talking quietly, so as not to disturb Lillian.

"I've been told hearing is one of the last senses to go. Let's make certain we don't say anything that would be difficult for her to hear," Cora told Warren.

"This is so unfair," Warren said. "She gave up everything for me, and now her life is over long before her time."

"Lillian told me she used to be a teacher."

"Yes, we met at college. She started teaching, and I went to law school right after we were married. Money was so tight we lived on potatoes one whole winter."

"I know what it's like," Cora said.

"Once I passed the bar, I decided to start a private practice here in Springfield. Lillian wanted to stay in a small town. But getting enough business was more than challenging. I worked ungodly hours searching for clients, preparing for trials, even doing my own accounting. Sometimes when clients had no money, they'd pay me in eggs or chickens."

"I had to take food payments also when I worked as a midwife. Somehow we survived the difficult years."

"I felt guilty when Lillian had to keep teaching after our first son, Matthew was born. We needed the income. But when our second son came along, she resigned to take care of the family. It was her decision."

"She told me she was happy to stay at home."

"Did she also tell you she raised the children alone?"

Cora shook her head.

"Once my practice started growing, it was all I could think about. I brought work home and even worked on Sundays. Lillian and the children rarely saw me." Something was driving Warren to bare his soul.

"You were doing it for the family's security."

"Yes, but you only have one childhood. And my children grew up barely knowing their father."

His words struck a painful chord. "I'd better check on her," Cora said.

When she came back into the living room, she shook her head. "No change."

"I'm sorry if I burdened you with my guilt," Warren said.

"I'm surprised. I always thought you two must have had the perfect family."

"No such thing. I see a lot of broken families in my practice. In the past ten years, I've worked to build relationships with my children – and with Lillian. I was hoping we'd have more time so I could make it up to her. I don't know why I'm telling you all this."

"In the midst of sorrow, it's sometimes easier to share at deeper levels."

They both knew a train of sorrow was bearing down on them, but talking seemed to hold it off for the moment.

"I'll miss her too. I know my emotions can't compare with yours, but Lillian is very special to me."

"She always speaks very highly of you, Cora."

She bit her lip to keep from crying and looked away. Another silence. When she looked back at Warren, he was studying her.

"Cora, what happened with your marriage?"

"It's not a very interesting story."

"You weren't sorry when he left you?"

"I never wanted to marry him."

"It's not my business, but why did you get involved with him?"

"I was working as a teacher in a small mission in Kentucky. He wanted help to learn to read. I worked with him several times. He always made me squirm when he was around."

"I'm sorry, I don't understand. You didn't like him, but you agreed to marry him?"

Cora looked into his warm brown eyes and felt safe.

"I was alone with him one evening, and he…he forced himself on me." Her cheeks flushed, and she looked at her hands twisting in her lap.

"I'm so sorry, Cora. And from this you got Helen?"

"No. Months later I found I was expecting and went to his father for advice. I was afraid I'd be thrown out of the community for being an unwed mother. His father tricked me and called for a preacher and insisted we get married right then. I didn't have time to think, and I was terrified. I was ashamed and embarrassed, feeling somehow responsible. Months later I delivered my first daughter, Ruby."

"Ruby? I didn't know you had another child. Is she still living?" Warren's voice was warm and low, without a trace of judgment.

"Yes. But she lives in Kentucky. It's not a pretty story, Warren." Tears were filling her eyes. "Are you sure you want to hear this?" She searched his face for signs of disgust.

"Only if you want to tell me, Cora." He took a monogrammed handkerchief out of his pocket and handed it to her. She wiped her eyes.

She hesitated, dabbing her eyes and then twisting the kerchief in her hands. "We'd better check on Lillian."

Lillian's hands had curled inward, and her body was moving into a fetal position.

"I think the end is very near. Shall we pray together Warren?"

"Yes, thank you!"

They prayed together quietly as Lillian passed into another world on a bitterly cold February morning.

"She's gone, Warren. "I'm sorry."

Warren collapsed on a chair and stared into space. Cora stood by silently. Tears streamed down her face, but she stood near Warren as he came to grips with her death.

"She has no more pain or sickness. Lillian's spirit is free now." Cora said.

"Yes, I do believe that. I'm relieved her suffering is over, but I'll never see her again."

"Not in this world, Warren. But in the next."

They sat at Lillian's side with their private thoughts for a few minutes. Cora stayed until the funeral home came to collect her. They wrapped her body in a sheet and carried her out with a casual efficiency that belied the enormous event which had just occurred.

Cora turned to Warren before leaving. He reached for her and pulled her into a powerful hug. She felt like melting into his arms. The closeness surprised her, but no doubt the emotion of the moment was carrying her.

On the way home, she regretted her unprofessional behavior. What was she thinking burdening him with her loss? What a terrible time to discuss her past. She hoped he wouldn't despise her when he reflected on what she shared with him. Better still she prayed he'd forget.

Ma was already awake when Cora trudged in from her long night.

"Ya helpin' with a birth?"

"No, Ma, I was with Lillian Frantz. She died a few hours ago."

"A few hours? What took ya so long gittin' home?"

"I was helping her husband, Warren, to make some arrangements."

"Ya was there all night?"

"Yes, Ma. It's my job."

"Seems to me that was beyond what yer job requires."

She sighed. Why did she always have to needle her? "It was a long night, and I'm going to get some sleep."

Warren called Cora in the afternoon and asked her to come over. She worried he might remember some of the personal items she shared during the long night.

When he opened the door, the dark circles under his eyes were evidence of little rest.

"Cora, thank heaven. I'm overwhelmed with all the decisions and the people to notify. I didn't know who to ask. I don't have any close friends."

"What can I do to help?"

"I've called my children, and they're arriving tomorrow, but the minister wants me to help plan the funeral."

Together they worked on funeral arrangements, choosing hymns and Biblical readings.

Days later, the Frantz children each played a role in their mother's funeral. The two oldest sons, Matthew and Andrew, read scripture passages. The youngest, Cecelia, played a special piano selection dear to her mother. The grandchildren drew pictures which they used to adorn a poster of photos. Friends, family and business associates of Warren filled the pews. Cora remained in the back of the church.

When the service was over, they formed a solemn procession with their cars to the local cemetery. Headlights on, they slowly moved through town to Lillian's final resting place. A tent was set up directly over the ground where her casket would be lowered to keep the snow from falling on those present. Cora stood in the back behind Warren as he watched his beloved wife's body swallowed by the frozen ground.

Why are winter burials so much more painful than summer ones, she pondered?

After the burial, there was a luncheon in the church basement. Parishioners brought casseroles, Jell-O salads, and pies to feed the crowd.

Later, after the luncheon, when other guests had gone, Warren and his children prepared to go back to the Frantz home.

"Cora, can you come back to the house with us?" Warren asked when he saw her leaving.

"Thank you, but this is your private family time. I don't want to intrude."

A week later, she stopped in his office for a brief visit. After his secretary brought them cups of warm, fragrant coffee, he shut the door to his office.

"I thought you might want this back." She reached into her bag to retrieve his clean and pressed handkerchief. "How are you coping?"

Warren was sitting behind his formidable desk laden with piles of paper. "Not well. I'm in a dense fog. Nothing seems to be in focus."

"It's no wonder. I knew Lillian less than a year, and I miss her. I can't imagine what you're going through. Are you ready to be back at work?"

"The last of our, or rather, my family left a few days ago. I'm trying to catch up, but I'm finding it difficult. My office is my domain. The place where I can shut out the world and sink my teeth into interesting cases, but I can't concentrate."

"Sounds normal. Give yourself time, Warren."

"The house is so quiet I can't stand to be there alone. And when I try to sleep all I can see is Lillian lying in our bed... dying."

She watched him in silence, not sure what to say to ease his suffering.

Warren stopped. "Sorry, that was too personal."

"I don't mind. Death is very personal and painful. I think time is the only medicine to help ease the pain."

"Thank you, Cora. Kind of you to stop by."

"I just wanted to see if there was anything I could do."

"I appreciate it."

They shook hands cordially and then he reached across the desk and gave her a quick hug.

She had no advice to offer him and realized he alone had to travel his journey of pain. Of course, she loved her daughters, but it was a different love. Children eventually grow apart to live independently. She loved her parents, even with the tensions that sometimes built up. But she had never given anyone her whole heart and tried to truly live as one. In her brief marriage, she fought to maintain her independence and to keep Frank at a distance. She never respected him and certainly didn't love him. When he ran off, she found she could breathe again. She never had a moment when she missed Frank.

How different from the love she witnessed between Warren and Lillian. They were a unit. A team. Inseparable. And yet now separated. Torn apart by death. Her heart grieved for Warren, but he alone had to find his way through the fog.

*Helen

"I'm thinking of getting a job, Mama," Helen said.

Mama was lost in her thoughts.

"I need more independence and less time at home with Grandma. Now that we're living in town I want to earn my own money."

Cora shook off her daydreaming and looked at Helen.

"Wonderful idea, as long as it doesn't interfere with your studies. Have you thought about where you want to look?"

"Somewhere I can get a discount on clothes."

"Clothes is it? You were never interested in them before," Cora teased.

"I want to have store-bought blouses and new sweaters. I have clothing rations, but no money to use them. Sure, I can make my skirts, but I need money for fabric."

"What's brought this on?"

"I know you've done your best, Mama, but I feel out of place around the other kids." She didn't want to complain, but her blouses were tattered and faded, her sweaters sagged. "I'm sick of being that poor little farm girl."

"And you want to look your best in history class. Is that it?"

"Maybe," Helen smiled. "That's part of it."

Helen went to the stores in town after school and inquired about a part-time job. She landed one at the local five and dime store selling items ranging from socks to kitchen gadgets. She dashed home to tell them the good news.

"Grandma, I won't be home for dinner until late on Monday, Wednesdays, and Fridays," she explained. "I've found a job at the five and dime."

"Well if ya ask me, it's bout time ya did somethin to help this household!"

"I'm hoping to buy a few new blouses with my earnings."

"Ya got plenty a clothes! Don't be spendin' money before ya earns it. They might not keep ya on for long, with the war and all."

Helen thought she noticed a faint smile. A rare sighting. *Was Grandma pleased for her? Or just happy she wouldn't be home as much after school?*

Grandma was full of surprises. The following Wednesday, she visited the store while Helen was working. *Checking up on me?* Helen introduced Grandma Gertrude to her supervisor, then turned her attention to a customer. At the end of the week, Helen expected to receive a pay packet. Instead, her supervisor told her that Grandma said the wages needed to be sent to her. Helen hid her anger and embarrassment but confronted her Grandma later.

"Grandma, why did you tell my supervisor to send my pay packets to you each week?"

"I figured ya'd just squander the money, child, so I'm savin' it up for ya. This way when ya needs somethin' you'll have enough."

"Why won't you let me save it up myself?"

"Yer a minor, missy. I tolds ya what we're doin, and that's that!"

Helen stomped up to her room. No point arguing with Grandma. The money was safe. At least she hoped so. Besides Helen had other things to think about. Like how to catch the eye of a boy in her history class.

*Cora

Weeks after Lillian's death, Cora was driving to Springfield to see a new patient, an elderly woman who had fallen and broken her hip. The drive to Springfield brought with it a flood of emotions and Cora realized the gnawing empty feeling inside her was both grief over Lillian's death and the loss of the friendship she had forged with both Warren and Lillian. After she made her house call, she took a short walk in the park where she used to take Lillian and sat on a park bench. The last of the winter snow was melting.

Cora almost felt Lillian's presence. She remembered her promise to help Warren, but as much as she liked him, she didn't want to appear forward. Or to send the wrong message. As she drove out of town, she passed his house…slowly. She longed to stop to see if he was home but kept driving.

She drove back home and reflected on the endless bitter winter which was finally giving way to spring. Ma's energy was flagging, leaving Cora to do most of the housework now that Helen had a job. Her sweet, talented Helen. Ma had fostered her interest in needlework and sewing, and Helen was developing quite a talent for it, even if there was little money to purchase fabric or embroidery threads. Helen was growing quickly, and Cora wanted to spend more time with her before she slipped away into adulthood. No, she didn't need any more complications in her life.

Chapter 22

*Cora

Weeks later, Cora ran into Warren at the grocery store in Greenberg. Her heart fluttered at the sight of him.

"What are you doing in our little city?" She smiled hoping her question didn't seem too nosy.

"I had some business here, so I thought I'd take advantage of your grocery store. Better fruit selections." He smiled as he held a bag of oranges.

"Good choice. How are you doing?"

"Keeping busy with work. It helps. So does this spring weather."

"Always a relief when the last snow melts. It'll be a beautiful Easter," Cora said.

"Yes, Cecelia and her husband and daughter are coming. First holiday without her mother."

"I'm glad you'll have company. It's so important." Carts were crowding around them with impatient shoppers. "I'd better go," she said.

Warren reached out and squeezed her elbow. "So good to see you again, Cora."

She smiled, and they both moved on.

A few days after Easter, the phone rang. Although she had originally thought a phone wouldn't be much help, she was surprised at how quickly others were installing them and now it made it simpler for clients to reach her.

"Cora, there's a man on the line. Sounds too old to be calling 'bout a delivery," Ma hollered.

"Mother!" She darted in from the living room, hoping the caller hadn't heard her mother's tactless remark.

She chatted quietly for a few minutes, then replaced the phone in its receiver on the kitchen wall.

"So, ya got a baby to deliver?"

"No, mother, not tonight."

"Well, what was all that about?"

"I'm meeting a friend for coffee tomorrow, that's all."

"That's all, huh? Better tell that to yer face! Yer grinnin' like a Cheshire cat!" Ma cackled.

Cora turned away from her mother's piercing spotlight. Why were her cheeks flushed? She supposed she was looking forward to their date. Date? No, certainly not. Just friends checking in on each other.

The next day she bounded out of bed with an enthusiasm she hadn't felt in years. What to wear? Look nice, but not too dressed up. A simple navy shirtwaist dress with a narrow belt and strappy blue shoes with a chunky heel were perfect. She brushed her long dark hair and pulled it back with a ribbon, rather than her usual bun. She didn't want Warren to think she was hoping for more than a friendly chat, but she had to admit she was eager to see him again.

They met at Auntie Annie's Café on Main Street. Ducking inside, she spotted Warren waiting by the door. He showed her to a quiet table.

"I missed having coffee with you in the afternoons," Warren said.

"Yes, I missed seeing you and - Lillian each week. How are you doing?"

"Better. The fog is lifting, and I'm learning to be alone in my home."

Any hesitation in their conversation soon lifted, and they chatted comfortably for an hour. When they got ready to leave Warren surprised her by asking her to dinner the following week. They shook hands amiably.

"Ya keepin company with that widower?" Ma asked Cora a few days later.

"We simply met for coffee. In a public café. No laws were broken."

"Seems to me it's too soon for him to go chasin after another woman."

"Honestly, Ma! He's not chasing after me. We're friends."

"Well now, ya don't want to become the center of town gossip."

"I don't care what people think of me," Cora said.

But when she found a moment alone, she called Warren.

"Are you backing out of our dinner?" Warren asked.

"No. I thought perhaps we should try the new Chinese restaurant in Fairview." Cora said.

"A bit of a drive, but sounds interesting."

"Perfect, I'll meet you there."

"Why don't you drive here and then leave your car so we can go together?"

"No, Warren, neighbors would talk. I'll just drive separately."

Once at the restaurant, Warren teased. "Are you worried about spies?"

"Yes, but not German spies. Mother's spies."

Warren burst out laughing. "You're still worried about your mother?"

"Yes, isn't it ridiculous? Why does she still have the power to make me feel like I'm doing something wrong?"

"Because you let her."

"What do you mean?"

"You control your feelings. Not your mother."

"I'll remind you of that if you ever meet her," Cora said.

"Sounds like a challenge. Next week, let's plan another dinner rendezvous and this time I'll pick you up at your home."

"Risky."

"What could go wrong? Come on, Cora. Your parents have to meet me sometime."

"They do?" She laughed. "OK, but if you stay longer than five minutes my mother will have you under cross-examination."

"Something I'm familiar with. But I consider myself warned."

The next week, Helen saw her mother brushing out her hair and adding a touch of lipstick. "Big date?"

"You're not the only one who can have a bit of fun," Cora teased back.

"I didn't think fun was a word in your vocabulary."

"Neither did I." She smiled at Helen. "Warren and I are just friends having dinner. What did you and Emily do the other night?"

"Went ice skating. Some of our school friends were there too. It was the best! But Mama, my clothes are dingy. I'm embarrassed. They saw the holes in my socks when I put on the skates. I wanted to use some of the money from my job to buy new clothes, but Grandma told my manager to send all my paychecks to her. It's unfair."

Cora sighed. Must her mother interfere in everyone's life? "I'll speak to her. You may use some of your wages for clothing, I agree."

"Thanks, Mama. When will Warren be here?"

"Any minute."

"Oh good, I want to check him out."

"Don't embarrass me."

"Do you think you'll marry him?"

"No, dear one. I'm just helping him through the first year after his wife's death."

"But you like him, don't you?"

"Yes, very much. Warren's a great friend."

"Well, I've never seen you this happy. I hope he sticks around."

The doorbell rang, and Cora hurried to open the door with Helen at her heels.

"Warren, this is Helen," Cora said, and Helen gave him her most charming smile.

"So, this must be the widower," Ma said coming from the kitchen.

"Mother, this is Warren Frantz," Cora said trying to keep a light tone.

"So sorry about yer wife. Ya must be devastated," Ma said.

"Yes, it's difficult, but I'm lucky to have Cora's friendship."

"Mmm huh," Ma retorted.

Pa was quickly introduced when he came out of the living room.

"We'll see you all later," Cora said, and they headed outside.

When they were safely in Warren's car, Cora said, "You escaped just in time!"

"I had the feeling she was ready to spear me with more comments."

"She was just getting warmed up." They laughed.

"Are you embarrassed to be seen with me? So soon after Lillian's death?" Warren asked.

"We're just having dinner. Since when does a person have to stay in solitary confinement after the death of a spouse?"

"Well put, Cora! It does me so much good to see you and to forget - everything."

During the summer, Warren came to get Cora on most Sunday afternoons. They went for walks or had picnics in parks. Occasionally they went out to dinner.

Handshakes turned into hugs, but nothing more. One August evening, they were having dinner alone in Warren's home.

"I'm better at grilling. No fancy cooking for me," he told Cora as the smoke alarm went off.

"I can help. I know a few things about kitchens," Cora said and opened the doors and windows to let the smoke out. She put on an apron and helped finish the meal.

As they were sitting at the table, Warren reached over and took her hands in his. "I miss you when I don't see you often."

"I miss you too."

"It feels so natural to have you around, Lillian."

Cora looked horrified.

"Did I say, Lillian? I'm so sorry, Cora. Just force of habit."

"Yes," she said and looked at her plate.

"Cora, you know it was just a slip."

"I know…but…"

"But? What are you holding back?"

"I'm not sure how to put this."

"Put what?"

"I need to be certain it's ME you miss and not just a substitute for Lillian."

"Ouch. Where did that come from?"

"I enjoy you so much, but I'm afraid you're going to wake up one day and realize I'm not Lillian. I'm not pretty like Lillian and sweet like her. I'm independent and plain."

"So, you think I'm spending time with you because you're here? Convenient?"

"Are you? I'm not used to being around men. I don't know how they... think."

"Cora, I took my wedding vows very seriously. I was always faithful to Lillian and never even flirted with another woman. But she's gone now, and she's not coming back. Yes, it's only been six months, but there's no law saying I can't appreciate your company. And I do. I enjoyed your friendship when Lillian was alive, and I'm drawn to you now as we spend more time together. I love your independent nature, and you're not plain!"

"I want to know you like me for who I am."

"What more can I say? I care about you." Warren reached for Cora and tried to kiss her, but she pulled away.

"I'm sorry, I'm just not ready. I think I need to leave."

"Cora, I didn't mean to offend you. Please stay."

"No, Warren. Thank you for dinner, but I need to go."

When she got to her car, she berated herself for being so hasty. On the drive home, she wondered if she put a dagger in their relationship. Tears filled her eyes. What was wrong with her? Why wasn't she thrilled to have the attention of this dear, caring man?

Three long weeks with no word from Warren. Every time Cora drove to Springfield to see a patient, she thought about calling him. But it felt too brazen. She was stalled out emotionally.

Finally, Warren phoned in early September. "Have dinner with me. I promise I won't cook," he said.

"I'd love to."

When he picked her up, she noticed a large basket in the back seat of the car. "Picnic food. Prepared by a local restaurant."

"Sounds delicious!"

"So, you won't run out on me tonight?"

"I'm sorry, Warren. It wasn't your cooking. I'm a bundle of conflicting emotions."

They drove out of town to a secluded park and enjoyed the picnic food.

"Fancy a walk?" Warren asked Cora.

"Yes, it's such a beautiful evening. We never know how many warm days are left before winter comes pounding in."

"So true."

Days were getting shorter, but there was still plenty of sunshine, and Cora wanted to capture the day and hold it in her heart. Warren reached for her hand as they walked. She enjoyed his touch and accepted the warmth of his large hand in hers. They stopped for a few moments in an abandoned shelter and let their senses drink in the pleasure of the beauty around them.

Warren reached for her and pulled her into a hug and then brushed his lips against hers.

Immediately she stiffened. Didn't push him away, but her body tensed. Still a prisoner of her past. Unused to kisses and fearful of letting anyone get close to her.

Warren let go of her.

"I'm sorry. I'm still so afraid."

"Of me?"

"No. Yes. Of getting close. Getting hurt."

"Cora, what happened to your marriage? I'm not pressuring you, but there are clearly parts of your past that still trouble you."

She searched his eyes. The two of them had developed a deepened affection and friendship the past few months she had never experienced.

"Warren, you're right. Parts of my past are ugly. Painful. I'm afraid you'll think less of me if you know the truth."

He reached for her hand. "I can't imagine how that'd happen. But if you keep this bottled up, you'll never get beyond it. I see painful situations in my practice on a weekly basis. Whatever you say won't shock me."

"But I'm not your client."

"No, you're a woman I care for deeply. But something is keeping you bottled up."

She hesitated for a moment and then unlocked the door to her past. At first, just a crack and then the floodgates opened. She told him of the rape, pregnancy and forced marriage.

"I was horrified to have Frank move into my cottage. The place where I felt safe. Sharing it with someone I didn't like was torture."

"Did you ever grow to love him?"

"Love? No, never. I tried to find things to like about him. But he never respected our marriage vows. I tried to be a wife to him."

Cora let go of his hand and paced around the small shelter as she poured out her poisonous past.

"When did you come back to Iowa?"

She told Warren about the fire, the hooligans who set it and the fear that they would strike again.

"I had no idea! What did you do?"

"I contacted my parents, and they sent us the money for the train back to Iowa. We had nothing left, no money, clothes or furniture. Nothing! And no other option, so the four of us took the train back to Iowa, but Frank was miserable." Her mouth was dry as she struggled to continue. Warren handed her some water.

"So, you decided to divorce?"

"No. I didn't feel I had the luxury of divorcing him. And in a small community, divorce is scandalous, as you well know."

"Yes, I've had to help a number of couples with divorce decrees and I know it's not an easy decision."

"I would've been happy to divorce him. We were stuck in a terrible situation. Neither of us had a job. My teaching credentials weren't good enough in Iowa. I felt guilty knowing we were a burden to my parents, adding four more mouths to feed."

"Did they know the truth about your marriage?"

"Not at first, but it didn't take long for them to figure out something wasn't right."

Warren nodded thoughtfully. "What happened?"

Tears spilled down her cheeks as she relived the night Frank disappeared with Ruby.

"He just left you?"

"No note. Just an empty bedroll where my two-and-a-half-year-old daughter slept. I was devastated."

Warren listened intently, his serious brown eyes filled with compassion and his eyebrows furled in concentration. He took his handkerchief from his pocket and pressed it into her hands. While she wiped her eyes, he rested a gentle hand on her shoulder, shook his head and said, "So sorry, Cora," over and over.

She tried to regain composure.

"What did you do?"

"Do you really want to hear this?"

"I think you need to get this out."

"When I found he was in Kentucky, I contacted him. He said the only way I could see Ruby was to go back and live in Kentucky with him. I knew he was bluffing. He had made no effort to contact me."

"Did you want to restore your family?"

"I wanted Ruby back, but not Frank. It was the most torturous decision of my life." Again the tears flowed much to her embarrassment. "I kept trying to find a way to regain custody of her, but I seemed to fail at every turn."

"I had no idea you were living with all that pain." He gently placed his hand on her back as she took a deep breath and tried to shake off the cobwebs of grief.

"For years I've carried this guilt knowing I gave away my daughter to escape a bad marriage. At night, when I can't sleep, I ask myself – 'What kind of woman gives up her child?'"

"You did what you thought you had to do, Cora. What you felt was best. Don't continue to question your decision because you can't go back and change it."

She nodded and wiped her eyes and nose. Yes, he was right. Her head knew it, but her heart never got over it. It felt liberating to know someone understood and didn't condemn her. But no one would completely understand the depths of the pain this decision caused.

When she stopped crying, she looked at him and saw compassion in his eyes. He pulled her into a hug again and held her close. "This wasn't your fault. You got caught in a web of difficulty you didn't ask for and couldn't stop."

"Thank you, Warren. Other than my family, you're the only person who knows my whole story. I've worked for years to rebuild my life, but the grief of my past haunts me."

"Thank you for trusting me enough to tell me. I felt there were circumstances you were holding back, but I had no idea the extent of it." He held her hand and then brought it to his lips and kissed it. "So how did you become a nurse?"

"Another difficult, but necessary decision. I knew I needed a way to support myself and Helen, so I enrolled in a nurse's college. I had to leave Helen with my parents all week. I'd come home weekends, and she'd cling to me. Once I got my education, I worked as a midwife, and I'd be gone for hours at a time, day or night. So, we stayed with my parents, and they watched Helen when I was working."

"You were fortunate to have their support."

"Yes – and no. My mother made it clear she wasn't happy about helping to raise another child. She can be cruel and rather cold. It was hard on Helen and painful for me to see that Helen often felt pushed aside. But once again I couldn't find a way out of the situation. I tried to make it up to Helen when I was home."

"What about your father?"

"My dad is a gentle soul, but he is ruled by my mother's temper. If Ma lays down the law, Pa won't cross her.

Helen is much closer to him, although he's not a very affectionate person. It's not been an ideal childhood."

"And what about Ruby? Did you ever see her again?

"When she was 13, Helen and I took the train to Kentucky, and the girls got to meet. She visited us on the farm later that summer. But she was too entrenched in the mountain ways. She quit school at 13 and married her teacher who was eleven years older. I lost her all over again. She writes now and then, but I haven't seen her in over five years." She pressed her lips together to stop them from quivering. Then took a deep breath and looked into Warren's eyes. "So now you've heard all my ugly secrets, Warren. Have I shocked you?"

"It takes a lot to shock me. But I'm saddened to think you've carried these burdens alone. Did you ever think about getting married again?"

"No. Never. After my taste of marriage, I haven't wanted to get close to anyone again."

"Do you think you might reconsider – getting close to someone?"

She looked at him and softened. "Maybe." He wrapped his arms around her, and she let herself lean into his strength. She rested her head on his chest and listened to his heartbeat. Then nuzzled his neck as he stroked her back. Finally, she looked into his eyes, put her hand on his cheek and pulled him into a kiss. Gentle at first, then stronger. It left her breathless and surprised. "So, that's what I've been missing."

After their emotional encounter at the park, Cora felt she still wasn't free of her past. She phoned Sylvia one afternoon when she was alone in the house and could speak without being overheard. They rarely spoke on the phone, but when they did it was as if they were picking up the conversation from the day before.

"I'm so happy you've found someone, Cora. I've been praying for this."

"But I feel so conflicted. Afraid I'll be hurt again. Afraid he'll dump me once he's over the loss of his wife."

"Does he seem like an impulsive fella?"

"No."

"Does he show signs of insincerity?"

"No."

"Infidelity?"

"No."

"Shiftless wanderer without a job?"

"Okay, Sylvia, I see your point. But it's as if there's a knot inside of me I can't untie."

"Have you ever prayed to forgive Frank?"

"Yes, of course, but as soon as I think of him, I'm furious again. The prayers aren't working."

"Why not seek the counsel of a professional."

"Like a shrink? If word got out, I'd never live it down. And I'd lose my patients."

"How about your pastor?"

"Wasn't Pastor Rehmann part of the gang that forced me to marry Frank?"

"Yes, but think of it. Out of that unholy union, you got two blessings – Ruby and Helen."

"And the heartache of my life was losing Ruby. Was it worth it?"

"You still have Helen. No one can deny you've had a difficult life. But Cora, it looks as if the next chapter will be a happy one. If you can let go of the pain."

"I miss you. I know you're right."

"What's the next step?"

"I'll think about calling my pastor."

"Let me know how it goes."

Cora stood by the phone and chewed on a fingernail. Finally, she opened the phone book and looked up the number for her pastor before she lost her courage. Pastor LaPatka answered, and they set an appointment for the next day.

"So how can I help you?" Pastor LaPatka asked after they chatted about the weather.

"I'm stuck emotionally. Angry at people who hurt me years ago."

Chapter 23

*Cora

Cora poured out the circumstances that changed her life. Pastor LaPatka said little as she gave the bare bones version of the last 20 years.

"What a lot of suffering in one lifetime. No wonder you're angry. What's brought this to the surface now?"

"I've found a man who seems to care for me. But I'm hesitant to get too deeply involved."

"Afraid he won't return your love?"

"Yes, I suppose. It's hard for me to understand how he can love me."

"You don't feel worthy of his love? Perhaps because you were never told that God loves you unconditionally. If you don't believe God loves you, how can you imagine a mere human loving you?"

Cora nodded, listening, soaking in his words.

"Is it possible you never felt the love of your parents?"

"My mother is a very difficult woman and rarely expresses any emotion other than anger. My father and I are closer, but neither of them showed much affection.

Intellectually, I knew I was loved, but I never felt it deep in my soul."

"This is a good place to begin. Accept God's love and focus on it. Meditate on God's love for you daily."

Cora wasn't sure how to do it, but she left encouraged that he listened to her and gave her homework for the week.

When they met again the next week, Cora told him, "I'm trying to focus on the fact that God loves me, but it feels so remote. Distant. I'm not sure I'm making progress."

"Feelings are unreliable. Thank God every day for his love."

"How can I thank him when I feel he's abandoned me over and over?"

"It wasn't God who abused you, but he can help you find grace by working through the pain."

"I'm still so angry."

"That's a good place to start."

"Why?"

"Admitting you're angry is a step toward rooting it out."

"But it won't change the circumstances."

"No, the past is finished. Nothing can change that. But to enjoy the present and your future, you have to forgive."

"Forgive my ex-husband?"

"Yes."

"Do I have to speak with him?"

"No, Cora, you never have to speak to him or see him again. Forgiveness is for your benefit."

"I feel if I forgive him, I'm saying what he did to me was okay. Like I'm letting him off the hook."

"Forgiveness isn't about a feeling. And it isn't for his good. It's for yours."

"But it's as if there is a knot inside me. I'm not sure I can untie it."

"Scripture is filled with passages that tell us to forgive. But Jesus knew it wasn't easy. In Matthew's gospel he told Peter that we have to forgive not seven times, but seventy times seven. He meant an infinite number."

"Where do I begin?"

"First, realize that you have the power to forgive."

"Power?"

"Yes, find the power of the God within yourself."

"But how?"

"Cora, pray to God for the desire to forgive. Sit in prayer and ask God to help you want to forgive him. Then repeat that you forgive him. Do this every day, whether you feel like it or not."

"But I always hear, 'forgive and forget.' Do I have to forget?"

"No, that won't happen. How could you possibly forget your past? You only have to forgive. This is between you and God alone."

"You make it sound easy," Cora said.

"I don't mean to. Forgiveness is difficult work, and it takes time. Be patient, Cora and God will help you replace the anger with love for your new life. Remember, you already have the power within you. Claim it."

Weeks later Cora was languishing in a big rocking chair in the living room, letting it soothe her as it swayed back and forth. A cup of hot tea and a delicious mystery were on the table next to her, but thoughts kept intruding on her concentration. The new house in Greenberg was comfortable but didn't feel like home. She had hoped she and Helen would someday have a place of their own, but the timing and the finances never seemed right. She missed the rolling fields where she strolled and cleared her head. Walking around the Greenberg town square didn't offer the same effect.

In spite of this, she continued to work on accepting God's love and forgiving those who hurt her. Mostly Frank, but as others came to mind, she prayed to forgive them as well.

She and Warren spent a great deal of time together throughout the fall. Their conversation in the park created deep-seated security as her trust in him developed. He didn't treat her as damaged goods – a woman cast aside. Her parents and Helen needed to get used to the idea he was in her life.

"Ma, I've invited Warren Frantz for Sunday dinner. I'll do all the cooking, so you don't have to fuss. I just wanted you to know."

"Don't ya think it's a little soon for Mr. Frantz to be steppin' out? His wife's been gone less than a year."

"It's just dinner, Ma. The man's got to eat."

"Humph. Seems like you two've been keepin' company plenty of late. Town's people are startin' to talk."

"We're not breaking any laws Ma. I just want him to come to dinner, and I want you to be polite."

Sunday evening, Cora opened the door and whispered to Warren, "Let the games begin."

"Good to see you too," he whispered back as he kissed her cheek.

"Ma, Pa, you remember Warren," Cora said bringing him into the living room.

"Course we remember! We just seen him a few months ago," Ma said.

"Hi, Warren," Helen called as she came down the stairs and into the living room.

"How is high school, Helen?" Warren asked.

"She's got herself a job now," Ma piped in.

"Yes, just part-time, but it'll help," Helen replied. "And Grandma, I'll need some of my pay soon."

"Not now child! We has company," Ma said.

"Good for you, Helen. I got my first job when I was a teen too. Good preparation for college," Warren said.

"Hmph! No need to talk about college. She's just a young girl," Ma said.

"Now, Gertrude, Helen's a good student, like her Mama," Pa said. "She might go to college."

"Yes, Grandma. I could be a lawyer like Warren!" Helen responded. "Warren, what exactly does a lawyer do?"

"Why! That's none a yer bizness young lady," Ma said.

Helen looked away and shook her head.

"I think dinner's ready," Cora cut in and rolled her eyes at Warren.

As they said a prayer of grace before the meal, Ma inserted an extra one. "And we pray for the soul a poor Lillian Frantz."

"Thank you," Warren said to her amiably.

"She had the cancer now, ain't that right? How long was she ill?" Ma asked Warren.

"More than a year. But her suffering has ended," Warren replied.

Ma looked down, ready to reload her questions.

"Pass the meat around, everyone," Cora said a little too brightly.

The clatter of silverware against plates was the only sound for a few minutes.

"Delicious roast, Cora," Warren said.

"Rather tough, if ya asks me?" Ma said chewing with her mouth open. The sound of Ma's ill-fitting dentures clacked as she worked on her pot roast.

"Helen, please pass the potatoes," Cora said.

As they passed the pottery dish of mashed potatoes around, Warren showed great interest in them. "Bless him," Cora thought.

"So, Helen, did you get into the high school chorus?" Cora asked.

"Yes, Mama! I thought I told you that. I'm a soprano."

"Hmph! Just like your daddy. Musician!" Ma sniffed.

"I have other talents, Grandma. But I also like to sing," Helen said.

"Don't ya go bragging child," Ma said and waved a fork in her direction.

Helen looked down and pushed peas around her plate.

The ticking of the mantle clock seemed magnified. Was it always that loud? Cora wondered silently trying to think of something to say.

"So, Mr. Frantz, how long has your dear wife been gone?" Ma asked.

"Lillian died last February," Warren said.

"Not long. Still in your year a mournin then," Ma said.

"Yes, although I don't think it's possible to put a time limit on mourning," Warren said.

"And here ya are with Cora," Ma shot another arrow.

"Cora's been a lifesaver," Warren said.

"I'll bet she has!" Ma said.

Cora's cheeks flamed. "Ma!" Cora glared at her and then looked down at her plate unable to think of what else to say. She endured another silence and pretended to be overly interested in chewing.

"Looks like it's goin to be a long war. Any of your boys fightin in it, Warren?" Ma asked.

"No, thankfully, not yet anyway."

"Well, they ain't gunna shirk their duty if they're called, are they?" Ma asked.

"Certainly not," Warren said. "I just meant they're safe for now."

Pa sighed. "Cora, did I hear ya say there's pie for dessert?"

"Yes. Apple pie. I'll get it." Cora went into the kitchen and didn't know whether to laugh or cry. Why did her mother have to dominate every conversation with doom and gloom?

She brought out the pie and coffee. For a few minutes, there was a contented silence.

"Delicious, Cora! I had no idea you were such a fine baker," Warren said.

"Hope ya didn't use the last a the apples," Ma said.

Plates scrapped clean. Coffee slurped. It was over at last.

"Helen, would you please do the dishes? Warren and I are going for a short drive," Cora said as she ushered Warren out of the house.

"I'm so sorry," she said when they were alone in the car.

Warren laughed. "No need to apologize. But everything you told me about her was true! I understand now why you escaped at 18."

Cora started each morning with the homework Pastor LaPatka gave her. The morning after the disastrous dinner, she thought about her relationship with Warren. Was it love? She wasn't certain. Her experience with it was vague. For the first time in her life, she felt comfortable with a man. Was it enough? Lillian's death was a fresh wound for Warren, but Cora was happy to accept whatever friendship he offered.

She worked each day on forgiveness. She was starting to feel lighter, happier. Perhaps the knots were untying at last. At least the ones that involved Frank. He was firmly in the past. Forgiving her mother was a daily battle. Difficult to heal when fresh hurts popped up.

Cora went to see the manager of the store where Helen worked and explained that she was Helen's guardian and asked that Helen be the one to receive her pay each week. Then approached her mother as she was resting in the living room. Cora sat down.

"Ma, I want you to return the money to Helen. She needs to learn to handle her own finances."

"She owes me that money."

"Did she borrow from you?"

"No. But she's been freeloadin here for most of her life."

"She was a child! And I helped with household expenses and bought her whatever she needed. Not you!" Cora stood up, furious.

"You dumped her on me sos you could go off to college. I told ya I was done raisin children, but you and your Pa pushed me into it."

"And you made her life miserable! You never let her forget she was a burden to you. Why, Ma?"

"While you were off feelin so high and mighty, I was the one wiping her bottom and nose."

"College was the only way for me to support myself and Helen. And I have done that all while helping you and Pa."

"No one asked for your help."

"Why are you so unhappy?"

"Maybe cuz no one asks me what I want. I never wanted to slave away on a stinkin farm."

"But you married a farmer."

"He was supposed to be an engineer."

"What? I've never heard that. He didn't get into college?"

"Got accepted, but had to change his plans."

"What happened?"

"You happened."

"Me?" Helen sunk into a chair. "You got pregnant."

"You ain't the only one who got ahead of your vows."

"Don't start. You know darned well what happened to me. To think you resented me my entire life because I got in the way of your plans."

"Life woulda been a lot easier married to an engineer."

"Yes, but that was your fault, not mine!"

"More like John's fault," Ma said.

"And yours. So, you both gave up on your dreams and moved to a farm?"

"We didn't have a choice. Times were tough."

"Yes, I lived through many of those tough times. But it doesn't excuse you for taking Helen's money."

"I don't have it."

"What did you spend it on?"

"Groceries. It's gone."

Cora shook her head and went upstairs to speak with Helen.

"I'm sorry sweetie, but your money is gone."

"What? She stole it?"

"I asked Ma, and she said she spent it on groceries. How many weeks did you work?"

"About ten."

"Figure out how much you lost and I'll repay you."

"Why does Grandma hate me?"

"She doesn't. But she never stops worrying about money. I'm so sorry she did this to you. I have spoken to your manager, and from now on, you'll get your pay each Friday."

"I asked Grandma several times for some of my wages, and she kept telling me I couldn't have them because she was saving them for me. I trusted her."

"She's a wily one. I'm sorry I didn't intervene sooner. But I'll make it up to you before Christmas."

Cora reflected on her mother's revelations. Cora couldn't change Ma's bitterness, but she understood it better now. At her next meeting with Pastor LaPatka, she relayed her progress.

"And have you been able to forgive your offenders?"

"To some degree. I think it would help to hear Frank say he's sorry."

"I think we both know that's highly unlikely."

"What do I do?"

"When you're meditating on the hurt, imagine Jesus intervening and healing you."

"I'm not sure what you mean."

"Think of the worst day of your life. And then instead of the pain, imagine Jesus is there, and he saves you from that situation. Visualize him hugging, healing and rescuing you."

Cora nodded, trying to imagine it.

"Would you like me to pray with you now?"

At first, she was nervous but decided to trust him. "Yes, please."

Pastor LaPatka held her hand and prayed aloud. As he was praying, Cora felt a lightness in her heart. As if a door swung open. She couldn't explain the almost giddy feeling.

"Thank you. I feel so much better," Cora told him as she left.

"That's wonderful, but don't rely on feelings alone. While you're working on forgiveness, include yourself for any missteps you may have made."

Cora impulsively hugged him and floated to her car.

As she drove down Main Street and saw the Christmas decorations in the store windows, Cora realized she was looking forward to her first Christmas with Warren. After what seemed like a lifetime of pain, was it possible God was smiling on her? Their romance wasn't full of youthful passion, but there was a deep affection between them that was soul satisfying.

Warren asked her to have Christmas Eve dinner with him and his children and grandchildren as a time for them all to get acquainted. Would they accept her? Especially so soon after Lillian's death?

Chapter 24

*Cora

Dark skirts and plain white blouses were scattered all over Cora's bed as she dug through her closet and pulled out more clothes.

Helen, dressed in a flannel nightgown, peeked in. "What's going on?"

"I'm trying to find something a bit festive to wear for Christmas."

"Tired of dressing like a nurse or a nun? Why the change?"

"My first Christmas with Warren and his children. I want to look presentable."

"Not sure what you mean by 'presentable,' but I'd love to help you."

"Thank you!"

"We can go to Wilson's Store. Don't need ration books for used clothes."

"Right, let's start after breakfast. I think I smell coffee."

Wilson's was a short walk. They dug through racks of dresses until Helen spotted a red dress with a tailored bodice with shoulder pads. The skirt had a fitted waist and a slight flare. She held it out to her mother.

"Just your size, Mama."

"I can't wear red!"

"It'd look great with your dark hair. Please try it on."

The dress fit her perfectly but showed a bit more leg than Cora was used to.

"Oh, Helen, I don't know about this. Warren will think I've gone off the deep end."

"Warren will love it. Just add a bit of rouge to your cheeks and lips."

Cora decided to take a risk on the dress and even wore her hair loose. Helen helped her wrap it in rags to create soft curls and later checked her mother's makeup.

"I feel as if I'm losing you, Mama."

"I'll always be your mother, Helen. Just because I'm spending time with Warren doesn't mean I don't have time for you. Besides you're the busy one lately with your job, choir, and school. I'll celebrate Christmas Day with you and Grandma and Grandpa. Promise."

Cora went to Warren's home early to help him with preparations. She was nervous as she knocked on his door. Did she look silly dressed up so fancy? He opened the door, and his eyes lit up when he saw her. Warren took her coat and then twirled her around.

"Cora, you look beautiful!"

Her cheeks flamed, and she whispered. "No one's ever said that to me before."

"Well, I'm telling you now. You are beautiful. Let's have a glass of mulled wine, Cora, before everyone gets here." Warren poured warmed spicy wine into two small crystal glasses and set them on a small wood table. He kissed her forehead, and she caught the scent of cherry tobacco from his pipe.

"Before the pandemonium sets in, I want to give you something." Warren reached into his breast coat pocket and handed a tiny box to her.

She opened it and stared wordlessly at the diamond ring.

"Cora, we've been through a difficult year together. But now is our chance to find happiness. You have been a faithful friend to me, and I'd like you to be my loving wife."

"This is too extravagant, Warren."

"Nonsense, Cora. I love you, and you deserve a proper engagement ring." Warren placed the ring on her finger. "What do you say? Will you marry me, Cora?"

She kissed him and tears filled her eyes. "Yes, Warren. I'd be honored to be your wife."

Warren pulled her into a warm embrace and then kissed her passionately.

"I'm dizzy, and I haven't even had a sip of wine," She looked up at him and touched his cheeks and the deep cleft in his chin. "I look forward to seeing this face every morning for the rest of my life."

Warren smiled and hugged her, the soft fibers of his wool jacket caressed her cheek.

"Let's not wait too long to marry, Cora. With the war and all, life seems unpredictable. Let's be brave and reach for happiness while we can."

"Warren, I never thought I could be this happy. You've awakened my stony heart."

"Your heart wasn't stony, Cora. If it had been, you never could have provided such tender care to Lillian. And what about all the mothers you helped to bring life into the world? You've always been a giver of love. Now's your time to receive love."

"You have the sweetest way of putting things, Warren. I hope your children will accept me so soon after their mother's death. I know I can't replace her, but I will do my best to love them."

"And I hope your Helen will accept me and not feel as if I'm taking you away from her."

"Helen's so busy with her own life, I don't think she'll even notice!"

"A toast. To our future happiness," Warren said, and they sipped the sweet wine. "Before everyone gets here, let's choose a date so we can share our news. I've been thinking about May 1. It's the Saturday after Easter."

"It's perfect. May first sounds like a beautiful day for a wedding."

Christmas morning, she awoke, and for a moment she thought she'd dreamt about the engagement. She looked at her hand, and the twinkling diamond assured her it was real. She and Warren were to be married. Cora carefully put the ring back in its' tiny box and hid it in her dresser. This surprise could wait.

Now to face Ma, Pa, and Helen. Prepare for resistance. Warren was joining them for Christmas dinner, and Cora needed to cook dinner and bake cookies.

Helen came into the kitchen for breakfast and saw Cora poking cloves into a ham.

"Merry Christmas everyone. No turkey this year Mama?"

"Merry Christmas, Helen! I thought we'd have a ham."

"Pa, do you remember the year I helped you hunt a turkey for Thanksgiving?"

"Sure do, Ole Bean. That was one huge bird."

"Yes, and if I recall, I had to prepare that bird at the last minute with all the other dinner preparations!" Ma said, splashing cold water on warm memories.

"Now Ma, you had plenty of help with dinner. And the turkey was delicious! I hope this ham is tender. Warren is coming for dinner, and I'm going to make my pinwheel date cookies."

"You already made sugar cookies," Ma said.

"Yes, but you know I love those date cookies and Warren's never tried them."

"Can I help you bake them?" Helen asked.

"'May I' dear, not 'can I.' And yes, I'd love your help."

Warren looked subdued and happy at dinner. Cora was a nervous wreck. As she served a tray of cookies for dessert, Warren produced a bottle of sweet wine. He poured wine into everyone's glasses. "I'd like to propose a toast to Cora."

"Cora? What on earth for?" Ma said.

"Cora has helped me through the most difficult year of my life."

"Uh huh!" Ma grunted.

"Ma, let him finish," Pa said.

"Thank you. Cora and I have developed a deep friendship and companionship through the sorrow of this past year. And now she has turned my sorrow to joy. She has agreed to marry me on the first of May!"

"Marry? What in tarnation? It's not even been a year since yer wife died!"

"The first anniversary is coming in February. I feel blessed God has brought such a wonderful woman into my life once again and I want to live the rest of my days with her."

For once, Ma was speechless. Pa lumbered to his feet and raised his glass.

"Let me be the first to congratulate you both. A toast to Cora and Warren."

Cora pulled the box out of her pocket and put the ring back on her finger to show them the engagement was official.

Later, after Warren had gone, Ma and Pa went to bed, leaving Helen and Cora with a few moments alone together.

"How do you feel about my engagement?"

"I like Mr. Frantz, and your ring is really pretty, but it seems kinda... sudden," Helen said.

"I've known Warren for a few years. As I helped care for his wife, I saw such a tender side of him."

"But, Mom, his wife's been dead less than a year. Won't this cause a scandal?"

"Helen, as a single mother in a small town, many have found me scandalous for years. I finally will be a respectably married woman. And the wedding won't be until the spring - after the first anniversary of Lillian's death."

Helen nodded thoughtfully.

"I didn't expect to marry again, but this relationship has been a blessing. Warren has helped me work through some of the ghosts of my past."

"You mean like my father?"

"Yes, when he ran out and took Ruby, it nearly killed me. And leaving you to go to school when you were so young was also painful. For both of us."

"Yes, Grandma Gertrude was never happy with me. But I knew you loved me and Grandpa loved me, even when he didn't say much."

"And now you're nearly grown. I'm so proud of the young woman you're becoming."

"Thanks, Mama." Helen reached out and hugged her. "But I don't want to lose you."

"You won't be losing me. And it'd make me very happy if you'd agree to be my maid of honor."

"Oh, Mama! Yes! What should I wear? What colors have you chosen? What flowers do you want? I can design a dress for you."

"Whoa! Slow down, Helen." She laughed at her enthusiasm. "I promise to let you help me with all the decisions for the wedding. But there is one more thing we need to discuss."

"This doesn't sound good."

"After I marry, I plan to live in Warren's home. If you move in with me, it'll mean you'll have to change high schools."

"So, you want me to stay with Grandma and Grandpa? Don't you want me to live with you?" Helen bit her lip.

"I'm just being practical. Warren lives in a much smaller town, and you'd be better off graduating from a larger school even if it means staying with Grandma and Grandpa. Besides Grandma is mellowing a bit in her old age, isn't she?"

"She may be mellow, but she's still up to her old tricks!" Helen said.

*Helen

"Mama's getting married – and moving away from me," Helen told Emily when she visited on New Year's Day. This sweet-sour news reawakened Helen's feelings of rejections. Most of her life had been a struggle for Mama's attention. She didn't remember the three years when her mother was away working on her nursing degree, but the scars were there.

"Where is she moving?"

"Springfield."

"Missouri?"

"No, Iowa."

"That's not far. Why aren't you moving with her?"

"I'd have to change schools, and Mama says Greenberg has a better high school."

"Well, I'm glad you aren't moving. I'd miss you!"

"Thanks, Emily! You're a great friend."

"And what about Joseph? You don't want to move away from him."

"No. He's so dreamy! I hope he asks me out soon."

"Then why the grumps?"

"I have to stay under my Grandma's thumb. And I won't see Mama as much. Her husband's going to get all her attention now."

"Come on. Maybe he can be like a father to you."

"I hope so. I am happy for Mama. She's had a difficult life. Marrying Warren will give her someone who'll care for her. They'll be here on Sundays."

Helen sighed, resigned to another two years under Grandma Gertrude's thumb. Mama was right. She did want to stay with her classmates – especially the dreamy boy in History class.

*Cora

As the first anniversary of Lillian's death approached, Warren and Cora made plans to attend church together and then to visit Lillian's grave. At first, Cora wondered if Warren wanted to mark this date alone. She wanted to give him time to grieve without worrying about her feelings. But he insisted he wanted her with him.

They stood in the snowy cemetery for a few moments holding gloved hands. "Lillian, you know I miss you every day. This was a difficult year, but I believe God sent Cora to help me find my way through it. I hope I have your blessing because Cora and I plan to marry."

The silence encompassed them as Warren struggled with his emotions. After a time, he turned to her.

"I believe Lillian would be happy to know I'm to marry again."

Cora knew it too. "Let's go have a coffee. We'll get frostbite if we stay out here much longer."

Warren agreed. They went to his home for privacy. Warren made coffee, started a fire in the fireplace, and they settled into the cozy living room.

Cora blew on her hot coffee, and while she waited for it to cool, she knew it was time to share her conversation with Lillian.

"I've never told you this, but Lillian and I spoke about you last January."

"What do you mean?"

"A few weeks before she died, you had gone to your office and Lillian and I were visiting. She asked me to help you through your grief. She even said she hoped you'd marry again."

"Help me? You ignored me for months. I think you shirked your duty?" Warren teased.

"I did visit you after the funeral, but I realized only you could heal the grief and separation."

"And what was this about her wanting me to marry again?"

"That's what she said. Of course, I didn't think she meant me. I had no plans ever to marry again so I promised her I'd think of someone I could introduce you to."

"Ah ha. And did you think of someone?"

"Apparently not. So, I avoided you. I decided you'd have to find someone on your own."

"A fine friend you turned out to be!" Warren smiled.

"Well, you found someone!"

"Yes, I certainly did. In fact, we found each other." He reached for her hand.

"As difficult as the year was, dealing with your grief, you helped me face my past."

"And how did I do that?"

"Last fall, when we walked to the park shelter, you asked me about my marriage, and I poured out the details of what went wrong. As difficult as it was sharing my secrets with you, it started the healing process."

Warren nodded. "By getting it out into the open?"

"Yes, but it also made me realize I was a prisoner to my bitterness. The anger I felt toward Frank was not only holding me back, but it was sinful. I realized I needed to forgive him."

"Did you call him?"

"No, I met with my pastor several times and confessed my inability to forgive Frank. I blamed Frank for stealing not only my innocence but my freedom and my ability to direct my path. For years I felt as if he stole my life from me. He stole my oldest child and the opportunity to teach. He forced me to raise Helen without a father."

"Your feelings were accurate. He did steal your innocence and your child."

"Yes, but Pastor LaPatka helped me see that by holding onto the anger, I was allowing the circumstances to keep me hostage. I needed to forgive Frank to move on emotionally."

"What did you do, my dear?"

"It took me a long time. I prayed and asked God just to help me want to forgive him at first. Then finally I felt ready to let go of the anger. The last time Pastor LaPatka and I were praying, I felt as if the door to a cage in my heart swung open. The relief was almost physical."

"Cora, I prayed you'd be freed from your past."

"Thank you, Warren. I didn't realize I had the power to forgive."

"Power?"

"Yes. When I realized I had control over the anger and resentment, it was powerful. I decided to let it all go."

"How courageous you are."

"Along the way, I also realized I needed to forgive myself."

"For what?"

"For not fighting harder to get Ruby back. It's my deepest regret, but I realized I couldn't keep punishing myself forever."

"You've faced a great deal, Cora."

"Thank you for pushing me to rid myself of this poison. It feels as if a weight has lifted."

"I'm so deeply proud of you. But also, a bit hurt. Why haven't you shared this with me until now?"

"The timing was never quite right. You had your own grief to deal with, and I didn't want my problems to overshadow yours."

"I think God has been working overtime in both of our lives. And of course, he has our matchmaker, Lillian, helping him." Warren winked at her. "You couldn't find another woman for me, eh?"

"No, you'll have to settle for me," she grinned.

"And you will have to settle for me."

"Happily, Warren. Happily."

Life was a bundle of activity in the spring preparing for their wedding. Because it was the second wedding for both of them, Cora wanted to keep things simple. She found a cream-colored suit she'd be able to wear again. Helen sewed a pastel blue dress that looked beautiful against her auburn hair and mirrored her blue eyes. Helen was not only her maid of honor, she also planned to sing a solo after their vows.

Only their immediate families and a few friends were invited. Of course, Ruby wouldn't be able to attend. The long drive with little ones was too much. Even if she could scrape the money together, she wouldn't have enough gas ration stamps. Ruby sent Cora a long letter of congratulations and filled with news of Cora's grandchildren. Sylvia sent a telegraph with her sentiments.

The day of their wedding was sunny and warm, to Cora's relief. She and Helen scouted Ma's flowerbeds for iris and daffodils and made two small bouquets to carry.

"Are you ready for this, Mama?"

"Yes, my dearest. I feel at peace. I love Warren, and I believe we'll have a wonderful life together. And I pray you'll find this someday. Someone who'll love and cherish you. A man you can share your faith with and your life."

"Someday. But I'm in no hurry. I want to enjoy life for a while, Mama."

She kissed her on the forehead. "That's what I want for you too, Helen. Now, let's head to the church."

And they did.

Acknowledgments

I was standing at a gravesite when the elderly relative next to me revealed a shocking detail about her mother. She had never told anyone and as we spent time talking, she revealed more and more of the horrific life of her own mother. Over the course of several months, I later interviewed her by phone and she relayed the events that shaped her mother's life, as well as her own, and gave me permission to craft them into a novel. My deepest gratitude to "Helen."

By adding a few characters and letting my imagination fill in other areas, I was able to flesh it out. But the story skeleton is hers. I merely put meat on the bones.

My sincerest appreciation to those who read early drafts and encouraged me to finish Cora's story. Namely, my daughter, Rose, and my seven sisters. (Yes, really! I have seven sisters:) Holley, Katie, Cecelia, Patty, Theresa, Caroline and Peggy.

I'd also like to acknowledge Anne Fleck for her guidance in helping me edit and shape the novel.

To you, dear reader, my eternal appreciation for taking the time to read about Cora and the struggles she faced and the strength she conjured to finally find peace.

About the Author

Clare Bills considers herself a "nearly normal" writer. She admits some eccentricity and has made it her New Year's Resolution every year to foster this quest. It's going swimmingly.

She's been married longer than most readers have been alive, however, she can still recall her first kiss, the year she baked her first chocolate-chip cookies, and her crimson two-piece swimsuit with the pineapple on her butt.

In spite of the serious nature of Mountains of Trouble, Clare also enjoys writing humor and nonfiction and has been published in numerous magazines, newspapers and newsletters, as well as online sites.

Clare shares recipes at clarebills.com.
Follow Clare as Nana Clare's Kitchen on:
Pinterest, Facebook and Twitter
On Instagram: clarebills2711
Email: clarebills@live.com

Questions to Ponder

1. When we first meet Cora, she doesn't yet have the right to vote nor does she have any college education. Yet she is responsible for teaching a room full of minors. What gave her the courage and confidence to leave home and take on this challenge?

2. If Cora's mother had been kinder, would Cora have stayed on the farm in Iowa?

3. Was Cora right to leave Helen with her parents when Helen was one?

4. Do you see Cora as a victim or a survivor?

5. Are there qualities in Cora you admire?

6. Cora was stuck emotionally for many years. Was she afraid to seek help out of pride or fear?

7. The friendship of Cora and Sylvia was one of the joys in Cora's life. How important are the friendships in your life?

8. If you were Helen, would you feel angry that you saw so little of your mother growing up?